THE BOWMAN

A DCI EVAN WARLOW NOVEL

DCI EVAN WARLOW CRIME THRILLER # 15

RHYS DYLAN

WYRMWOOD
BOOKS

COPYRIGHT

Print ISBN 978-1-915185-39-6
eBook ISBN 978-1-915185-38-9

Published by Wyrmwood Books.
An imprint of Wyrmwood Media.

EXCLUSIVE OFFER

Please look out for the link near the end of the book for your chance to sign up to the no-spam guaranteed VIP Reader's Club and receive a FREE DCI Warlow novella as well as news of upcoming releases.

Or you can go direct to my website: https://rhysdylan.com and sign up now.
Remember, you can unsubscribe at any time and I promise I won't send you any spam. Ever.

OTHER DCI WARLOW NOVELS

THE ENGINE HOUSE
CAUTION DEATH AT WORK
ICE COLD MALICE
SUFFER THE DEAD
GRAVELY CONCERNED
A MARK OF IMPERFECTION
BURNT ECHO
A BODY OF WATER
LINES OF INQUIRY
NO ONE NEAR

THE LIGHT REMAINS
A MATTER OF EVIDENCE
THE LAST THROW
DRAGON'S BREATH

PROLOGUE

Nock Nock

Nock ... to fit (an arrow) against the bowstring.

CHAPTER ONE

LATE MARCH, and a rare dry spring day.

The clouds were driven off overnight by an easterly wind that dried up the paths and brought walkers out to their parks and woods. But Ali and Simon Creighton chose to celebrate the spring with an altogether more challenging adventure. They'd come across from Moseley in Birmingham in their motorhome for a long weekend, which, this time, included Monday, both having wangled the day off hoping they might make a fist of it.

And, for once, the gods smiled down on them. This was the last day, and their gamble to walk the Cambrian Mountains and fit in a visit to the Nant-y-Gro Dam was being met with a no-rain day.

Or at least a no-rain-yet day.

Simon suggested they drive up, park at the Visitor Centre at Caban Coch, part of the Elan Valley reservoir system, visit the remnants of the dam, and then strike out across the open country towards Y Gamriw and its cairn at six hundred metres before heading to somewhere unpronounceable called Llanwrthwl and back along the lanes to the car park. A good twelve miles across difficult terrain once they left the paths around the dam.

Simon practised his pronunciations and had tried, gamely, to get Ali to give them a go.

'Caban Coch is easy,' he'd said. 'Caban is as in English, and Coch is Caw-ch as in loch said the Scottish way. Gamriw is Gam as in gamma, and riw goes r-yew. Gamm-r-yew.'

'What about the other place?'

'Ah, Llanwrthwl. Okay, we can't do the double ll's. Takes years of practise. The best way I've found is by making an L sound and then softly blowing air out to create vibrating cheeks. So, it's LL-ann-oo-r-thule. But don't forget to enunciate the 'r' as in roar.'

'I think I'll let you do the map reading,' Ali said, dropping one eyebrow.

'No, you can do it.'

Simon had the dam on his agenda for a good while. And they'd have gone there, rain or shine. The visit was a kind of pilgrimage for Simon. His grandfather had worked on designing the revolving depth charge that became known as the bouncing bomb, made famous by the Dam Busters.

But what a great many people did not know was that a small masonry dam built on the Nant-y-Gro stream, originally used to make a reservoir to supply the construction workers building the much larger Caban Coch Dam site, ended up being chosen as a top-secret test site for the bombs, designed to strike the dam wall, roll down to a specific depth, and explode at that depth.

Simon made Ali watch the Dam Busters film of 617 Squadron as they flew in to destroy the Ruhr Valley dams in Germany under heavy fire more than once.

His grandfather hadn't been with the squadron to see how devastating that raid had been, but he'd been to the Elan Valley to watch the spectacularly successful test run.

And so, on this March morning, after strolling around and viewing what little there was to see, Ali hung on to Simon's arm as he stared down at the lumps of concrete and the remains of the dam wall.

'At least I've been here now. To see what he'd done,' he said. 'I promised him that.'

Wilbur Creighton passed nine months before, and it had been a blessing, but Simon had given his word. 'I mean, what he did was only a small thing, but I suppose it's part of the reason we're standing here today, and there isn't a swastika flying over the Houses of Parliament.'

Ali had heard him talk like this before and, at first, it shocked her. All a bit too dramatic and not the usual conversation she or her millennial friends normally had. The Second World War was something from way in the past.

But Simon had been close to his grandad and was rightly proud.

'Let's take some pics to show your mum and dad,' Ali said.

She took some of Simon, and a few selfies, making sure that Jasper, their Springer Spaniel, appeared in most of them; a difficult task given that Jasper was allergic to sitting still. And then, they'd walked up the steep ascent and across the Nant-y-Gro stream and headed south along the eastern bank of the Caban Coch reservoir before striking off southeast, away from the trees and on to the open moor.

'First stop is a cairn almost directly south.'

'Ok to let Jasper off, you think?' Ali put a hand on the dog's collar.

'I detect no sheep,' Simon said.

Ali slipped the choker lead off Jasper, and the dog ran ahead, never more than twenty yards away, covering the ground, nose down, at breakneck speed. Ali kept the map in a waterproof map case around her neck. Simon manned the compass.

'Not much of a path,' Ali said, looking out over the treeless expanse of rolling hillocks ahead.

'That's what the trail description said when I downloaded it yesterday. Map reading an essential, it said.'

'Lucky we brought a compass, then.'

Jasper disappeared over a ridge, and Simon whistled him back. He returned immediately. The only way Ali and Simon could consider letting him off was the certainty of their recall. Jasper, even if he saw a sheep, would ignore it.

Despite the clarity of the day, they moved over the open moor in and out of a sharp wind, bitter enough to make Ali lift up her neck warmer to cover her chin. 'God, what the hell did people do up here?'

'Grazing for sheep and maybe cattle when the monks owned all the lands. Before that, in the Bronze Age, I think they started clearing the land. What's that? 3000 years BC?'

'They must have bloody frozen up here.'

'Ah, that's where you're wrong. The climate was much warmer then. This might have been good grazing. Some of the cairns are Bronze Age burial mounds.'

'Lovely. Let's hope Jasper doesn't disappear down a hole and come up with a Neolithic femur.'

Simon let out a derisive roar. 'You've been reading too many cheesy crime novels, Ali Creighton.'

The going was difficult. Though too early in the season for the tough moor-grass to have grown, it still clung, winter-brown from hibernation, cloaking the landscape. They'd made good progress by half eleven. Jasper raced in and out of the gulleys as the Creightons followed sheep tracks and avoided the bigger peaty pools. The wind remained a constant presence, and as they gradually climbed, the view opened out all around them. Mile after mile of emptiness, stretching in all directions as they walked deeper into one of the remotest areas in the whole of the UK.

And then the cairn came into view. A solitary monument, a sentinel guarding the secrets of this unforgiving land.

Ali stopped for another photo, using her selfie stick to take some snaps. But when she took her phone out of the holder, she looked up.

'Jasper? Jasper? Where's Jasper?'

Simon looked around. No sign of the dog. They were on the up slope of a small hill that ran down towards a stream on their left.

'Probably getting a drink.' He sounded like he was reassuring himself. 'Jasper? Jasper?'

The dog did not appear.

Simon reached for a whistle. The dog always returned on the whistle.

Two short blasts. But for once, no Jasper.

'Oh God, please don't say he's got a sheep?'

Simon blew another two blasts. And then from above them, not below, the dog appeared. Brown and white but with something in his jaws as he peered at his owners, wondering what all the fuss was about.

'Jasper. What have you got, there?' Ali shouted up.

The dog ran down. Jasper was a bird dog, trained to retrieve. And what Jasper had retrieved was a woollen hat and some silver paper, still with sandwich crusts inside them.

'Wow, Jasper. You won the lottery there,' Simon said with a grin.

Ali reached down and took the hat and the wrapper.

Jasper promptly sat down, waiting for a reward.

'What's this on the hat, Jasp?' Ali, her own hands gloved, passed the headgear to Simon.

'Oh dear. It's wet.' Simon looked at his hands and lifted his fingers to his nose. 'Oh, shit,' he whispered. 'This smells like blood.' He began to stride up the hill to the ridge.

'Simon,' Ali called after him.

But he only got as far as the top where he stood to stare, Jasper at his side, sturdy on four legs. Man and dog were still standing as Ali arrived and followed Simon's gaze to what lay halfway down the slope on the other side.

'Oh, my God. Is that a—'

'Stay here, Ali. Keep Jasper with you.'

Simon walked down towards a crumpled figure on the ground, calling out, 'Hello? Hello?'

No response.

Simon found that very unsettling, and he paused in his approach to call out again, 'Hello there, are you alright?'

As he got closer, he took in the weathered but good-quality hiking gear in muted colours, waterproof trousers, and a spilled backpack. A telescopic walking pole lay close by. When he was ten feet away, and approaching from the rear,

Simon made out clumps of peaty soil clinging to leather boots.

And then he saw it. Another pole perhaps? Something upright protruding from the brown anorak stained darker by water or–

Simon stopped there to peer in disbelief at the thing sticking up vertically. A thing that was definitely not a walking pole.

A noise. A grunt that was part horror, part plea for it not to be true, escaped his lips. He'd have to get closer to be certain, check for a pulse, make sure his eyes weren't deceiving him. But his feet seemed frozen, unable to stride the twenty feet to the figure.

He turned a pale and fearful face back to Ali.

'Call the police. And an ambulance, though I doubt … Oh, Christ, Jasper might have licked … Oh, Christ.'

'Simon, what's wrong?'

'It's a bloke, and he has an arrow in his back, Ali. Call the police. Now.'

CHAPTER TWO

JESS ALLANBY STARED at the remains of a barn at the outskirts of Rosebush in the Preseli Hills.

'What's it called again?' she asked.

She got a reply from Bryn Davies, the senior of the two builders that DCI Evan Warlow had brought with them to look at the property.

'Ty'r Cloddfa.'

'Clod-far?' Jess read the sheet from the estate agent again.

'Clo as in Claw, dd pronounced as in 'the,' and fa as in van.'

Jess tried again. 'Cloddfa.'

'Spot on,' Warlow said, stepping back around from where he'd been inspecting a stone wall. 'Comes with a couple of acres.'

'And why is it for sale now? I mean, it's ancient,' Jess asked.

'Smallpox outbreak in 1924. They abandoned a few places around here, then. Obviously had something to do with the quarry, hence the name Cloddfa—'

'Which means quarry.'

'One word for it, yes,' Bryn said. He wore a trademark watch cap, and his thick glasses were speckled with dry plaster. 'They came back to farm here, but no go. No one has been living here since the war.'

'Looks like it,' Jess said.

'So, yes, it has been on sale for a while,' Warlow said. 'But it's a doer-upper, alright. And whoever owned it has dropped the price.'

'So, within budget,' Jess agreed. 'But how much would it cost to make it habitable?'

'Good question.' Bryn's jaw jutted sideways. 'With my Davies and Clough hat on, I reckon whatever an architect tells you, add thirty per cent.'

Alwyn, Bryn's much younger partner, spoke up, 'That's the beauty about this, though. The planning restrictions aren't that bad. Nothing stupid, though they'll want the walls stone and the roof zinc. They stipulate that. But that's a modern look now. And it's cheaper than slate.'

Alwyn had a floor plan and opened the sheet out on the bonnet of Warlow's Jeep. He had a full beard on his weathered face, and the plans looked small in his big hands as he smoothed out the paper. 'Two tidy rooms downstairs, three bedrooms above, and the long extension with oak and glass, which might be a kitchen or another bedroom and shower. I think it would be stunning. The stream is nearby at the bottom of a sloping garden. Patio down there for the summer. If you didn't live in it yourself, you'd have people flocking to be here.'

'You reckon?' Jess asked.

'We're what, a ten-minute walk from Tafarn Sinc?' Alwyn said. 'Famous pub that's been here since the year dot. There's a restaurant in Rosebush, walks, and the coast is half an hour at the most.'

'Okay. Can we walk the boundary of the property?'

This proved to be not as easy as it sounded. The place was overgrown with piles of stones on the path.

They were at the verge of common land here, on a private road running up from the village of Rosebush itself past the quarry, and then right towards the forest and open moorland. The house was not visible from the road, but down a short curving track. The cleared land on which the building was constructed needed some TLC, but the potential of this location, so close to facilities and walks in the Preselis, made it an attractive prospect.

They didn't walk the whole of the two acres, but Bryn pointed out the boundaries as they crossed the coarse grass, until they eventually returned to the parked cars.

There, the builder stepped back to study the building. 'Mr W mentioned you were on the lookout. This was bought at auction five years ago, and the owners got planning. Then Covid hit. Someone in the family died, and their project died with it. Takes an age for stuff to work through. Bank auctioned the place, and we've bought it. The option is there for us to do the thing ourselves, but it would require working on weekends, and the time it would take before we saw a return is too long. Then we thought of you.'

Jess nodded. A grateful nod. One that failed to hide a sliver of terror.

'I hadn't really considered something this ... decon-structed.'

Alwyn laughed. 'Evan's place was worse than this.' He grinned. 'The previous builder made a start. Foundations, damp proof course. I mean, they had to start from scratch, and the plans and internal breeze-block walls are all sound. Material costs have gone up, of course, but the amazing thing is, they've left a lot of materials here. Blocks and such like. Enough to finish the walls.'

'But someone in the bank had the sense to refresh the planning application. The previous builder tore the worst of it down. Better than potching with some of these old places where they make you keep this wall and that,' Bryn added.

'Potching?' Jess asked.

'Half-arsed meddling,' Warlow explained.

Jess turned to survey the building. The original part now had modern concrete blocks added on and an additional layer inside. But everything looked a mess.

'Do you think we could end up with something like Evan's place?'

'Better,' Alwyn said. 'Skimped a bit on the garden walls, did Mr W.'

'Oy,' Warlow said, but without rancour. 'They were a labour of love for two summers; I'll have you know.'

'I suppose it's not bad for two acres,' Jess said.

'We keep the stone, of course,' Bryn said. 'For the external walls. But it's a bargain with loads of potential. And we'll sort a staged payment. Fifty per cent and then as we go. All official, like.'

Jess let out an enormous sigh. 'Could I have a couple of days to mull things over?'

'No problem,' Bryn said.

Warlow and Jess had met Alwyn and Bryn in the middle of the working day, and now the afternoon beckoned.

'Fancy a quick one in the pub?' Warlow suggested. 'My shout.'

'No. Mine,' Jess said, turning to Bryn. 'It was good of you two to come and meet us.'

The pub, called Tafarn Sinc because its walls and roof were clad in reddish corrugated galvanised iron – Sinc, of course, was Welsh for zinc, there being no Z in the language – had been bought out by the community when closure was threatened in the 1990s. The menu was in Welsh with English translations.

Warlow liked that. If you were in France, they wouldn't put the English translation first. In fact, in France you were lucky to get an English translation at all.

He and Jess shared an *Afocado a wŷ wedi'u ffrio ar rholyn ciabatta*. Jess translated the fried egg bit with ease, the avocado and ciabatta roll spoke for themselves. When it came, the portion probably would have fed most of Dyfed Powys HQ, too.

Alwyn and Bryn had *Tato phobi gyda tsili pum ffa*. Jacket potato with five-bean chilli. The place was heaving.

'This is popular,' Jess said.

'Should see it in the summer.' Alwyn blew on a chunk of potato speared on his fork.

'And well within walking distance from Ty'r Cloddfa.' Her pronunciation was spot on. 'Molly'd love this.'

'Exactly,' Bryn said. He'd already been outside for a cigarette. 'Secluded Pembrokeshire cottage near the Preseli Hills, wild quarry walks, and a pub. Estate Agents can only dream of such things.'

Arwel finished his chilli and wiped his beard. 'As I say, only thirty minutes from the coast, too.'

'And from Nevern. I could supervise the building works,' Warlow said.

Bryn shook his head. 'One garden wall, and now you're an expert.'

Jess and Warlow's phones rang at exactly the same time. They both knew what that meant. Warlow took it outside and left Jess to talk with Davies and Clough.

The man on the other end of the phone needed no introduction.

'Gil. I'm guessing this isn't me winning the raffle.'

'You guess correctly. Very nasty one up on the edge of the Elan Valley. Walker found dead. Shot with an arrow.'

'You did say arrow?'

'I did. I'm on the way. When things kick off, I'll take control of the office. But I thought I'd take Gina up with me. It'll be her first. Rhys can stay behind and set up.'

Warlow had asked Gina Mellings if she'd like to take Catrin Richard's place while the sergeant enjoyed her maternity leave. Gina had sat and passed her National Investigator's Examination in November but had told no one, except her partner, Rhys.

As a trained uniformed liaison officer, she'd been involved in several of the cases Warlow and the team had investigated. Catrin's absence now offered her an opportunity to expand her portfolio of investigation experience, and she'd jumped at the chance. It meant Rhys Harries taking on the temporary rank of sergeant, too. Much to his delight.

'Text me the address.'

'It's a mountain. Bring boots,' Gil said.

When Warlow got back inside, Jess sent him a questioning

glance. He nodded in reply. 'Gentlemen, thanks again for the show home viewing. Unfortunately, we have to get to work.'

'I will be in touch,' Jess said, getting up. 'By the day after tomorrow at the latest.'

'Thanks for lunch, Jess,' Alwyn said, also standing. He was old-school. 'Evan never bought us lunch while we were working on Ffau'r Blaidd.'

'No, because I was too busy mixing cement and carrying bricks.' Warlow had taken very much a hands-on approach to the renovation of his own place during a period when he'd been officially retired from the Force. When he'd woken up most mornings to a breakfast of doubts and worries over his health and the choices he'd made.

'I think we all agree you make a better policeman than you do a labourer, mind.' Bryn added a teasing grin.

'Second thoughts.' Warlow turned to Jess. 'I hear the circus is in Haverfordwest. We could probably find a couple of cheaper clowns there.'

They left the pub to hoots of good-natured derision from the builders.

CHAPTER THREE

THE DRIVE UP to the Elan Valley on any day, even one where the reason for that visit was murder, ranked as spectacular. A journey Warlow had made several times over the course of his career. Both as part of his work, drawing him to far-flung corners of the Dyfed Powys patch, and with his dog Cadi, purely for leisure.

'I never tire of this run,' Jess said as they left Carmarthen and the A40 ran east with the river. 'How many castles are there again?'

Warlow glanced across at Jess. She looked bright eyed and good in a lilac sweater and dark trousers. But then, she'd look good in a burlap sack.

'You're as bad as Rhys,' Warlow said.

'Come on.' Jess wasn't about to let him off the hook. 'You're always waxing lyrical. And please don't say you've got some ointment for that.'

'Tablets, actually.'

'You're avoiding the question.'

'Okay. There's Llansteffan, at the mouth of the estuary, then Carmarthen itself.'

'And I've never visited that one, even though it's the nearest to work.'

'Just the gatehouse and a few walls to examine, but on

your next visit to town, you ought to pop along. Only take you five minutes.'

'Right, that's two.'

'Then there's Dryslwyn. The one we're coming up on now. Sitting right in the middle of the valley.'

Warlow pointed towards the small hillock and the remains of the fortification. 'Easy access from a car park opposite. Beware, though, sometimes there are goats.'

'Sure you don't mean ghosts? And please don't say, only kidding.'

'You are no fun, do you know that?'

Jess held up three fingers. 'Three so far.'

'There's Dinefwr Castle, on the outskirts of Llandeilo. That's impressive.'

'Another one I haven't seen.'

'So, that leaves Llandovery. After that, it's the badlands.'

'That's where we're going, is it?'

'Afraid so.'

'Okay, so let's do a Towy Valley Castle run this summer. Molly might even want to come. But if she doesn't, you, me, and Cadi,' Jess said.

'Love to. Lunch in Llandeilo and a walk up in Cilycwm.'

'Date,' Jess said.

They fell silent, enjoying the undulating ride with the views of the Black Mountains ahead. Jess, noticing Warlow's grin, eventually felt the urge to comment.

'Why are you grinning?'

'Because I'd always wanted to suggest showing you these places, but I was too …'

'Repressed?'

Warlow shrugged. 'One word for it. There are others. Out of my league, depth, place. All of the above.'

'But not anymore?'

'Not anymore. Not since you succumbed to my puppy-dog eyes.'

'I'd say, sympathetic old-dog eyes.'

Warlow threw her a glance. 'I'll take that. We both realise that with age comes wisdom and maturity.'

'And perhaps an inflated sense of ego?'

Warlow switched on the radio and, much to his delight, The Doobie Brothers weighed in with *What a Fool Believes*. He left it at that.

Once past Llandovery, Warlow steered the Jeep northwards towards Rhayader and the Elan Valley Visitor Centre beyond.

A familiar face met them in the car park. Sergeant Tomo Thomas, one of Dyfed Powys's rural crime sergeants, raised a hand in welcome.

Warlow reciprocated.

He and Jess got out of the Jeep and zipped up their jackets as Tomo strode towards them.

'We meet again,' he said.

'I didn't know this part of the world fell under your purview,' Jess said.

'Everything south of the dark side of the moon, ma'am. At least it feels like that sometimes.'

Though this was uttered with a gruff tone of complaint, both detectives had Tomo down as a lifer who would probably die with his Hi-Vis jacket on.

'Missing Hannah?' Warlow asked.

He and Tomo had worked on several unpleasant cases. Most of which had also involved another rural crime officer, PCSO Hannah Prosser, who had recently become a fully-fledged Uniform.

'Always,' Tomo said. 'But we have fresh blood.' He pointed towards a tall female officer, explaining why the car park was half full of police vehicles to bewildered visitors who had come to bike or fish.

'Pryia Sharma. Fits right in, except no one understands a word she says.'

That drew a razor-wire glance from Jess. But Warlow stifled a grin. He knew Tomo of old.

'I appreciate it's rural here,' Jess said. 'But surely, in this day and age—'

'It's her North Wales accent, ma'am. When she speaks Welsh, I have no idea what the hell she's saying.'

Jess let her shoulders slump in defeat.

'You're a wicked man, Tomo,' Warlow said.

'She's a great kid.' Tomo grinned. 'Sharp, but still learning the ropes. Still says "aw" when we see bloody lambs.'

'What can you tell us about where the body was found?' Jess asked.

'Middle of nowhere. No roads near. In fact, I've given Brecon Mountain Rescue a shout. When we move the body, it'll be by stretcher to where they can get a Gator in. Should be here any minute.'

'Gator?' Jess asked.

'It's an all-terrain buggy, ma'am. We could take the Explorer up some of the way, but the Gator is better suited. Once we get the body onto a road, it'll be up to Cardiff for slicing and dicing by the HOP.'

'Make sure Pryia introduces herself. I have a hunch that we will need her and your help in this particular case. Like we have in the past,' Warlow said.

'I warned her this job was low on glamour when she applied.' He turned to look at his recruit, who flashed a smile in return.

'And still she wanted in? Must be your charm and reputation, Tomo.'

'Of course, there is that,' Tomo agreed. 'Your lot are inside the Visitor Centre. In the warm, as always. When you're done, let me know. Mountain Rescue will be here in ten. They'll have the Gator here. We can run you out on that.'

The Centre, run by a water company, had once been a workshop for the dam and was stone-built and renovated. A couple of Uniforms directed them to a room at the rear of reception, one of three sometimes used for visiting school children to write up work after visiting the exhibition full of information on the reservoirs, including a looped video.

Warlow wondered if he ought to linger and bone up. All he remembered about it, picked up from the odd articles he'd read over the years, was that construction began late in the nineteenth century and that the complex supplied a significant area of the Midlands across the border. That in itself was a cause of continued debate between hot-under-the-collar nationalists and profit-making Utilities companies that still raised its head at election times.

But there were no school children today. Only the newest member of Warlow's team and two tired and frightened-looking people sitting around the desk at the front of the room.

Gina Mellings stood up as Warlow and Jess entered, all smiles. Her default expression.

'Here we are. I was just telling Simon and Ali you'd be along.'

'Sorry we kept you,' Warlow said and let Gina make the formal introductions to the Creightons. Once that was done, he took a seat along with Jess.

'You've had a hell of a day so far,' Warlow commiserated with them.

'It was meant to be a visit to the dam and a pleasant walk in fine weather. Instead, it's ended up being a scene from *Cabin In The Woods*,' Ali said miserably, burying both her hands between her thighs.

'I've not seen it,' Jess admitted. 'But I can fill in the blanks. We'd like to record this chat, if that's okay?' She held up her phone.

Simon nodded and explained their movements up to and including finding the body.

'So, only you touched him?' Jess asked.

Gina turned to her senior officers. 'I was just explaining how we'll need some DNA to eliminate Simon from the enquiry.'

'I'm cool with that,' Simon said.

'I'm not,' Ali interjected.

'By touching the body, Simon's DNA will have contaminated the scene,' Jess explained.

'Makes sense.' Simon turned to Ali.

'I don't like the idea of your DNA on a police computer. You read about cases where mix-ups happen all the time.'

'All the time?' Simon looked sceptical.

'Well, I do,' Ali said, sounding increasingly irate.

'Ali's into all the true crime stuff on TV,' Simon explained.

'Don't patronise me, Si. There was a guy not that long ago. In Newcastle I think it was. An entirely innocent man—who lived over 200 miles away and had never even visited Newcastle—was wrongly accused due to a mistake in a lab. A sample used to analyse his DNA from a minor incident was accidentally reused in a rape case, leading to the wrongful accusation..'

'That's a one-off, though, right?' Simon looked at the officers for reassurance.

'Incredibly rare. And non-DNA evidence exonerated that man. I remember the case,' Jess said.

Ali was less convinced. 'Once your DNA is on the database, it's difficult to get it off there.'

'That is true.' Warlow was honest.

'Doesn't matter,' Simon said. 'I've got nothing planned.' He was trying to defuse the situation, but Ali just shook her head.

'What choice is there, though?' Simon asked.

'I still don't like it.'

'Just do it,' Simon said.

'When are we going to be done here?' Ali diverted her anger back towards Warlow. 'We've got a dog in the van. He's been in there hours now. Can we at least take him out?'

'What is his name?' Jess asked.

'Jasper.'

Gina, an expert at pouring oil over troubled waters, took the opportunity for the change in tone to say, 'I said I didn't think you'd mind, not when there's a dog involved.'

'We will not keep you much longer,' Warlow promised.

They talked a little about where they were from, what they were doing there, and Warlow recognised Ali's agitation as a common reaction. Many people experienced anxiety as a result of undergoing police interviews. But he wanted to keep things light and friendly. Getting entangled in this situation was not these peoples' fault.

Gina had already taken a full statement, but he and Jess liked to talk to the first on the scene whenever they could.

'What about the arrow? You're sure?'

'No.' Simon shrugged. 'It looked a bit stubby, if I'm honest. But then I'm no expert. The last time I shot a bow, the arrow had a rubber sucker on the end. I must have been nine.'

Bottom line, these witnesses had not seen, nor heard anyone on their walk that would be of any help.

Warlow thanked them and let them get out to see to Jasper. Once they'd gone, he spoke briefly to Gina.

'Once Povey's taken samples from him, they can go. Make sure you have their address and phone numbers for both of them.'

'Already done, sir.'

'Course it is,' Jess said.

'I can stay with them until they're done with it all,' Gina offered.

Warlow shook his head. 'No. There's a new PCSO out there working with Tomo. Good experience for her to stay with witnesses. You, on the other hand, need to come with us to the scene. We've done all we need to do here.'

CHAPTER FOUR

WHAT WOULD HAVE TAKEN several hours of difficult walking took half an hour on the ATV.

Povey had set up tents. Warlow put a bet on with Jess how long it would be before Gil, because of said tentage, referred to an Apache village, at the same time adding with sardonic aplomb that other First Nations' tribes were available. There was never any element of implied bigotry or racism in this; simply a say it as you see it, humorous referencing of a cinematic history of traditional Westerns.

And, in Gil's case, a refusal to be cowed by the powder keg of cultural appropriation for the sake of it, added to the hope it might trigger a Gen Z into apoplexy.

Gil was old-school, too.

They'd cordoned off a corridor with fluttering tape. Gil, having been there for a good hour, was ruddy in the cheeks from the wind. He met them some twenty yards away from where Povey's crime scene protective tent canvas drummed in the wind which, out here, raced across the expanse.

'Afternoon,' Gil said. 'Welcome to my office.' He had donned the snowsuit and overshoes required at the scene.

'Povey here?' Jess asked.

'She is. Out and about if she isn't in the command centre there.' He pointed to a separate tent off to one side.

'What does this cordoned-off area mean, sarge?' Gina stared at the seemingly random arrangement of blue and white tape fluttering between the stakes that secured it to the ground.

'Excellent question. We've gone back fifty yards from where the body was lying. There is no path as such. But the dogleg, and excuse the pun, is where the Creighton's were coming from and where Jasper returned to with the bloody hat and sandwich wrappings.'

'Do we know who it is?' Gina asked.

'We have a name. Or at least we think we do. Because of the wounds, Povey does not want to move the body until the HOP gets here.'

'How long?'

'Half an hour, according to him. A Dr Gordon Bryers. In for Sengupta, who's on maternity leave. So, we haven't retrieved a phone as the body is face down, but there was a backpack that spilled open. Let's go to the evidence tent. The fancy dress is in the second tent.'

The new arrivals suited up, and he, Gina, and Jess entered the evidence tent to find a table with several items bagged up for protection and a small green rucksack stained dark with fluid.

'All we have so far is a guidebook with a name written on the inside,' Gil explained. 'Gerald Nash. We won't know much more until we get a driver's licence or something like that once the HOP is happy for the body to be moved.'

'Is that blood on the rucksack?' Gina asked, her voice a little cracked.

'It is,' Gil said.

'Okay. Let's have a peep at him.' Warlow turned and exited.

Gil led the way back outside the cordoned-off area to a point where they accessed the corridor. All around the body, numbered tags showed where blood had spattered the grass. A black shaft with orange flight protruded from the man's back at an acute angle.

'Ten inches protruding,' Gil said. 'Povey estimates another eight or so at least in the body.'

The brown anorak around the shaft had a geographic dark-aubergine stain. Much like the rucksack.

'Shot in the back,' Jess muttered grimly. 'Do we think he was running?'

'Can't say, yet,' Gil answered. 'Povey believes it's a crossbow bolt, judging by the thickness.'

Warlow bent down to get a better view, being cautious to keep a reasonable distance of four feet. 'Show me where they think he was coming from, Gil.'

The team walked back outside, and Gil led the way to where a faint sheep track led up a rise. Warlow walked up, outside the cordoned corridor, for a few hundred yards on his own.

The others waited, everyone preoccupied with thoughts of what kind of horror had transpired here.

Twenty minutes later, Warlow rejoined them outside the evidence tent.

'We'll get some bodies out here and do a proper search,' Gil said. 'It'll take a bit of organising. I'll talk to the PolSA.'

The tent flap opened, and Alison Povey, head of Crime Scene Investigation, appeared.

'There you are,' she said, her demeanour unusually dour.

Warlow spoke her name by way of acknowledgement. 'Alison, can you tell us anything?'

'About this? No, not yet.'

'What's up?' Warlow tried to read her expression and failed.

Povey's experience and prowess in the field was second to none. You developed a hard outer shell in this kind of work.

But now he detected a crack in Povey's.

She slid off her hood and ran a hand through her short black hair. 'I've just taken a call from a CID colleague of yours about a missing surveyor north of Abergwesyn Common.'

'Why are they contacting you about a missing surveyor?' Jess asked.

'Because they've found her, and she's dead.'

'What?' Gil barked out the question in dismay.

'Initially, they believed she had fallen, but the arriving paramedics confirmed she had been shot.'

'Oh, *mam fach*.' Gil's oath spoke for everyone.

'Rural crimes are on the way.'

'Tomo?' Warlow asked.

'It's an hour and a quarter's drive from here,' Gil said.

'He's left his PCSO at the Visitor Centre and cadged a quad bike from the Rangers at the reservoir. He's gone cross-country.' Povey had her finger on the pulse here.

Jess looked bemused.

'He knows this patch better than anyone,' Gil explained. 'He'll get there in no time. Probably only eight or ten miles as the crow flies from the reservoir—'

Gil's phone interrupted his words.

'Tomo,' Gil said as he read the caller ID before lifting the phone to his ear. 'Where are you? Lost?'

Gil listened to the reply and handed the phone to Warlow. 'Wants to speak to you.'

'Tomo,' Warlow said. 'You there?'

'Where they found this poor girl, yes. I can see the cairn on Abergwesyn from here.'

'What do we know? Are they getting her off the mountain?'

'No. That's why I'm ringing. Bryers, the HOP, is here. It was closer to him than where you were. He stopped here first.'

'Any details yet?'

'That's just it. Lot of blood. But I've had a scout around before the circus arrives. I found something. About fifteen yards from the body. I'm sending Gil a photo. I've had to go up to higher ground where there's a signal. Let me know your opinion.'

Warlow handed the phone back to Gil and waited. A ping told him a message had come through. He stood next to the sergeant as a blurred image developed into something that caused the breath to seize in the DCI's chest.

There on the grass, in contrast to the natural browns and greens of the vegetation, sat a black crossbow bolt with orange feathers and a wicked-looking three-edged steel arrow tip smudged with something dark.

Warlow and Gil exchanged a prolonged moment of eye contact that came to an end only when Gil shook his head and shifted his focus back to the image. Only then did Warlow turn to the expectant faces around him and showed them. Povey first. She squeezed her eyes shut and looked away after a long five seconds. Then Warlow showed the others.

'Same colour on the shaft and the flights,' Gina said.

'Agreed.' Warlow handed Gil his phone. 'Let's split up. Gil, you stay here with Gina. I want to know what Bryers thinks. Jess and I will get down to Tomo. Back to HQ tonight for a catch-up. That okay?'

Everyone nodded.

'Feed everything you learn straight through to Rhys,' he added as he turned towards where the Gator was parked. 'Alison, can you get a team down there?'

'Tannard is on her way.'

'What is on your mind?' Jess asked as they slid into the ATV's seats.

'It's more akin to a supplication than a thought. Don't let there be three.'

———

WARLOW SAID little as they drove out in the Jeep, retracing their route. In no small part, his silence stemmed from the harrowing nature of what he'd just witnessed.

On top of imagining what kind of death Gerald Nash might have suffered came the frustration of no direct route to where they now needed to be. Abergwesyn sat at the southern end of the empty rolling moorland of valleys and ridges that had once been a temperate forest but had now been choked by the coarse moor-grass.

To get to where Tomo had rung him from meant travelling first south to Newbridge-on-Wye before heading west to their goal, circumnavigating the unspoiled, unpopulated landscape.

Jess had her eyes on this very landscape as they drove. 'Well, I recall reading somewhere that some environmentalists advocate for the complete re-wilding of this area. Trees planted to make it like it was before farmers stripped it bare for livestock.'

Warlow had heard the argument. On one hand, he enjoyed the rolling moors cut through by deep glacial valleys. But the grass here, the Molinia, choked out many life forms, rendering it almost a desert. When he didn't respond to Jess's conversational gambit, she waited a long minute before shifting her gaze from the window to him with an expression of amused exasperation.

'Well, are you going to spill those beans or not?'

'About what?'

'Oh, come on. The nonverbal communication that you, Gil, and Alison Povey exchanged. Loaded doesn't even come close. If it had been carrying any more weight, the three of you would have collapsed under it.'

Warlow let out a suppressed sigh. 'I saw the same notion flash through both Gil and Povey's minds. Like minds. Twenty something years ago, when I was working my way up the ranks just after leaving the Met, I worked in Swansea for a short while. Dyfed Powys had a case that I wasn't directly involved in. Two people shot with a crossbow. Both walkers. I can't remember the exact details, but it was somewhere in this neck of the woods.'

'When were you going to tell me?' Jess, obviously affronted, almost crossed her arms over her chest.

'When I got this clunky brain of mine in gear to remember enough detail.'

'Really?'

'The silence you suffered was my brain doing some sieving.'

'Trying to recall?'

'The thrill of it all.'

'What?'

'Old Frank Ifield song. My dad loved him. A yodeller he was. Ask Gil—'

'See this?' Jess held up her phone. 'It has more computing power than the Lunar module that took a man to the moon. Just give me some details and I will Go-ogle it.'

'That's a Gil-ism.'

'Yes, well, *mea culpa*.'

Warlow sent her a look.

Jess nipped it in the bud. 'And don't you dare say, culpa cabana, please. Not in the mood for Manilow this morning.'

'Oh, Mandy.'

Jess sighed.

'Okay. But I'm warning you. If you look up the Bowman Murders, you might be glad of the distraction.'

CHAPTER FIVE

THE SCENE AT ABERGWESYN, when Warlow and Jess arrived, was very different compared with the one they'd left at the Elan Valley.

A Uniform standing behind a response vehicle directed them into a farm entrance and another in the yard waved them towards a track leading up to open land beyond. Already, the wet ground showed signs of vehicular ruts, and if more rain came, which was an inevitability in this remote area, the access would deteriorate quickly.

Warlow relayed his concerns to Jess, and she agreed. But for now, the Jeep made it safely to a staging area. They were on higher ground, with police vehicles and one non-police vehicle beside the Crime Investigation vans. The blue Land Rover had a company logo: Redoubt Energy.

Another Uniform holding a clipboard acknowledged their presence.

They walked towards a ridge and took in a vast sweep of open land, sloping down to a distant stream on the valley floor a good mile away.

Halfway down stood some more tents.

This time, they were met by Jo Tannard, Povey's deputy. A formidable investigator in her own right, with a methodical approach and an athletic build that contrasted sharply with her superior's. Her striking features, particularly her perfectly sculpted eyebrows, caught Warlow's eye. Her coolness in the face of gruesome crime scenes spoke volumes about her professional calibre. She'd also learned from a master and applied an equally scrupulous and thorough approach to any crime scene.

'HOP still here?' Warlow asked after they exchanged the briefest of greetings.

'No. You will have passed him on the way down. We've hung on for you before we move the body.'

Warlow gave her a prim nod and followed her down to the tents.

'Who is she?' Jess asked.

'Kirsty Stuart. She worked for Redoubt Energy.'

'We saw the van,' Jess said.

'She was up here surveying. There are plans to develop some of the land as wind farms.'

That did not surprise Warlow. Several areas already had the giant windmills spread over many acres. But he had not heard of any developments in this far south.

'Isn't this National Trust land?'

'It is,' Tannard said. 'I don't consider it to be imminent. The van you saw is a colleague's. He told us she's been up here a few times before.'

'Alone?'

'Yes. She was an experienced hiker. The company had a failsafe. They'd set up check-in times. When she did not check in, someone came up to look. That's when they found her.'

Tannard stopped twenty yards from the biggest tent and pointed to a marker in the grass.

'We've identified some blood here. The grass is flattened. My impression is that this is where she fell after being struck. She then crawled forward and stopped where the tent is positioned, probably losing consciousness.'

Warlow followed the line of markers to the tent. 'Before we look at her, where did Tomo find the arrow or bolt or whatever it is?'

'Definitely a bolt.' Tannard walked past the tent by some

fifteen yards. 'We've removed it, but the position and length are indicated.'

On the grass, markers pinned with metal stakes showed the find. Warlow looked back to where Tannard suggested Kirsty was shot, then beyond to a small elevation in the land.

'Someone might have been lying in wait,' he said.

'Are we assuming the bolt went through her and out the other side?' Jess asked.

'That's my interpretation. We've found no other weapon or ammunition.'

'Are crossbows that powerful?' Jess wondered.

'They can be. Of course, it depends on which one, but they can be lethal.' Tannard stood over Warlow as he crouched near to where the arrow was found. He stood up.

'Okay, let's have a look at her,' he said.

Kirsty Stuart lay on her back under the protection of a tech tent, where she'd fallen. Her face chalk white in death, blood congealed in a rivulet from the corner of her mouth. She wore a Patagonia coat, light blue originally, now stained purple in patches, mainly on the left side of her chest. The coat had been unzipped.

'We think the bolt entered behind on the right-hand side, travelled up, and out on the left just above the diaphragm.'

'And who was it that found her?' Jess asked.

'Her colleague. He's back up in the car park.'

'Right. Let's get her moved. Meanwhile, we'll need a quick word with the colleague.'

THE MAN who found Kirsty had been put in a response vehicle to protect him from the weather. Robin Lipton looked fit. Like Kirsty, he was kitted up with a RAB coat, Rohan trousers, and Keen boots. He'd unzipped his coat to reveal a blue fleece.

They'd put him in the passenger seat.

Jess was behind Warlow in the driver's seat. Once again,

she'd asked and been given permission by Lipton to record the conversation. She led the interview.

'In your own words, Robin, tell us what happened.'

'Kirsty went out early. Before the rain.'

'To do what, exactly?'

Lipton, for a second or two, didn't seem to understand the question.

Jess couched it in different terms. 'Why was she up here, Robin?'

'It's a complicated job, assessing the impact and positioning of a construction like a wind farm. It is necessary for us to consider access and construct roads. The effects can be widespread. Both on landscape and water courses. That sort of thing. Kirsty was also looking at the biosphere. There are some protected species that might be affected up here. At least for access to the proposed site. Plus, there's the blanket bog and sustainable management scheme. It all has to be considered.'

'Okay,' Jess said. 'And Kirsty was meant to check in every couple of hours?'

Lipton let his chin drop and nodded, but he looked up again to explain. 'There are communication black spots. But that's our arrangement. We are a team of surveyors. Three of us. If one or two of us are out, someone always stays accessible within signal on lower ground. That was me today. The company has an office in Cardiff, but we have a few meetings coming up locally, so the three of us were on site.'

'What meetings?' Warlow asked.

'Open evenings. Consultations where residents meet the developers, local planners, and Assembly Members. It's protracted, the process.' Lipton was calm and collected, but it was taking a lot of effort.

'So, that's where you were? Doing paperwork?'

'There's a coffee shop in Lanwrtyd Wells.' He defaulted from the double l that so many English people had trouble pronouncing to the single in Llanwrtyd. 'I sat there with a nice coffee and worked.'

He dropped his chin again. 'I keep thinking, what if I had

gone with her? I could have done something. I mean, if she's fallen and cracked her head or suffered some kind of internal bleeding …'

Warlow flicked his eyes across to Jess. Not exactly a glance, more a signal of awareness that Lipton had not been let in on the cause of death here.

Jess picked up on it but decided not to explain. Not yet. 'Is there much opposition to what you're planning?'

'There always is. It will not be soon, but consultation sometimes starts years before we ever get there, and the Assembly will need to give permission. We all know how much of a green agenda there is these days. And, to be honest, where we're thinking of citing this one, it's way off the beaten track.'

'Not where Kirsty was found?'

'No. She must have been coming back out.' He delivered this with an unhappy expression clouding his forehead. 'Can you tell me what happened? There was blood, but I couldn't see where it was coming from. The ambulance people made me check her pulse, but I couldn't …'

His voice dropped to a whisper. 'So much blood.'

Jess persisted with her line of questioning. 'There have been some meetings already?'

Lipton nodded.

'And how did the meetings go?'

'Not too bad. These are early days. There will be opposition—'

'How much opposition?'

'A vociferous few.' Lipton's frown deepened. 'Why are you asking me about meetings? What aren't you telling me?'

Warlow spoke. 'We think Kirsty was shot, Robin.'

Lipton's mouth crept open. 'Wa-wa-what?'

'The blood you saw came from a wound in her chest and abdomen. It's likely she bled to death long before you arrived.' Warlow had no idea if this was true, but added it as a platitude, anyway.

'An accident?'

'We don't know yet,' Jess said.

'But shot? What is there to shoot up here?'

'Good question,' Warlow said. 'Do you hunt, Robin?'

The question sucker-punched Lipton. He looked like he might be sick. 'My God, you don't think … Christ, I've never even shot a gun.'

'Did Kirsty?'

'No, she never said … no. Who could have shot her?'

'That is what we are going to find out,' Warlow said.

'It's important that, at this stage, you say nothing about this to anyone. Okay, Robin?' Jess's request was met with a series of rapid nods. 'You've had a shock. Is there anyone we can contact? Probably not the best idea in the world you drive yourself home to Cardiff.'

'I'll be fine.'

'I doubt that,' Jess said. 'Where did Kirsty live?'

'Bristol. She drives over the bridge every day.'

'Is she in a relationship?'

'She is. I've already given all this information to one of your officers.'

'Good. Now I suggest you contact someone in your organisation and ask them to come and pick you up. Was Kirsty in the van this morning?'

Robin nodded. 'I drove her up here, dropped her off.'

'Then we'll need to keep the van for forensics to look over. Sorry about that.'

Robin nodded. 'I'll ring my colleague. He's in Cardiff. He'll have to come and get me.'

They took more details, handed him back to the Uniforms to wait it out, and Warlow took some photos of the geography on his phone before they got back into the Jeep and headed for Carmarthen.

'What a mess,' Warlow said.

'I'll give Avon and Somerset a ring. Someone needs to tell Kirsty's family.'

Warlow didn't argue. Normally, he would have done this sort of thing himself, but the logistics were against him here. Bristol was hours away, and someone would already be worried about Kirsty. They deserved to know.

'I know someone in serious crimes there. Bob Marston.'

'Okay. Apologies on our behalf.'

'He'll understand.'

Someone was going to see a response vehicle turn up on the street and hear Uniforms knocking on their door. Open it to see someone with an unsmiling face deliver news that would alter their life in a matter of seconds. He'd been that unsmiling face too many times himself to know it was everyone's worst nightmare.

'Any news from Gil?'

'Bryers, the HOP, is there now. He hadn't much to say. Wants the body in Cardiff, but they have confirmed the identity, Gerald Nash, retired doctor from Pershore.'

'Out making the most of his time,' Warlow muttered out the bitter words. 'Already I hate this case.'

CHAPTER SIX

As JESS and Warlow headed back through Llanwrtyd, they stopped at the café Robin Lipton had spent the morning in. They pulled in. Warlow stayed in the car while Jess ran a quick check. She was back in under three minutes.

'I showed a nice kid the photograph of Lipton from the Redoubt website. She confirms he'd been there most of the morning.'

Warlow drove off.

'Have you noticed, half the shops here have women's names? Myrtle's, Lorraine's, Elizabeth Ann, Janet's.'

'Is that significant?' Warlow asked.

'Refreshing. Change from Bob the Builder, or Williams and sons. I may have asked you this, but the wells thing, you know, Llanwrtyd Wells, Builth Wells.'

'Blame the Victorians. They were all for taking the waters once the railways were built and it didn't mean three days by pony and trap to get here for the well-heeled city dweller. Now people come here to escape city dwelling. For long walks in the hills.'

'And look where that can get you,' Jess muttered. She watched as the street slid by and they headed south again before stifling a yawn.

'Tired?' Warlow asked.

'All this fresh air. I'm sure it isn't good for you.'

'Never mind. Text Rhys and tell him we're on the way, and we will expect refreshments.'

'Done. What did you make of Lipton?'

'He's a man who's just lost a colleague under the worst kind of circumstance.'

'You don't think he might be involved?'

'The double bluff? Murder her in the worst possible way, then pretend to find the body? No. Too convoluted by half. Why? Is he on your radar?' Warlow asked.

'No. But I keep seeing that poor girl crawling across the grass. Whoever shot her will have seen it, too. Probably enjoyed watching it. This greatly increases my level of suspicion for anyone within a ten-mile radius.' Warlow took a breath. 'Gil on the way?'

'Ten miles behind us.'

'Good. I hope Rhys has put a lot of water in that kettle.'

———

A FEW MILES to the north, Gil and Gina were driving through the small hamlet of Beulah.

Gina peered out of the window as they drove past the one pub and the one shop in the one garage and felt the need to comment. 'I always get the impression Beulah should be somewhere in the Deep South of the USA, from the name.'

'There is one.'

'Really?' Gina asked.

'There is also another in Ceredigion. The Methodists were up here, and probably in Georgia, where your Deep South Beulah is situated. Someone told me it means heaven.'

'It's astonishing to realise the importance of religion to the people here.'

'Long time ago, mind. Two centuries. The times, they are a changing. Or, the answer, *mon ami*, is wafting on the breeze, as Mr Zimmerman once said.'

'Who?' Gina asked.

'Bob Dylan.'

'Oh, I've heard of him.'

'Thank God for that. For a moment there, I thought I'd slipped through an inter-dimensional crack into another universe. Anyhoo, that's why I teach the girls – my grand-daughters – to always shut the toilet door so that no one will guess what they've eaten the day before.'

'You've lost me, sarge,' Gina said.

'Because the answer, Gina, is often blowing in the wind.'

'Ah, right, got you.' Gina's smile was less than effusive.

'You realise my clumsy attempts at comedy, albeit toilet humour, are designed to try to distract you from the horror that you've witnessed today.'

'I do.' Gina's smile never quite managed to peel her lips back far enough to show any teeth. 'Rhys does the same. He always jokes when he sees that I'm a bit down, bless him. But when they flipped that poor man over today … I … I almost lost it.'

Gil nodded. 'You can never unsee that, sorry. But it fades. Right now, it's all a bit too fresh. However, I have found that half an hour of *Frozen* with several under-eights dressed as princesses belting out the chorus of *Let it Go*, with me conducting, banishes most things of an unpleasant nature.'

Gina's swallowed-a-fly expression changed to momentary confusion. All she could do was nod quickly. But gradually, as her brain assimilated Gil's words, a smile flickered and broad-ened into a grin. 'I'd like to see the video.'

'Careful what you wish for. I think I have Elsa on a playlist in the vehicle. But there is one other thing that helps get you through this,' Gil added.

'Tea?'

'Tea goes without saying. No. It's a promise to yourself that you will find the miserable toahb that did this and make sure they pay. That they get their freedom taken away. Their hopes and wishes. Because that's what justice is all about. We don't kill people anymore in the name of retribution, but we take their lives in other ways. Some people think it's cruel. But they are usually people who never see what we have to see.'

'Toahb?'

'Turd of a human being.'

'I'm going to write that down, sarge.'

'You do that, Detective Constable Mellings. And under-line the bloody thing in red. Tidy.'

———

DETECTIVE CONSTABLE RHYS HARRIES had both the Gallery, showing early crime scene photos that Povey and Tannard had sent through, and the Job Centre, the board they used for posting actions and other important bits of paper, including, in this instance, victim profiles, updated.

He'd drawn a vertical line down the Gallery and, at the top of this hived-off area, he'd written THE BOWMAN – March 2001. Beneath that were two images of the victims. Not from the crime scene this time, but snaps offered up by the families to be used by the press in their reporting twenty-odd years ago. Two smiling faces, which is how the families had wanted to remember them by.

Rhys took his responsibilities seriously, and Catrin, in the weeks before her maternity leave, had schooled him in the dark art of arranging the boards. The key, always, was to try and illustrate patterns.

There'd be obvious links from the outset. Groupings, as in victims or family relationships. But eventually, he'd be able to draw a line linking names, or ideas, which might not appear obvious to begin with, but would eventually lead to better understanding or the small triggers that could some-times lead to unlocking the puzzle. A puzzle often constructed of lies, or withheld information, or malevolence.

He'd always appreciated Catrin's approach to this aspect of any enquiry. He'd also been a willing pupil. This case would be the first test of how well he'd listened.

Warlow and Jess arrived first, Gil and Gina eight minutes later. He'd timed the tea making such that he had a tray ready as the last of the team entered the Incident Room. And though he did his utmost to be professional, he couldn't help but notice Gina's slightly haunted look as he handed around the mugs.

Everyone else raided the array of biscuits laid out on a plate, this time including some Jammie Dodgers Rhys had been unable to resist as a special offer in the garage he'd filled up in that morning. There because their sell-by date was imminent. However, as he'd taken them to the counter to pay, Rhys knew that there was little danger of that date being breached. Not with this team. Everyone indulged in a biscuit except for Gina.

There was no ignoring her drawn expression. As the others attacked the baked goods, Rhys stood with his back to them, in front of a seated DC Mellings.

'How was it?'

'Two dead,' she replied.

'Did you stay for the HOP?'

Gina nodded.

Rhys put her tea down on the desk. She made no effort to reach for it.

'It was … horrible. That poor man.'

'Dr Gerald Nash.' Rhys filled in the blanks.

'When they turned him over, and I saw his face … His eyes were open. The grass had made an impression on his skin and on the corneas—'

But she got no further as Warlow called things to order.

'It's getting late, I realise that, but I think it would be useful to pool our findings while everything is still fresh.' He glanced up at the boards. 'I see you've been busy, Rhys.'

'I've posted up what Tannard and Povey sent through.'

'Any news from the HOP about postmortems?'

'He's going to do them both tomorrow, sir. Early start is what I've heard.'

'Earlier for us, then,' Warlow muttered. He glanced over at Gina. 'We will need to get you to a PM, but I'm going to spare you this time, you'll be delighted to know. We're going to need our resident expert.' He nodded towards Rhys.

It did not go unnoticed by him nor the rest of the team that Warlow had not used the words "resident ghoul" which had entered into the team lexicon given Rhys's enthusiasm for want of a better word, for all things pathological. The fact was that he was skilled at listening and at interpreting at a slice and dice.

Some, Gil especially, twisted that into morbid curiosity. However, it remained true that Rhys had never been discouraged by the most gruesome of findings. He'd become their man in the mortuary.

'Rhys and I will go up to Cardiff tomorrow. That will leave Gil running the office and Gina and Jess to run down the victim profiles.'

Everyone nodded at that.

'Let's quickly run through what we've learnt this evening.' He threw Gina another glance. 'It might be difficult, but I am going to ask you to regurgitate the findings up at Elan Valley. Talking it through will help, believe me.'

He glanced at her mug. 'Have you drunk your tea?'

'No, sir.'

'Eaten a Jammie Dodger?'

'No, sir.'

'Both things need to be done. Sugar helps. It may be bad for you, but the time for worrying about all that will be tomorrow. Now I need you *compos mentis* and functioning.'

'And there is nothing better than a shortcake with a raspberry-flavoured jam filling to get those synapses firing.' Gil gave Rhys a thumbs up. 'Stroke of genius there, sergeant.'

'Special offer in the White Mill garage,' Rhys said.

'What's this, then, Rhys? Bringing in treats for no reason?' Gil asked, eyeing the box with interest.

'Don't spoil the magic,' Jess said.

But Warlow had one eye on the younger officer, noticing the way he shuffled his feet.

'We haven't forgotten your birthday, have we?' He glanced over at Gina who managed to hide most of her face behind a mug.

Gil, never one to beat around the bush, cut to the chase. 'Come on, out with it. You're practically bursting.'

Unable to contain himself any longer, Rhys blurted out, 'Alright, alright. I ... I passed my step two sergeant's exam.'

The office erupted in congratulations.

Jess, first out of her seat, gave him a hug.

Warlow held out a hand and grinned, genuinely pleased. 'Well done, Rhys, no small feat.'

'There's no denying that,' Gil said. 'What are you, size thirteen?'

Gina looked on, oddly subdued. 'I told him he'd have to tell you.'

Gil clapped him on the back. 'Congratulations! I know you've been hitting the books.' Gil reached for a biscuit, a smile playing on his lips. 'This calls for a proper celebration. Once this case is over.'

Rhys laughed, clearly relieved by his colleagues' reaction.

Gina looked on, her expression betraying her confusion.

'You okay, Gina?' Jess asked.

'Yes, ma'am. It's just ... I mean, you're all being so normal and ... making jokes ... I mean ... It's not normal, though.'

'It's a coping mechanism, Gina,' Jess said.

She nodded, unconvinced.

Warlow walked over and sat next to her. 'Gina, in a minute, once you've finished your tea ... and that's an order, by the way ...'

Reluctantly, Gina picked it up and sipped.

' ... In a minute,' Warlow continued, 'we will discuss the details of the worst of all crimes any human being can commit. That's our job. Previously, you, as a Family Liaison Officer, will have been surrounded by the fallout and the aftermath. It may seem like there's little or no room for humour there. But here, we have to take these brief moments of lightness and hold on to them, otherwise we'd all go stark-raving mad. It's not disrespectful. It's not in any way flippant. There'll be no jokes about the dead, the victims, or the monsters. Don't forget, we have to build psychological armour. A way of letting this stuff not penetrate too deeply into our heads. If we didn't, we'd get no sleep. Tea and biscuits are the nuts and bolts of that armour. So are Gil's puns, Jess's occasional use of mithering for my procrastinations, Rhys's addiction to crisps, and my perfect nature.'

'Curmudgeonly nature,' Jess said from behind her mug.

For the first time since entering the Incident Room, Gina smiled. As brief as the flutter of a nesting bird's wing. But a smile, nonetheless.

'Now, drink your tea and eat a biscuit. Then put on your armour, stand up and tell us what you and Gil found up at the reservoir.'

CHAPTER SEVEN

GINA STOOD AT HER DESK, well, Catrin Richards's desk, but Gina's for the foreseeable while the erstwhile team member Sergeant Richards and her traffic officer husband, Craig, got to grips with a three-and-a-bit-month-old baby. Notebook in hand, Gina went over what they'd found on the path to the Gamriw.

'The victim is sixty-six-year-old Gerald Nash, a retired GP from Pershore, near Evesham. He'd driven over this morning, having left his wife in Worcester on a shopping trip with their daughter. This was not an unusual thing for him to do since he retired three years ago.'

'You got that information from the officers who spoke to his wife?' Jess asked.

'Yes, ma'am.' Gina paused to see if there were any more questions at that point. None came. 'From what Povey and the HOP could work out, Mr Nash was shot with a crossbow bolt at relatively close range, from behind. The bolt remained in place and had penetrated to a depth of some six to eight inches through the rear of the chest wall. Dr Bryers said he'd haemorrhaged and probably lost a great deal of blood internally as well as externally.'

'Timeline?'

'He left Pershore at eight, via Worcester. His wife said he

dropped her off at half-eight. Assume two hours' travel time. That would take it to ten-thirty. We've traced his car. He parked in the Dol Mynach parking area.'

'Show us,' Warlow said.

Gina walked to the posted-up area map and pointed to a spot at the very bottom of the long, thin arm of the reservoir complex at its southern tip.

'He could have crossed the river here, sir, and set off east towards y Gamriw.'

'The Creightons approached from the north.' Warlow pointed with his finger. 'Let's say he set off at eleven. How long would it have taken him?'

'I'm not sure, sir,' Gina said, looking uncomfortable.

'Of course, you're not. But you will find out.'

Gina nodded, realising that this was not a rebuke, but an action that needed to be taken.

'Thank you, Gina.'

'Tomorrow, we'll see if we can set up a meeting with Gerald Nash's widow,' Jess said. 'And get more information on the walk.'

Gina began writing it down, but Rhys had already posted the action on the board. He smiled and pointed at it.

'Jess?' Warlow let her take the lead.

'As an addendum to Gina's report, we interviewed the Creightons, the couple, and their dog, who found Nash. They check out as weekend walkers who cadged an extra day to make this a long weekend. Simon Creighton's grandfather had something to do with designing a bouncing bomb that they mocked up at the reservoir as a test run before being used against the Nazis.'

Rhys perked up. 'Amazing, ma'am. Barnes Wallis and the Dam Busters.'

'The Creightons were heading towards—' Jess's turn to check her notes. '—Y Gamriw.' Her pronunciation came out as "Gamroo".

'Not bad,' Gil said with half a smile.

'They found Gerald already dead. Simon Creighton checked for a pulse. The HOP will probably give us more.'

'Hopefully,' Gil said.

'The Creightons reported not seeing any other walkers during their time on the hills. But we may have to appeal for witnesses,' Jess added.

Warlow stood and pointed to the image of Kirsty Stuart, a head shot taken from the Redoubt Energy website.

'Kirsty Stuart. Thirty-six years old. Not married, but cohabiting. No children. Surveying the area for a possible wind farm development. She'd been further north than where she was found and began her walk early, at around eight-forty, according to her colleague who'd driven her up to Abergwesyn Common using a company vehicle via a farm track. From there, the colleague assumes she would have headed north, and that she was on the way back when the attack took place.'

Warlow pointed to a second point on the map, already marked with a red-topped pushpin. 'In her case, the arrow penetrated her body and exited intact. The bolt, found by Sergeant Thomas from Rural Crimes, may or may not have been left deliberately. Tomo'd gone cross-country to where she'd been found from the Elan Valley Visitor Centre. It looks as if Kirsty did not die immediately but crawled several yards before collapsing. The bolt sat some fifteen yards beyond where she'd crawled from. We'll understand more about how she died after the postmortem. But, so far, preliminary reports from Povey's team indicate the bolt used was identical in both instances. Eighteen inches long, orange and pink flights, a steel trefoil arrowhead.'

Rhys had a photo of the bolt that had exited.

'We'll need to do a more formal interview.' Warlow turned to look at the images of Kirsty Stuart's body. Rhys had posted the crime scene photo on the Gallery already.

'Obviously, we'll need to find out where this came from, who made it, who bought it, the kind of weapon that fired it.' Warlow pondered his words and then sipped his tea before continuing, 'As soon as Gil and I heard the MO here, we immediately considered the possibility that this might be linked to a cold case. One I was aware of because it gained significant attention when it occurred. Gil?'

'March 2001,' Gil began. 'It says something about the state of our civilisation that not everyone in this room can recall the details of this case. And that's accounting for age, too. Because there have been so many other horror shows in between. And that despite a TV special about eight years ago. Bloody hell, Rhys, you would have still been in short trousers.'

'Still am on weekends, sarge,' Rhys said. On seeing Gil's questioning tilt of the head, he quickly qualified that with, 'On the rugby field, I mean, not pretending to be a schoolboy or … anything.'

Gina shook her head slowly.

'Nicely put away there,' Gil said. 'As a DC based out of Aberystwyth, I got involved a bit. DCI Warlow, were you a sergeant then?'

Warlow nodded. 'With South Wales Police. Not long after leaving London. Swansea based.'

'You've been around, sir,' Rhys said.

'Similar pattern. Both victims lone walkers. One an author who wrote books about bagging hills by the name of Heather Messenger. Shot and killed at Abergwesyn. Bit of a loner, so no one knew she'd gone missing for a couple of days. The second victim, a man by the name of Coombs, was also someone who enjoyed wild camping. These days, no doubt, he'd have been vlogging his adventures. But, back then, YouTube was a more fat-shaming insult than a social media channel. Found dead after not checking in with his wife or girlfriend. Spotted by a search party in a gulley between the Elan Valley reservoir and the Drygarn Fawr cairn.'

'We walked that last year for a charity gig,' Rhys said with a glance at Gina, who nodded in response.

Warlow noted with satisfaction that the business of investigation was slowly overcoming the numbing horror of the subject.

'Goes without saying that it triggered massive press interest,' he continued, 'and Dyfed Powys began probably the biggest and most extensive investigation it had ever been involved in up to that point.'

'Were you involved, Gil?' Jess asked.

'Only peripherally. Various tips suggested certain vehicles had been seen in the area. I helped in chasing these down. Nothing ever came of it.'

'From what I remember, forensic evidence was sparse,' Warlow took up the narrative.

'Both victims were killed within a few hours of each other. No witnesses. The bodies had not been hidden but left to be found, one by rescuers, one by a farmer.'

'But both shot with crossbow bolts,' Gil said. 'We recovered one. Made in France. The investigators could not establish how it came to be in this country. Lyons-based manufacturers with no records of sales of that bolt to the UK.'

'What about crossbow ownership? Don't you need a licence?' Gina asked.

'You do not. You can legally own a crossbow and use it in areas designated for its use,' Gil answered. 'That does not mean in your own back garden. It was then, and is now, illegal to hunt any animal with a crossbow or bow in the UK. It is also in the EU, but then, the EU is a big place and traditions can sometimes be a hard thing to eradicate.'

'Are we saying that the bolt we found near Kirsty Stuart was the same as in the Bowman killings?' Rhys asked.

'Povey is checking on that detail. Even if it isn't, there are similarities between the cases,' Gil said.

'Are we thinking it's the same person?' Rhys asked.

'As I say, you can't ignore the similarities.'

'The obvious next question is, who was in charge of the Bowman investigation?' Jess asked.

Gil was ready with the answer. 'That was Superintendent Tim Leach. And he ran that with DI Pauline Garston. Leach was mid-fifties then. He retired not long after. But Pauline progressed to greater things. Ended up being Deputy Chief Constable of North Wales Police.'

'I reckon we might have to pick their brains. But first things first,' Jess said.

'Agreed,' Warlow said. 'We need the case files for the Bowman. And I think we might need a bit more room.'

'Why is that, sir?' Gina asked.

'There will be a pile of evidence somewhere. An enormous pile for an investigation of that size. We'll need room to sort it all out. Let me speak to the Buccaneer about that. In the meantime, we stick to the plan. Gil, find out where Tim Leach and Pauline Garston are now. I need to make a quick call.'

———

WARLOW MADE that call in the SIO cupboard. Superintendent Sion Buchannan was his line manager. The man responsible for enticing him back after a premature retirement. The man who acted as something of a foil between the higher ups and people on the coal face, like Warlow and his team.

'Sion, feet up in front of Eastenders, are you?'

'Just in after another budget meeting. So, not Eastenders, but almost as much of a bloody soap opera.'

'We've just had a team meeting after being up in the wilds most of the afternoon.'

'And?'

'Two dead. Possibly by the same hand.'

Buchannan's silence told Warlow that he'd just put a tin hat on what sounded like a very imperfect day. 'How?'

'Are you sitting down?'

'That's never a good question at the best of times. Coming from you, it puts me into a cold sweat and means put on your seat belt. Come on, then.'

Warlow saw no point in pulling his punches. 'Cause of death is likely a crossbow bolt. One was left in the body and one passed through the other victim, found nearby.'

'Oh, God.' Buchannan breathed out the words. They emerged as almost an appeal to an uncaring deity.

'Postmortems on both tomorrow. No witnesses. Significant

enough similarities to the Bowman to merit a chat with the SIOs.'

'I didn't know Tim Leach well, but I know Pauline pretty well.'

'Then maybe you're the man to break the ice. I think I'd like to talk to her if not both of them.'

'Of course.'

'And then there's a little matter of the case files.'

'You are going to need a removal van.'

'I was thinking where best to move the removals to. We don't have room here.'

'Right. Let me mull that one over.' Buchannan paused before going on, 'I was going to try to go without a drink tonight, but you've put paid to that. A half inch of Penderyn is called for and smartish.'

'I didn't know you were a Welsh Whisky man like Gil?'

'The kids got me the Patagonia blend for a birthday. Halfway through it already. I'll have an answer to the files problem by the morning.'

'I'll be on the way to Cardiff with Rhys Harries.'

'Your man in the morgue?'

'The very same. Who, by the way, just passed his step two NPPF exam.'

'Brilliant.'

'You already know he's acting sergeant on this one. To cover Catrin and only for the duration of the case. It'll look good on his work-based assessment and scenario presentation.'

'Just for the case, right?'

'Yes, I know there are others in the wings, and I don't want an apple cart upset.'

'No, it's a done deed. And try and get some sleep. You ought to try a snifter before bed.'

Warlow smiled. 'You are my favourite kind of doctor, Sion, you know that? I'll bear that advice in mind.'

CHAPTER EIGHT

BOTH GINA and Rhys were at the breakfast table at 6.30am. Warlow was picking Rhys up at seven, and he was showered and dressed for the day. Gina was still in a dressing gown, hair tousled, looking a little the worse for wear.

On the kitchen table, two Weetabix floated in a small lake of milk in a bowl. Two rounds of toast had knobs of rich yellow butter slowly melting on their surface on a plate nearby.

Gina, however, had nothing but a cup of tea in front of her.

'Did you sleep at all?' Rhys asked.

'Took me ages to get off. I stopped looking at the clock after half one.'

'It gets easier,' Rhys said.

'I don't know how you do it.' Gina glanced down at the food. 'I can't face anything this morning.'

'Thing is, I might not eat again now until lunchtime.'

'Like a normal person, you mean?'

'What I mean is that having a low blood sugar in a post-mortem is not a good idea. Gil said he's seen more than one poor sod faint as they were leaning over a body to fall head-first into someone's intestines.' He levered another table-spoon's worth of breakfast cereal into his mouth.

Gina squeezed her eyes shut. 'I keep seeing Gerald Nash's dead face.'

Rhys put down his spoon, swallowed his food, got up from his stool and came around the table to give Gina a hug.

'You smell nice,' she said.

'You feel nice.'

She laughed gently.

'Thing is, Geen, if you didn't feel like you do, there'd be something wrong with you. And that's important.'

'Is this Gil again?'

'No, this is the Wolf. He told me this not long after I'd started. Some people we deal with feel nothing. And that's what separates us from them. He says you should take that disgust and that horror and turn it into something hard and cold. It's okay to be angry. It's better to be determined. But a bit of both works best. No one else needs to see the anger. You keep that inside.'

Gina didn't need to ask him who he was referring to when he said, "the Wolf." Evan Warlow led the pack she was now a member of.

'So, he doesn't think I'm a complete wuss?'

'You would not be sitting in the Incident Room with the rest of us if he did.'

She pushed him away and put a finger up to the corner of his mouth to wipe a morsel of cereal away. 'Eat your breakfast. I don't want you falling into anyone's intestines this morning.'

'I'll do my best.' Rhys grinned and went back to his food.

Half an hour later, as Gina showered, he was downstairs waiting when Warlow pulled up in the Jeep.

———

Jess dropped Cadi, Warlow's black Labrador, with the Dawes, who looked after her when Jess and Warlow were at work, and had done ever since Warlow had recommenced his career. They were dog people, with a Lab of their own. Cadi simply jumped out of the car and straight into the house to greet Bouncer. Most often, the door was already open with one of the Dawes waiting to greet the dog and wave at whoever was driving the car.

It had panned out that way this morning, and Jess had gone only a couple of miles when she took a call from one of the Uniforms working in the Incident Room to tell her that Gerald Nash's daughter was on the line and would it be okay to give out Jess's work phone number. She said it was.

Five minutes later, it rang.

'Hello?'

'This is Detective Inspector Jess Allanby. Who am I speaking with?'

'I'm Vicky Statham. That's my married name. I was Vicky Nash. Gerald Nash is my father.'

No "was" yet. Too soon for that, thought Jess.

'Mrs Statham. I'm sorry we have to speak under such awful circumstances. I am on the way in to work, and I intended to give you and your mother a ring this morning.'

'Thank you. I'm a teacher, but I'm not working today. I'm bringing Mum across. I'm ringing to find out what you can tell us.' The strain was clear, but you had to admire this grieving daughter for keeping it together.

'What is it you know already, Mrs Statham?'

'Please, call me Vicky.'

'What have you been told, Vicky?'

'Only that there's been some kind of terrible accident—'

'Right.' Jess pulled in to complete the call.

'She wants to go to where it happened.'

'There will not be much to see. They've moved your father's body up to Cardiff for the postmortem.'

'Yes, I know. But Mum ... she feels she has to do something. We can't go to the postmortem, can we?'

'No.'

'Right, then Mum wants to see for herself.'

'As I say, I can't stop you,' Jess said. 'But where it happened isn't easy access. It's in the middle of the Cambrian Mountains. A good hour's walking from the Visitor Centre—'

'At Elan Valley. That's where we're headed. We're in the car—'

'I can't stop you going there, of course, but it's a fool's errand. There might still be some crime scene vehicles around, but they cannot talk to you.'

'But we can't just sit here.'

'No, I understand. I am on the way into the Incident Room at Carmarthen. Let me see what, if anything, has happened overnight. Then, why don't I meet you halfway? Are you familiar with Hay-on-Wye?'

'I've been to the book festival there. There's a Garden Centre and Farm Shop on the A438 a few miles from Hay on this side of the border. Why don't I meet you there at, say, eleven? It's halfway for you and me.'

'That would be … Thank you. It'll help if I tell Mum someone will speak to us.'

———

HER BRIEF DELAY meant that Jess got in just after Gina that morning, and the Incident Room had filled up with its co-opted extra staff of indexers, researchers, and support staff, including several Uniforms. Because of the lack of forensic evidence, other than the crossbow bolts, and the nature of the crime scene, Warlow had decided not to decamp closer to where the murders happened.

'Any news?' Jess asked Gil.

'I've had Superintendent Buchannan on the phone. DCI Warlow requested more room so that we can get to grips with the Bowman investigation files. He's found us somewhere in Johnstown. An old industrial unit that became a gym for a while but is now empty.'

'I hope it's heated,' Gina said.

'Oh, yes, all mod cons and lots of space. I'll send you both maps. The records are coming over sometime today, and I've got Sandra Griffiths in as a Receiver and Evidence Officer. She'll get desks for us. I'll nip down later and make sure it's all in hand. But you know Sandra … she's a terrier.'

'Good,' Jess said. 'Nothing else?'

'Not yet.'

Jess relayed her phone call with Nash's relatives. 'You and I have another road trip, I'm afraid, Gina. But it's all part and parcel of today's actions. And the relatives aren't yet aware that this is a murder investigation.'

'Why not, ma'am?' Gina asked.

'When does an accident become suspicious circumstances before leapfrogging into murder? That has to be done face to face, Gina. And before any official statement to the press. I'm also going to ring Kirsty Stuart's partner. If she's in Bristol, it would make sense for Evan and Rhys to pop over there since they are already in Cardiff.'

'Good idea,' Gil said. 'Bryers, the pathologist, is splitting the autopsies into morning and afternoon.'

'So, the dynamic duo should have some time in between. In fact, I'll make that call now.' Jess made another call to Amanda Beech, Kirsty Stuart's partner, and followed it up with one to Rhys.

'Okay,' she said when she'd finished. 'They're going to meet her in the Magor services. Halfway between Cardiff and Bristol. In between the PMs.'

Gina made a face. 'I forgot there were two. Postmortems, I mean. They can't do them at the same time, obviously. But one is bad enough.'

Gil picked up on her distaste. 'It isn't all that bad. Especially if you suck a polo mint.'

'I'm not sure I'd want to eat anything before or after. I'm not sure I could stomach it.' She was looking for reassurance. Unfortunately, she'd asked Gil.

'That, DC Mellings, remains to be seen.'

Gina stared, confused. 'Does it? Oh, remains, right, got it.'

Her smile, when it came, looked paper thin.

'Is that from a Christmas cracker?' Jess asked, thrusting her jaw to one side.

'No, this one is from a Christmas cracker. What is the commonest cause of death, at autopsy, of a duck?'

No one answered.

'Quack overdose. And don't blame me for that one. Serves the Lady Anwen right for buying crackers in March when they're cheap and obviously last year's rejects. I'm not going to begin to tell you how much fun I didn't have explaining that one to my granddaughter who would not let it go. At least she now knows another use for baking powder if it ever comes up in class.'

Still, no one so much as smiled. Not even the secretaries.

'Come on, work with me here. Rhys laughed when I told him,' Gil grumbled.

'Rhys laughs at dogs in Halloween costumes with pretend arms,' Gina said.

'A man with impeccable taste. I rest my case.'

Gina stared at the Gallery. When she spoke, it was to address Jess. 'I was thinking, ma'am, on the way in. Shouldn't we alert the public? I mean, it's likely that whoever did this is the same person. And they've killed two people. Is it safe to let people wander around?'

'There is a public safety consideration, and I know that Sion Buchannan is meeting with the Chief Super and the Assistant Chief Constable this morning. That's why we need to speak to the relatives. I suspect a press conference will be called at some point today. I doubt they can shut a mountain, but I suspect they'll caution against walking alone.'

'I've seen what news like that does to a family,' Gina murmured.

'You have. More than once. And it never gets easier. But talking to the relatives is essential in this early phase. And not simply for common courtesy. We will be there to gather intelligence. The first seventy-two hours yield the most useful information nine times out of ten. And the clock is ticking.'

'Yes, ma'am.'

CHAPTER NINE

WARLOW HAD BECOME USED to a hushed, almost ecclesiastic atmosphere in the pathology autopsy suite at the University of Wales hospital in Cardiff. So, hearing Fleetwood Mac coming out of the speakers came as something of a surprise both to him and to Rhys, who, gowned up and masked, had exchanged a few looks with the DCI already.

Tiernon, who, through fate, seemed to be the HOP most often assigned to the cases Warlow and team had investigated, liked quiet. Sengupta sometimes had music on, but very muted and usually sober and classical. So, having something even mildly upbeat was a major departure. Which, along with Bryers being open and chatty as opposed to dour and self-opinionated, was making today a fairly memorable event.

But even that could not detract from the horrors that Bryers had in store for them.

On the stainless-steel table lay Kirsty Stuart, naked in death, her inanimate flesh split open by Bryers's careful hand.

'Full confession, I have not seen many crossbow injuries, though they are well documented in the literature. Quite a few from Europe. Contrast that with gunshots, where one only has to look across the pond for a wealth of information. But here we are today and, of course with the added advantage of knowing the weapon used.'

The long cut in the thorax had already been made and the chest wall opened. Bryers used some forceps to illustrate his findings.

'The entry wound is star-shaped, consistent with a three-bladed arrowhead, seven centimetres in from the right axilla. As you can see, I've used a wire marker to demonstrate its passage. It penetrates the fifth intercostal space, notching the fifth rib. It continues a slightly downward trajectory and enters the sixth intercostal space, again notching the sixth rib. In between, it traverses the middle and part of the lower lobe of the right lung before exiting the back with an identical stellate wound. Gentlemen?'

Two of Bryers's attendants came forward and tilted Kirsty Stuart onto her side to reveal the wound and Bryers's wire exiting her back.

'Total length of the tract is 22.5cm.'

'These wounds are consistent with the broad head of the bolts found?' Warlow asked.

'Absolutely. These bolts have immense penetration capacity, and the arrowhead splits tissue. It's noiseless. I'm no expert, but I did a little reading last night, knowing that this was in front of me this morning. Know much about the crossbow, DC Harries?'

Warlow allowed himself a smile. Bryers had picked up on how interested Rhys was.

'Medieval weapon. Handheld.'

'Correct. But began life as a belly bow with the Greeks and who knows when with the Chinese. Of course, over here, we had the Welsh longbow, which was quicker to fire. But the crossbow didn't need strength like the longbow, so it remained popular in Europe because it could penetrate armour. Hand cranking the string, though, made it slow to load.'

'The bolt killed Kirsty Stuart, how?' Warlow asked.

'Haemopneumothorax. I aspirated 1.35 litres of blood from the chest cavity. She bled out internally. Not immediately.'

'That's how she crawled?' Rhys asked.

'A short distance, yes.'

'No other evidence of any violence?'

'No. Just the one strike from the bolt. That is enough to have disrupted vessels and caused the exsanguination as described.'

They'd been there an hour by now, and Warlow made his excuses with a promise they'd be back at one thirty for Gerald Nash. On the way back to where Warlow had parked the car, having long since learned that finding a spot on the hospital site was a nonstarter, Rhys looked pensive.

'Thoughts?'

'Pretty horrible way to die, sir. That's my thought. Drowning in your own blood. But what's worse is knowing that the killer would have watched it all happen. Know it was happening. That's an unusual degree of cruelty.'

'Malice aforethought,' Warlow said. 'I see nothing other than premeditation here. If we ever, for one minute, considered that some idiot wanted to shoot a crossbow out in the wilds and this poor woman got in the way of it, it would be insane to think it could happen twice. There can only be one motive here.'

'And what's that, sir?'

'Maliciousness. A killer's way of thinking, Rhys. That's going to be your homework.'

Rhys grimaced. 'I'd rather do an essay on flatulence as a means of crowd control, sir.'

'Ever looked up the phrase *non sequitur*, Rhys?'

'Is that Edward Scissorhand's Welsh sister, sir?'

Warlow counted to ten. 'I'll ignore that last remark, but as for the flatulence, please tell me that is a joke essay title. You've never had to do anything like that, have you?'

'Which bit, sir? Flatulence, or using it as crowd control.'

'I am well aware you've done the former. I've spent too long in the confined space of a vehicle not to have witnessed your … troubles in that regard.'

Rhys grinned. 'If you think about it, sir, could be a soft launch, in terms of crowd control. It works in a lift, sir. I've proved that to myself. And I mean, no one moves towards it, ever. Worth trying before the water cannon.'

'And you've put this on paper, have you?'

'No, sir.' Rhys grinned. 'But Sergeant Jones mentioned it in passing—'

'Wind?'

'Very good, sir.'

'I should have known Gil would not be far away if a topic like that crops up in conversation. Right. Forget I asked. We're heading to the services at Magor. Time to let your mind turn towards mid-morning coffee.'

'And a snack, sir?'

'Personally, I don't think my appetite is up to anything at the moment. But of course, knock yourself out, Rhys. And by that, I mean the American idiom pertaining to indulgence, not self-induced unconsciousness.'

———

The Garden Centre and Farm Shop had been easy to find. At 11am on a Tuesday morning in March, parking had not been difficult either. The farm food produce sat at one end, the plants at the other. In between, once passed the wines, it became a mishmash of random items. Soft toys, jostled with horse-riding equipment, fence paint, candles and, bizarrely, a whole section of wind chimes. 'Who are we looking for?' Gina asked as they made their way through the shop along a zigzag path, which meant running a gauntlet through shelves stacked with a cornucopia of goods.

'No idea,' Jess said. 'But my guess is that they're already here and will know us.'

She was right. As they entered the seating area, hived off from the large industrial space of the shop proper by four-foot-high trellis and faux ivy, an attractive young woman in her thirties stood up. She wore a camel coat and raised her hand speculatively.

Jess reciprocated and headed for the table.

An older version of the same woman did not get up from the seat she was sitting in.

'Mrs Statham? Mrs Nash?' Jess asked.

The younger woman stayed on her feet and nodded. 'You must be DI Allanby?'

'The same. This is DC Gina Mellings.'

Vicky Statham had chestnut hair and, despite the circumstances, a composed demeanour. But Jess wondered how thick that veneer was, and a puffiness around her darting dark eyes hinted at the psychological turmoil of being a murder victim's daughter.

'I'm Vicky, by the way.'

The older woman, still sitting, looked up at the two officers with a lost expression and a trembling lower lip. Her red eyes spoke of the tears that had already flowed that morning.

'This is my mother, Suzanne Nash.'

Gina immediately went to put a hand on Mrs Nash's arm. 'I'm so sorry about what's happened to your husband.'

Mrs Nash nodded and dropped her head at this sympathetic reminder.

'Can I get you some tea?' Vicky asked.

'That's kind of you,' Jess said.

While Vicky Statham went to the counter, Jess pulled out a seat and sat. 'Thank you for coming all this way, Mrs Nash.'

Suzanne Nash nodded. 'I wanted to see. I need to see where it happened.'

Jess did not reiterate her warning of earlier. It would make no difference for now.

Vicki Statham returned. 'They said they'd bring it.'

She sat, as did Gina, still with one hand on Suzanne Nash's arm.

'It's hard, isn't it?' Gina said.

Vicky nodded. 'Please, can you tell us anything at all?'

Jess took a breath. 'This will not be easy to hear.'

Vicky reached for her mother's hand and held it.

'Gerald died because he was shot.'

'What?' Vicky whispered, the disbelief causing the lower lip of her open mouth to wobble uncontrollably.

Next to her, Mrs Nash simply mumbled, 'Oh God. Oh God.'

Gina inched her chair closer and held on to Mrs Nash's arm firmly.

'How?' Vicky asked.

'He was shot with a crossbow, Vicky.'

'An accident?'

Jess felt as if she was on the first curve of a Helter Skelter and rapidly accelerating downwards.

'There will be a press release later today. There is a great deal of police activity on the hill where Gerald was found. People speculate. We consider it best to tell the press about findings, within limits, to avoid such speculation. And in this instance, we will be appealing for witnesses.'

'Why?' Vicky picked up on that. 'If it was an accident?'

Jess felt another curve on the slippery slope approaching. 'Your father was not the only one shot yesterday. Someone else died in a different place, but in the same manner. With a crossbow.'

Suzanne Nash seemed to babble, making noises with no discernible words inside them.

Jess heard her own breath stutter as she let it out. 'I am so sorry to have to tell you all this.'

'I don't know … what … what …' Suzanne mumbled.

Vicky shifted her attention to her mother. 'Mum, do you want to go back to the car?'

Whatever it was that Suzanne Nash was witnessing, it was no longer the farm shop. All she did was stare about vacantly.

'Give her a minute,' Gina said to Vicky. 'She's in shock.'

The café wasn't full. But the emotion on display, raw and visceral, was drawing looks.

Jess made a decision. She walked to the counter and spoke to an older member of staff there. Two minutes later, an anxious, but efficient-looking man with thinning hair and a badge on his polo shirt, appeared. He introduced himself as Ruben, deputy manager.

'Are you the police officer?'

Jess pulled her warrant card out on its lanyard from where she'd tucked it away.

'You can use my office,' Ruben said. 'Stay there as long as you need to. It's just behind the café.'

He led the way.

Gina had her arm looped in Suzanne Nash's on one side and Vicky had the other. The older lady was puffing, face red, her eyes glassy.

Gina kept talking to her, reassuring her, explaining.

The office was small. A desk with a computer, certificates on the wall pertaining to cleanliness and hygiene, and the odd award.

Suzanne Nash was the first to sit, followed by her daughter, and then the officers.

'There will not be a good time to ask these questions. But better here than in the café,' Jess said.

Vicky nodded. Her own shock seemed to firm up into an unfocused anger. 'Who would do that? Who would do such a thing?'

'We have no answers yet, Vicky. That's why we're here. Your father was a GP?'

'Yes.'

'Are you aware of anyone who might have wanted to harm him?'

'No,' Suzanne Nash moaned.

Vicky turned to her. 'Mum, DI Allanby is only trying to help.' She turned back. 'My dad had been a GP in the practice for thirty-five years. People loved him.'

'No conflict with any neighbours? Money problems?'

'No, nothing like that,' Mrs Nash answered. She looked better. 'Gerry was no trouble to anyone.'

'And neither of you know anyone by the name of Kirsty Stuart?'

'Is she the one—'

'She is the other victim,' Gina said. 'We don't think your father knew her, either. But we have to ask.'

Ruben brought a pot of tea. They sat. Jess talked, the Nashs listened. But how much of anything they assimilated was anyone's guess.

Half an hour after arriving, Jess and Gina handed over

their business cards, explained they would be in touch and that a Family Liaison Officer from West Midlands would be with them for the duration. They convinced Gerald Nash's widow and daughter to go back home and wait for the contact. Gina helped Suzanne out to their car and then came back to join Jess at the farm shop entrance.

'You, okay?' Jess asked.

'Yes.'

'Now you can see why we take our laughs when we can get them.'

'I can, ma'am. I most certainly can.'

CHAPTER TEN

ON THE WAY back in the car, Gina was pensive. Jess sensed some words of advice were needed.

'There can't be many worse things in the world than telling relatives that a loved one has been murdered. I can only think of one, and that's telling parents it's their child.'

'I've been a FLO in that situation, ma'am.' Gina shook her head at a best forgotten memory. 'But I was dealing with them after they'd been told, not actually doing the telling.'

'Now we do the checking. And much as it seems like a betrayal, it has to be done. Midday, Superintendent Drinkwater makes the statement. At five past, you ring Gerald Nash's old practice manager and double-check his daughter's story. Her impression of him may not be the same as other people's. We need to be sure. We need to determine if he had fans or if he had enemies.'

Gina had a notebook out, scribbling.

'They seem so nice, though,' she said.

'It's called due diligence, Gina. People may hate us for it. But we are not here to be everyone's friend, right?'

'I'll get hold of the practice number now, ma'am.'

'Good. And then, if you like, find out from West Mids who the FLO is. Have a word with them. It'll do no harm to establish a relationship from the start.'

Gina nodded. 'Good idea. I always found it nice to talk things through.'

'You're on the other side of the revolving door here now. But you bring all that to the table, so let's make use of it.'

———

WARLOW AND RHYS, like Gina and Jess, had chosen a public place to meet with Amanda Beech, Kirsty Stuart's partner.

But, less optimistic than Jess, Warlow's experience of breaking the bad news of a suspicious death to a relative in a public place held no appeal. And, despite the chill of the day, he insisted on discussing the case at an outside seating area.

'Apologies for this,' Warlow explained. 'But what we have to say to you demands privacy. This is the best we can get here.'

Beech looked around. They were, apart from some tobacco addicts stomping their feet outside the automatic doors to the building, the only people in a block of six picnic tables.

A constant stream of hurrying people, either with full bladders or empty stomachs, crossed from the car park to the building a few yards away, but they paid the seated group no heed and were not within earshot.

Beech, not a big woman, looked diminished inside her coat with a striped beanie hat on her head, her face pale and makeup-free, contrasting starkly with the strands of dark hair visible under the hat. She eyed Warlow with a vacant glare, good cheeks hollowed out by the journey and the reason for the meeting, jaw clenched in silent pain.

'Your sergeant wouldn't tell me what happened,' she said. The truculent accusation coloured both the statement and suddenly the skin of her cheeks.

Warlow was unfazed. 'And with good reason, Ms Beech. Kirsty died from being shot with a crossbow.'

Beech stared at Warlow as if urging him to repeat the statement. Only this time with different words. Her pale features got paler, and she started to shudder before swinging away and retching. Something vaguely brown spattered on the floor at her feet.

'Shit,' she uttered, before retching again.

The officers waited.

Eventually, Beech looked up, wiping her mouth with the back of her hand. A hand that trembled almost uncontrollably. 'Who did it?'

'We don't know. But she was one of two victims.'

'Jesus Christ. I've been up there with her. It's empty ...'

'Can we get you some water, Amanda?' Warlow asked.

Beech shook her head, though they were more wobbles than shakes.

They went through the same apologetic ritual as Jess had done with the Nashs, explaining that the questions they needed to ask would seem harsh, but that there were good reasons for asking them.

Beech listened with a distant look in her eyes, her brain clearly numb already. But she muttered some answers.

She'd been at work all day yesterday. She and Kirsty were about to go away skiing.

Rhys wrote the answers down. Warlow offered to contact someone on behalf of Beech, to which she replied tremulously, only if they could contact the dead, because that was where her best friend was now.

They sat with her, answering as many questions as they could, knowing every one of those answers was unsatisfactory. After forty minutes, Beech left, looking forlorn and dispirited, but mainly bereft.

Warlow paid for Rhys's lunch inside the service station. They spoke about something non-case related as Rhys ate. Once again, Warlow used loss of appetite at the prospect of another autopsy as his excuse for not letting anything solid past his lips.

But his younger colleague made up for that.

At 1.45, they were back in the postmortem suite, gowned up once again, with Bryers about to cut into Gerald Nash. This time, Pink Floyd came at them through the speakers.

'Ah, gentlemen,' Bryers said, and Warlow suspected he

was grinning behind his mask. 'Immaculate timing once again. As you will see, we have the chest cavity open. An identical entry wound, same stellate pattern and, of course, it matches the found bolt, since we have already removed it. The tip was protruding from the anterior abdomen by three centimetres.'

Warlow walked over to a bowl where the bolt, a little bent, sat bloodied in a small pool of ochre fluid.

'The penetration this time is more vertical, reaching the thorax and abdomen. There is a tear in the pericardium, the diaphragm, and the liver, as well as the small intestine. Not so much of a haemothorax this time, though there is significant blood in the left lung cavity. We've weighed up a 600-gram clot in the left pleural cavity and nearly 450ml of blood in the abdominal cavity. Another 54 grams of clot in the pericardial cavity. The blood in the abdomen was a result of extensive damage to the liver. Once again, exsanguination and haemorrhagic shock would be at the top of my list as a cause of death.'

'Goes to show how lethal these things are.'

Bryers paused in his efforts to look at Rhys and consider the point of his words. 'I am not an arms expert, as mentioned, but it is interesting to note that the penetration of this bolt far exceeds that of a bullet, even though its velocity is nowhere near that of a gunshot projectile.'

'Why is that?' Rhys asked.

'There's likely a good maths or physics answer. Something to do with the mass of the bolt itself and the destructive nature of the hunting tip. It's designed for penetration, I would say.'

'Would it have been quick?' Warlow asked.

'Massive bleeding, but not instant. Far from it. These things were used in siege warfare, don't forget, fired from battlements into the poor beggars besieging the castle. Fish in a barrel, you might say. But designed for suffering and terror.'

Bryers began nodding his head to another track. Something Warlow found vaguely familiar.

'Midlake?' he ventured. 'But sounds older.'

Bryers's head shot up. 'Close enough. I am impressed. This is Harp. Ex Midlake. Few people in this building would have picked that out. You are a man of many talents, Mr Warlow.'

'I had some shoe-gazer mates when such a thing didn't exist. I spent my share of rainy Friday nights as a moody teen in a pal's back parlour with a smuggled in flagon of cider.'

'Lovely picture you paint,' Bryers said.

'The eighties could be full of flares and fun. I know Midlake was much later, but this sounds even earlier. And you say this album is new?'

'It is. Brand new but with a very early eighties vibe.' Bryers turned to the attendants. 'This lot think I'm a throwback. Never heard of Caravan or Barclay James Harvest.'

'You're young for prog and folk rock, aren't you?' Warlow asked.

'My dad is a big fan.'

Rhys coughed into his mask.

With Harp's album, Albion, playing in the background, the two officers hung on while Bryers checked for any other injuries. But, as with Kirsty Stuart, there were none.

In the car, before they started home, Warlow sat punching something into his phone for a few minutes while Rhys waited in silence.

'Right,' Warlow announced, finally looking up. 'I've just found a prog rock playlist. Be prepared for extended guitar and keyboard solos.'

'No, you're alright, sir.'

'I know I am. Consider this all part of your training.' Warlow put the car into gear as Yes's staccato opening to *Yours is No Disgrace* drifted up.

'Now, let the music take you, sergeant, and regale me with your initial thoughts on the fun-filled day we've enjoyed with Dr Bryers.'

Rhys pushed his head back into the car's headrest and exhaled. 'Well, sir …'

Warlow steered him in the right direction. 'What information do we have, and what information are we missing?'

'We know Nash was shot from behind and that the bolt entered from a high point in a downward direction.'

'Good, agreed. And what about Kirsty Stuart?'

'Hit the chest from in front. My guess, he was hiding and hit her at point-blank range since the bolt went through. Otherwise, she would've turned and run.'

'Good point. What about the weaponry?'

'You mean the type of crossbow used?'

Warlow sent over one of his appraising stares. 'I saw you when Bryers was going on about crossbows. You've done some research already, haven't you?'

'A bit, sir.' Rhys nodded. 'I suppose we need to ask an expert, but some of the modern models are a bit like pistols – one-handed grips and that sort of thing. But I don't think they would have enough power to shoot a bolt right through you.'

'There, that's more homework,' Warlow noted approvingly. 'Find someone who knows.'

They drove on in silence. Long enough for the Yes track to fade out. Rhys's pensive demeanour prompted Warlow to ask, 'How is Gina coping?'

Rhys pressed his fingertips together in an attempt at easing the subtle tension between the men. 'I won't lie, sir. She's finding it tough.'

Warlow grunted. 'That's because it is. But she will sort herself out.'

'At least she won't give me any more grief about always making jokes. Now she can see where it all comes from.'

'Yes, our daily routine is a bountiful source of comedy.' Warlow gave a subtle, approving huff. 'At least she's had a day with DI Allanby away from us. Let's hope they come through unscathed.'

'Does that ever happen, though, sir?' The skin around Rhys's eyes tightened. He was concerned. That was clear. 'Getting through it unscathed. I mean it's not like having to wear a stab vest, it's more the effect it has on you up here.' He tapped his head.

'Everything touches you. But it's a burden we all have to

carry so that other people don't have to. Like the sin eaters of old. Now that's a good old-fashioned Welsh reference for you.'

Rhys looked unconvinced.

'Gina will be fine,' Warlow elaborated. 'She's not made of Teflon, but I've seen her at work. Let her find her feet.'

Wishbone Ash's *Blowing Free* started up, and the Gibson Flying V made its presence felt from the opening bars.

'Now, this is what I call a tune.' Warlow grinned and tapped his fingers on the steering wheel in time with the music. 'Very underrated band. Should have been mega. I played some of my best air guitar to *Jailbait*.'

Rhys gave up a polite, if not entirely convincing, smile.

In response, Warlow cranked up the volume and gradually, Rhys's hand began to tap a knee, following the driving beat.

Warlow noted it but kept his smile very much to himself.

CHAPTER ELEVEN

VESPERS AT 4.15PM.

Gil had the usual sustenance on display from the Human Tissue for Transplant box and fresh tea prepared. The team was waiting for Warlow to emerge from the SIO office, where he'd been fielding another call from Tannard.

And while the cat's away …

Gina, whose afternoon had been spent doing background checks on Gerald Nash, eyed the black, blue, and gold packaging that held centre spot on Gil's tray.

'Are those dark chocolate Tunnock's teacakes?'

'Hmm, perhaps. Or are they a mirage stimulated by your craving for marshmallow and biscuit?' Gil said.

'But they're my absolute faves.' Gina threw Gil a look of wonderment. 'How did you know?'

Gil wagged his head jauntily. 'We like to make new team members feel special and at home, Gina. And let's just say a little bird told me.'

He pointedly did not look at Rhys.

Gina did, her eyes crinkling. 'That's the biggest little bird I ever saw.'

'Fair point,' Gil said. 'Gannet springs to mind.'

'You're a fine one to talk,' Rhys countered, emboldened,

no doubt, by his acting-sergeant status. But his bravado faltered at the last, and he added a coy, ' …sarge.'

'Fair point. So, how would you anthropomorphise me and the rest of the gathering?'

Rhys, never one to back down, even when he knew he was walking into a sprung trap, looked around. 'DI Allanby would be a raven.'

'Because her voice is raucous and brash?' Gil uttered this statement knowing full well it would earn him a Jess Allanby stare, and the only way of avoiding being turned into an icicle was to studiously not acknowledge it.

'No,' Rhys replied. 'Because of her, like, dark hair and that … and intelligence.'

'Nice save,' Gil said. 'I think. Gina? And please do not tell us you have a pet name for her, like *my little kookaburra*.'

'As if. I'd never choose anything that lived in a burrow, anyway.'

'Excellent point,' Gil said, po-faced, while Jess hid a chortle behind her mug.

'Gina, I'd say is like a cat. Friendly and cute, but occasionally lethal.'

'Thank you, Sergeant Harries,' Gina said, but the bunching of her eyes told him it was a qualified gratitude.

'Must be all those dead animals you bring in after relieving yourself in the garden of an evening, DC Mellings,' Gil said.

'It could be arranged,' she replied with a sickly smile.

'You …' Rhys looked at Gil. 'A bear. Definitely.'

'The friendly koala, or the angry grizzly?'

'More of a chunky brown.'

'I've told you already, just eat lots of kimchee and ease up on the processed foods,' Gil retorted.

'Bear,' Rhys said, exasperated. 'Chunky brown bear.'

'What about our leader?' Jess joined in.

'That's easy. He's already a wolf. Leader of the pack but likes to be alone.'

'And howl at the moon?' Jess asked.

'What he does in his own time, ma'am, is not for us to question.'

'Upon ·reflection, I have seen him show an unhealthy interest in lampposts.' Gil looked up as the SIO room door opened, and Warlow emerged.

On seeing them all grinning like a flock of Merinos, he asked, 'What?'

'Nothing,' Gil said. 'Only Rhys here claiming that you have the habits of a dog.'

'That's not what I said—'

'I'm sure it isn't.' Warlow sent him a glare. Not so much baleful as bale-overflowing.

'We were comparing our personalities and looks to animals. Gina is a cat, DI Allanby a raven, Gil a bear, and you, sir, a wolf …' The clarification petered out under Warlow's flat gaze.

'Sometimes, for the merest second when I open the door of that room and walk in here, I know exactly how Nurse Ratched felt unlocking the ward in *One Flew Over the Cuckoo's Nest*.'

'Bagsy Jack Nicholson,' Gil said.

'Surely, you would be Chief,' Jess contradicted him. 'Given your predilection for all things First Nations.'

'Right. Enough of the frivolity.' Warlow took a proffered mug and reached for a Tunnock's teacake. 'Hmm, dark chocolate. Glad to note that someone is taking this job seriously.'

He turned to Gina. 'I don't want you to get the wrong impression. We are all dedicated professionals. Once I give the nod, we'll catch-up on what we've all learned. But, as mentioned earlier, some sugar in the blood helps.'

'Want me to go first, sir?' Gina asked.

'No, we'll let Rhys show us … howwww.' He held the last note of the word in a passable, if muted, impression of a wolf's howl.

No one laughed, but he got acknowledging smiles from all.

As SUGGESTED, Rhys kicked off with a rundown of Bryers's findings at postmortem. He embellished nothing. The plain facts were horrific enough.

Gil was able to corroborate Beech's assertions that she was at work, though, since she worked from home, it had taken a little time corroborating via a supervisor at the tech firm that paid her.

In the same vein, Jess outlined the meeting with Gerald Nash's widow and daughter before Gina told them what happened when she contacted the practice manager at Nash's old practice.

'She broke down. This was five minutes after the press had been informed, but it was news to her. From what I can gather, Gerald Nash was an old-school GP. He'd retired almost reluctantly. But there had been no acrimony between him and the partners and certainly none between him and his patients.'

'No legal cases pending?'

'I've contacted the GMC, but they could not confirm or refute. I suspect they'll run it through their legal department before any formal response.'

Warlow glanced up at the Job Centre.

Gil had two timelines: one for each victim. Nash's they'd more or less established already by estimating driving time from Pershore versus the time that the Creightons had come across the body, which was 11.30-ish. That put the likely window of the attack to be between 10.30 and 11.30.

Kirsty Stuart's timeline was less definite. From Robin Lipton, they had a drop-off time of 9.30. Stuart failed to make a contact call at 12. Lipton came looking an hour later and found her just before 1pm.

'If we are to assume—' Gil held his hand up in apology to Warlow. 'I know how much you hate that word, but if we are to assume that the same person carried out the attacks, then we have a one-and-a-half-hour window. If Kirsty was killed first, let's say between 9.30 and 10.30, the killer would have needed to get across the distance between the two scenes of crime within an hour. That window applies equally if we assume Nash was the first victim and we assume Kirsty was killed before mid-day, which was her contact call time.'

'Which do you consider to be the most likely, Gil?' Jess asked.

Gil turned to the board to consider it. 'Nash would have begun his walk before eleven. And he was half an hour from where he'd parked his car. So, let's assume eleven. That gave the killer an hour to get across to where Kirsty was attacked, given she was killed before mid-day. The Creightons neither heard nor saw anyone, which makes me think the killer had not come back in their direction.'

'Is an hour long enough to walk between the two points?' Gina asked.

'I am told it is by Tomo.' It had not been the only thing he'd learned from the rural policing officer. 'Those mountains, they were used by drovers taking animals to England. And they would take the shortest route, always. Often over wild upland country, and you can come across pathways that look as if they have no right to be there. It would take weeks to fully cross. Remember the pub the MoD like to pretend still runs on the firing range near Sennybridge? The Drover's Arms? It's there for a reason. And there'd be ha'penny fields where sheep could graze along the way for a fee. Of course, if the killer had been on an ATV, it would have taken nowhere near that length of time to get across. The landscape is hilly, and the walking is not easy.'

'We'll need Povey to confirm it's the same type of bolt for both,' Warlow said. 'Then it comes to the why.'

Jess offered an observation. 'I realise we're looking at someone with a grudge against one or both. And that's fair enough. Perhaps it's only a grudge against one, and the other was in the wrong place at the wrong time as the killer tried to get away.'

Warlow nodded.

'Or it's random,' Rhys said. 'Which brings us back to the cold case. The Bowman.'

Warlow squeezed his eyes shut for a moment.

Cold cases literally sent an icy tremor down his spine. They were messy and overblown and full of other people's pulled threads.

'In which case,' Rhys continued, 'we have to consider that it's the same killer coming back for more. Or a copycat.'

'Or it might have nothing to do with the old case at all,' Gina said.

Warlow opened his eyes. 'We can't ignore any of those possibilities. The question is, how do we approach them in the most efficient manner?'

'Ah.' Gil reached out for some sheets on his desk. 'As already mentioned, Superintendent Buchannan's venue for the cold case notes. It's an empty factory space in Johnstown, and I was down there this afternoon. Sandra Griffiths is setting things up.'

'Okay. Let's not muddy the waters. It's what, ten minutes away? Let's keep things separate for now, at least in terms of paper trails. And there will be a lot of paper with the cold case. What about the original SIO?'

'Good news and bad news,' Jess said. 'I've spoken to Pauline Garston. She's agreed to meet us whenever we like. But it's not so good on the old super, Tim Leach. He was almost sixty when this case hit the headlines in 2001. He's in his eighties now and in a retirement home.'

'Locally?'

'Castleview Mansions. Garston says his mind isn't what it used to be.'

Warlow made his mind up. 'Let's set up a meeting with Garston for tomorrow morning at Sherwood Forest.'

'Where, sir?'

'That's the name I'm giving the old factory because it is where we'll be sorting through the Bowman's case.'

'Robin Hood. Bowman. I like it, sir.' Rhys looked pleased.

'Meantime, we gather as much background information as we can for the rest of what's left of the day. And Jess and I, since it's almost on our way, will call in on Tim Leach.'

———

THE NURSING HOME sat at the end of a track off the main Carmarthen to Kidwelly road. From the car park, a view of the estuary stretched out ahead of Warlow as he and Jess parked up. The entrance was a security door with an intercom access.

When a voice answered, Warlow explained why they were there.

'You're in luck,' the voice said. 'The lounge is free. We'll get Tim in there for you.'

Leach might never have been a tall man, but an aggressive form of arthritis had bent his cervical spine so much that his head was now constantly bowed. He was dressed in a clean but worn jumper with a Japanese golf-clothing manufacturer's logo on the breast. He wore corduroy trousers that ended in thick socks and large and swollen feet in protective shoes with Velcro straps.

The room was light and airy, with marvellous views and no smell of boiled cabbage, or worse. Warlow had to give the place credit for that.

He made the introductions. Leach peered up at them with yellow scleras and dried lips. His limbs looked stick thin inside his loose trousers.

Jess exchanged pleasantries, but her "how are you?" was met by a mirthless 'Eh?' and a grimace that showed teeth dry from lack of saliva.

'How are you?' Jess repeated.

'Prostate cancer,' Leach said. 'Lucky you came now. Three months, they say. I'd go tomorrow if someone brought in a bullet.'

Warlow saw no point in dallying.

'We're here about the Bowman, Tim.'

Leach's eyes looked up from his bowed head. 'I put that one to rest.'

'You remember?' Warlow's hopes went up.

Leach nodded. 'Yardley. I'll go to my grave happy that shit got what he deserved.'

'How's that, Mr Leach?' Jess asked.

'Yardley. That bastard is never getting out. He'd have killed more, there's no doubt.'

'You were convinced it was Yardley, then?'

'No parole. Whole of life sentence.'

'You had no one else in the frame?' Jess probed.

'No need. Vicious bastard killed his neighbours. Some nonsense over a fence. A bloody fence in the garden. Then he killed those two in the mountains. Like shooting rabbits.'

Warlow saw Jess fighting the urge to glance over at him, but Warlow resisted and simply smiled back at Leach.

'We sorted it,' said the ex-superintendent. 'Got the bastard.'

Warlow nodded. 'Okay. Thanks for that, Tim.'

He got up from his seat, and Jess followed.

Leach reached out a liver-spotted hand to grasp Warlow's. 'If you see my brother outside, tell him to bring in the good biscuits. These shortcakes are dry as dust. We're going fishing, and he's bringing the tackle.'

'I will,' Warlow said. He looked down. A plate, empty except for some crumbs, sat on the table in front of Leach.

Outside the lounge, Warlow noticed a staff member wearing a Castleview polo shirt in the corridor. He relayed Leach's message and got a rueful smile in return.

'Poor Tim, bless him. His brother died five years ago here with us. Tim's memory isn't what it used to be.'

This time, Warlow and Jess's eyes met in understanding.

They got back to the car, and Warlow headed back towards Carmarthen and the A40 dual carriageway that would take them back to Pembrokeshire and the cottage they shared.

'Ever thought about what you'll be like at that age?' Jess asked.

'You'll probably still be a glamorous gran.'

'I think that's a compliment,' Jess said. 'Come on, stop deflecting.'

'I don't know. Everybody's different. Somehow, I'd like to

think I had the gumption to plan ahead and aim for some kind of clean ending with no need to hang about.'

'That's—'

'Nihilism or pragmatism? It's a toss-up. Castleview seems like a good place. But I also realise that by the time you're Tim Leach, it hardly matters where you are because you can't appreciate it, anyway.'

'Makes you appreciate things now, though. I keep thinking I ought to make more of the time I have.'

'Difficult to do on a wet West Wales weekend.'

'Oh, I don't know. I've found some new things to do when the weather outside is foul.' She sent him a coy look.

'That is verging on the coquettish, DI Allanby.'

'It's the end of the day. Deal with it.' She waited a beat and then added, 'Shame about Leach, though.'

'It is. But not my job to upset an old man. Let him have his confabulations.'

'So, I am right, that was all BS, right?'

'Could not have put it better myself, Jess. Yardley may have been caught and imprisoned on planet Leach. But in the real world, it's what we in the biz call complete bollocks.'

CHAPTER TWELVE

By ARRANGEMENT, the team met at Sherwood Forest, or Unit 34 Cilefwr Road, according to the Satnav, at 08.30 the next morning. It was as described on the tin; a brick-walled, metal-profiled box in amongst the hotchpotch of other industrial units ranging from builders' merchants to welding shops.

Trestle tables occupied the space, already laden with evidence crates and, disconcertingly, cardboard files. Some boxed, some held together with string and elastic bands. The whole lot had the dog-eared appearance of having been looked at many times before hurriedly being bundled up and put away again.

Sergeant Sandra Griffiths had already arranged things chronologically. It was going to take a lot of work to go through everything. As such, the woman who shook his hand as soon as he walked in came as a blessing to Warlow.

'For those of you who don't already know Pauline Garston, she is the Ex-Assistant Chief Constable of North Wales Police, and, more importantly for us, a senior investigator in the Bowman case for Dyfed Powys.'

'It's Pauline now,' she said and held up her hand. 'And it was a very long time ago, but I am more than happy to do some Q and A.'

Warlow introduced the team and everyone shook hands. But Jess was the first to address the ex-detective.

'Some background would be useful, too, Pauline,' Jess said, 'for those of us not *au fait* with what went on.'

Pauline must have been about the same age as Gil, and though not having given up the battle with her weight completely, had clearly lost the last few skirmishes. She'd come in dressed in trousers and a knitted jacket; her hair grey but with the odd highlight that lent a touch of pride to her appearance. She had a pleasant face and exuded an air of competence about her. 'I was a wet behind the ears DI at the time. Tim Leach was the official SIO. Plus, there have been a couple of reviews since. I was not involved with those directly. Fresh eyes and all that.'

Warlow understood that all too well, having come up against raised eyebrows when he'd been brought back in to review a cold case involving missing walkers not that long ago, because of his previous involvement. Sometimes, that could trigger resistance and resentment. He'd met both. But that case, as harrowing as it had been, had also brought him back into policing from out in the cold.

'Who was it who ran the last one, ma'am?' Gil asked.

'North Wales Police ran the last review, and there was a liaison officer from Dyfed Powys involved in that one. A DI Caldwell, as I recollect.'

If a pin had dropped at that moment, no doubt it would have been audible in the next county.

Pauline Garston read the silence as the wrong kind of regret and felt the need to sympathise. 'I understand that Kelvin Caldwell has been lost to us. My apologies if that is still raw.'

'In a way, it will always be, ma'am,' Gil said. A statement that had the ring of truth to it.

But the regret Pauline Garston had read in the silence that followed the mention of Caldwell's name came from the members of the team having come across KFC – Kelvin Fucking Caldwell – in the first place, since he'd been a duplicitous snake. Still, he'd died in the line of duty – albeit trying to kill Warlow in the process – and that would ever be his obituary. But no one wanted to exhume that ghost in front of Pauline Garston.

'We spoke with Tim Leach yesterday, Pauline,' Warlow said. 'He seems convinced that he'd cracked the case before he retired.'

Pauline's mouth twitched into a wry smile. 'And yet, the case remains very much open, as you know.'

'So …' Rhys's question came with an accompanying half smile of confusion.

'It's fair to say that as far as Tim Leach is concerned, the Bowman case cracked him …' She paused and eyed Warlow. 'He still thinks Yardley did it?'

'Not only did it but is now serving a whole life sentence somewhere.'

Pauline nodded. 'It's a nodule of self-delusion that's grown over the years in tandem with his deteriorating mental capacity. All very sad and completely untrue. Tim had a huge buzzing bee in his bonnet about Yardley. Absolutely determined to make him fit when there was no forensic evidence linking him to the Bowman case. No one saw him near the mountains. He was never interviewed, and the crossbows found in his possession were not linked to the murder of Phillip Coombs and Heather Messenger.'

'Why was he so convinced, then?' Gil asked.

'Because a week before the Bowman killings, Yardley had shot and killed his neighbour in Chepstow and shot and injured his neighbour's wife with a crossbow. All because of a dispute about a fence line. Yardley went on the run and was found dead after overdosing on sleeping tablets two days after the Bowman murders.'

'But he didn't fit?'

'Only in Tim Leach's mind. I'm sorry to say that the original investigation was derailed by Tim's obsession with driving his theory that Yardley could have done this when everything pointed to it being someone else. The bolts used by Yardley when he shot at his neighbours were field arrows. Longer bolts with hunting arrowheads were used on Coombs and

Messenger. Vicious three-pronged things. Yardley's camper van ended up in a patch of wasteland near the Heads of the Valleys road. The time of death given by the pathologist gave a window of two hours in which Yardley might have been able to get from the Elan Valley to where his van was found, but there had been no sightings of that van at all for three days.'

'Sounds all a bit—'

'Nonsensical,' Pauline said. 'And a waste of resource. Both reviews said as much, though in both instances, they could not come up with any new leads to follow up.'

'We will need to sift through all of this,' Warlow said with a wave of his hand. 'But with the benefit of hindsight, and knowing what you now know, what physical evidence do you think is worth following up?'

'The weapons to start with. We had one partial crossbow bolt. The killer had removed one from Coombs, his first victim. But with Messenger, the second, it went through and in trying to remove it, we think must have snapped, or the impact itself broke it, and so we were left with the top half of the bolt and its flights inside the body of Heather. These were unusual in that they were of French manufacture. Some had been imported, but all our efforts at trying to find out who'd bought bolts like this came to nothing. Some were sold to clubs, some to individuals, but no one we interviewed in connection with those points of contact were considered suspects. We had a lot of help from a medieval expert. If he's still around, it would be worth giving him a shout. I'll chase that up.'

'Thanks.' Warlow saw Rhys making a note. 'We'll take another look at all that. And we'll tie that in with the recent evidence from our present case.' He paused before adding, 'We have two bolts to look at.'

'Two?' Pauline looked genuinely animated.

'Once they're processed, I'll be happy to share that detail with you, Pauline,' Warlow said.

'And I'll get you a copy of my thoughts on that review that my lot in North Wales did. I didn't influence it any way, but I was privy to it once it was done and filed away. Something I did for my benefit. It confirms everything that we found originally. It may save you some considerable time.'

'That will be very useful.' Warlow knew it would.

'So long as Kelvin Caldwell did not have too much of a say in it,' Gil said.

Pauline Garston's brows bunched. 'He did not. In fact. He was bordering on the useless, but I was not going to talk ill of the dead.'

'Talk away, Pauline,' Jess said. 'You will have receptive ears here.'

'Good.'

'You happy to hang around for an hour?' Warlow asked.

'As long as you want,' Pauline said.

'I won't keep you, but it might be useful for Sergeant Griffiths to get to grips with the evidence if she has someone to ask.'

'I'm at your disposal,' Pauline said.

'Excellent. That'll mean we can get on with the second lot of interviews. The original victims' families.'

'They'll be freshly traumatised by all of this,' Pauline said. 'I don't envy you that task.'

WARLOW DIVVIED UP THE INTERVIEWS. From Pauline, they learned that Phillip Coombs' death had significant repercussions for a young family who, with one deadly crossbow bolt, had become a single-parent unit and suffered as a result. The other victim in 2001, Heather Messenger, had left a boyfriend, grieving parents who would now be in their eighties if they were still alive, and siblings in their forties.

Warlow and Gina were heading for the Messenger clan in Herefordshire, so they set off first. Jess and Gil were setting off to visit Samantha Coombs, the daughter of the victim, who'd made herself available as soon as Gil had rung to ask if they could talk. Rhys was left to return to HQ and run the office.

. . .

JESS DROVE IN HER GOLF, and they headed north to an address near Builth Wells that Samantha Coombs had given them.

'What did you make of Leach, if you don't mind me asking?' Gil posed the question as he thumbed through his maps to punch in the address he'd been sent.

'Unfortunately,' Jess replied, 'not the first time I've heard that kind of story.'

'You mean Pauline Garston's version?'

'Exactly. Sounds like whatever Leach said went. Getting him to change direction would be like stopping the tide.'

'Did I detect a Canute reference there?'

'I've worked with a few Canutes in my time. Getting people like Leach to change their minds requires subtly introducing your idea and letting them believe it was their own. It's a draining process that wears down morale.'

'He sounds delusional,' Gil agreed.

'Delusions are the stories people like Leach tell themselves to whitewash over their bruised egos. It's a toxic combination.'

'Lucky our leader isn't an egotist, then.'

'He could try to be,' Jess said, 'but he knows he'd be cut down by friendly fire in an instant.'

'There is that.' Gil snorted his approval. 'You and Molly still looking for a new property?'

Jess brightened at that. 'I may already have found it. A half-finished place a builder has picked up after a repossession sale. He needs my capital to finish it.'

'Those can be dodgy, though, can't they?'

'Evan vouches for the builder. The same firm that built his place.'

'Ah, well. Sounds like a win-win. In the meantime, you'll continue to lodge at Ffau'r Blaidd?'

'Is this your unsubtle way of asking me if I've moved in, Gil?'

'Me? Unsubtle?' Gil's expression affected a picture of innocence.

'The answer is yes. As if you didn't know.'

'I'd guessed as much. Talk of your moving out has dried up. And Evan's ability to change the subject whenever it comes up is painfully obvious.'

'To everyone but him?'

'Of course.'

'And you keep probing?'

'Of course, again.' Gil grinned. 'But it's good to hear it from the … mare's mouth. And good to see him enjoying life a bit.'

'Isn't it just?' Jess allowed herself a smile and drove on content, knowing that they were two people, her and Gil, who in their very different ways had shared a rare opportunity to voice their appreciation of a man they both respected and wished only the best for.

CHAPTER THIRTEEN

MICHELLE MESSENGER HAD MARRIED and become Michelle Tudor. As they approached her door, Warlow toyed with quipping that he hoped she knew a good divorce lawyer and stayed away from axes. But, and no disrespect to Gina, who seemed to be blessed with a great dollop of common sense, you never knew what kind of history they were taught in schools these days.

He preferred the type based on scholarship and record, not the new type as seen on TV, colour-washed through the lens of modernism, which ignored facts if they were inconveniently triggering. And yes, of course he was aware that Henry the VIII was a murdering womaniser, and many other things. But when his kids did GCSE, the curriculum had leapfrogged the Tudors for the Elizabethan era.

If they were still doing that, his joke might fall on stony ground … again. Of course, Gina was likely well-informed about Henry and his wives. *Horrible Histories* portrayed him excellently, but it appeared safer to remain silent and adhere to the script instead.

Or, as Gil had suggested, simply walk around wearing a hat with "Trigger Warning" imprinted upon it and make the quip, anyway.

Life had the potential to be challenging.

Mrs Tudor opened the door of her house on the outskirts of Weobley after one ring of the doorbell. Her smile of greeting wore an air of inevitability. She'd opened this door, or doors like it, to police officers too many times in her life already.

'Mrs Tudor?' Warlow asked.

'Michelle will be fine.'

'Evan Warlow.' He held up his warrant card. 'And this is DC Gina Mellings.'

Gina responded with a restrained smile. They were here to talk about death, after all.

'Come on in,' Michelle said.

They'd run through the woman's details on the way up. That she was now forty-one and had two children aged thirteen and eleven. That her husband and brother worked for a company that built oak-framed houses. That she worked as a supply teacher now and again.

But an in-the-flesh meeting like this filled in many of the invaluable gaps. Like the fact that she survived the murder of her sister with enough resilience to trust another human being and begin a family. That spoke to Warlow of a strong character. Because much of the time, in the aftermath of the violent death of someone close, such survival skills did not always apply.

Michelle Tudor clearly looked after herself and her home, judging from what Warlow saw as he followed her in through the hallway of her detached property and its furnishings. They were in Leominster, and the house had exposed beams everywhere, with matching sturdy furniture. As for the woman herself, her fleecy top and jogging pants – not the skintight variety that left so little to the imagination – hinted at a fitness regimen which, to Warlow's observant, if untrained, eye, appeared to be working well.

Gina noticed the clothing, too. 'Is that a Betty top?'

'And bottom. Got it in the New Year's sale.'

'Great colours. I like this year's.'

'Thank you.'

Warlow let it all slide over his head. Gina was establishing a rapport and did it effortlessly and without artifice because it was simply her nature.

'Did you get hold of your brother?' he asked.

'I did,' Michelle replied. 'He's on his way.'

Warlow caught the tiniest of wary inflections in her answer, but it evaporated as she asked, 'Tea? Coffee?'

She sat them in a living room full of stylised art, quasi-architectural ink drawings that hinted at someone's subjective interest.

'Nice,' Gina said, her gaze scanning the room. From the kitchen came the clanking of cups and a whistling kettle. It was on the decrescendo when the doorbell rang.

They heard a door open and a voice say only, 'Where are they?' instead of a greeting.

The unsmiling man who entered the living room resembled Michelle by the shape of his mouth and eyes, larger now by dint of some restrained emotion simmering inside him.

'This is my brother, Chris—' Michelle began, but before she could introduce the officers, her brother waded in, metaphorical sleeves rolled up.

'I thought we'd heard the last of this bloody pantomime.'

Warlow narrowed his eyes. Gina stepped in.

'We appreciate you giving us your time, Mr Messenger.'

Chris Messenger shook his head, his mouth tight. 'Christ, you lot. Bloody clueless, I bet. Don't tell me you're here fishing like last time?'

'We leave no stone unturned, Mr Messenger,' Warlow said. Careful to keep his voice even.

'Do me a favour and spare us the bullshit.' Messenger's belligerence emerged both in words and in a spray of saliva that spattered Warlow's shirt.

'Mr Messenger,' Gina began. But Warlow quelled her with a hand on her arm.

No amount of Gina Mellings' oil would calm these troubled waters. They'd been churning in a whirlpool of resentment for too many years.

'Fair enough,' Warlow said. 'No bullshit. Your sister was killed by a crossbow bolt. Two other people suffered the same fate two days ago. We are investigating their death. It does not take a genius to recognise the similarities, even at that basic level. Given that the attacks took place in the same area, you will appreciate our need to look at this from every angle. I am not here to rake over old mud. However, we must consider the possibility, remote or otherwise, that it is the same murderer.'

'Come on, that was twenty years ago,' Messenger countered.

'Agreed. Therefore, we are also considering the possibility of a copycat attack. Both scenarios merit some re-evaluation of evidence and details surrounding your sister's death.'

Messenger stared back at Warlow, but his aggressive chest-out posture eased, and he stepped back in the face of the DCI's words. But his scepticism had not retreated fully.

'So, what? You're going to find the answers when no one else could? What makes you so bloody special?'

'Two people have died here,' Gina said.

'My sister died, too, remember?' He glanced dismissively at the DC. 'Christ, you probably weren't even born.'

But Gina was no pushover. 'And have you stopped to consider how the people close to Kirsty Stuart and Gerald Nash are feeling at this moment?'

Messenger glared at her but eventually looked away.

'Chris,' Michelle said softly, 'let them speak, please.'

Her brother looked at her, his animosity not easing, but exhaled loudly.

Warlow took it as a signal. 'As mentioned, there are obvious parallels. All I'm here to ask is that if there is anything you feel you want to bring to my attention regarding your sister's case, anything at all, we will listen.'

Gina held out a printed card.

'Promise us you will not drag my mother into all of this.' Chris Messenger ignored the card. Michelle eventually stepped forward to take it.

'Your father passed three years ago, am I right?' Gina asked.

Michelle nodded. 'He was never the same after Heather died.'

'But your mother—'

Messenger cut Gina off again.

'Is eighty-three and in a home. Early stages of dementia. She's emotionally labile. The bloody last thing she needs is some arse of a copper asking her questions about her dead daughter. The last one you lot sent was bad enough. Mr bloody personality. I nearly did for, the twat … Caldwell, I think it was.'

Warlow refrained from commenting, but it took some effort. Messenger had all his sympathy on that score.

'The offer stands. Anything you can think of,' Gina said.

'We won't be bothering your mother,' Warlow added.

'Your tea must be ready,' Michelle said with a smile.

'Christ, Meesh, why are you pandering to this lot?' Chris rounded on her.

Warlow made the judgement call. 'We'll forget the tea, Michelle. But thanks all the same. Perhaps the two of you could put your heads together. We'll give you some space. I can see that this is all still very raw.'

'Raw?' Chris spat out the word. 'You have no idea.'

'Actually, we do, Mr Messenger,' Gina said. Her words were calm, but her gaze was steely as it returned Messenger's pop-eyed glare.

'There is one more thing,' Warlow said. 'As unpalatable as it may seem, it'll be necessary for us to know your where-abouts over the period of Monday morning between eight and mid-day. A formality, but it needs to be done.'

'What?' A fresh surge of anger reddened Messenger's face. 'You can't be serious.'

Warlow, by now, had had enough of Messenger's bluster. 'Either supply us with details we can corroborate or we will get you in for a formal statement under caution. It's as simple as that.'

'Are you suggesting that I could have something to do with—'

'You're angry and uncooperative, Mr Messenger,' Warlow said. 'I recommend you drink some of your sister's tea.'

'Don't patronise me.'

Warlow made to leave. 'We'll need those details if you please. Plus, anything else you're happy to share.'

'You bastard,' Chris said.

'Chris!' This time, Michelle's voice rose as her own frustration at her brother's attitude boiled over.

'No, it's fine,' Warlow said.

All four of them were standing in the small living room, the tension crackling like electricity in the air.

'I hardly ever come with good news, and I have been called a lot worse. I hope you'll be in touch.'

With that, Warlow ushered Gina out and back to the Jeep.

Gina, flushed from the encounter, slid her seat belt on. 'That could have gone better, sir?'

'I don't know,' Warlow said with surprising equanimity. 'It could have gone worse. He could have walked in holding a crossbow.'

'You don't think—'

'Best not to conclude anything now. Better to write up the chat and zero in on the relationships between the siblings when we eventually get back to Sherwood Forest. I think a direct question to Pauline Garston on that front is called for.'

'But he was angry about his sister's death.'

'Angrier that we were there asking questions.'

That gave Gina pause.

Warlow expounded on his thinking. 'Let's just say that Christopher Messenger has every right to be mightily pissed off at us and the world. Then again, he might be a complete psychopath who is playing a really, really good game of hide in plain sight. In that case, he'd be doubly miffed at seeing us at his door.'

'But wouldn't he want to be calm? If he was involved, I mean?'

Warlow grinned. 'Now you're trying to second guess a psychopath. Not that he is one. Maybe he's an angry brother. Frustrated at the police letting him down. Perhaps he's as straight as …'

'Don't say it, sir.'

'Wouldn't dream of it,' Warlow said and brushed aside

the temptation to whistle the William Tell overture. Unseemly didn't come near. Not that it would have stopped Gil had he been here.

———

WARLOW'S PHONE rang ten minutes after they left Michelle Tudor's house. He channelled the call through the car's hands-free speaker system.

'Mr Warlow?' He recognised Michelle's voice.

'Mrs Tudor.'

'It's still Michelle. I wanted to apologise for Chris. He's like this whenever we mention the police.'

'He's had terrible experiences.'

'We all have. In all the years, only one seemed to really take the time. I knew her as Pauline. She was good and attentive and cared about us as a family. But some of them were … not like that. Now Chris doesn't trust anyone.'

Silence pervaded the static air as Warlow waited for Michelle to continue.

'Were you serious about us providing details for our movements?'

'I am. You and your husband, too. It's all a matter of routine.'

'I understand. But please don't think too badly of Chris.'

Another pause. One long enough to ponder how many times this big sister had needed to defend her little brother over the years. Unkind taunts and a wrong look going Chris Messenger's way might have been a spark too close to the petrol-soaked bonfire.

Warlow's patience was rewarded when Michelle spoke again. 'I am aware it's stupid of me to ask, but will this new case … might it help find who did this to Heather all those years ago?'

He sensed the desperation in her question. The daring to hope that yet again there might be answers to all those imponderables. He wasn't about to extinguish the flickering candle, but at the same time, the reality of the situation needed underlining. 'Your sister's case remains open, Michelle. Whatever it is we do or find here, it will, by necessity, involve looking again at the past.'

'I'd like to think … even after all this time … that there'd be a chance. And I've come to the realisation of how awful it is to have that mindset because other people have lost their lives. But I've spent countless nights awake, yearning to understand why it happened to Heather. To us.'

A rock in a pond. That's what a violent act always ended up being. Its ripples spread out in time and space, besmirching everything it touched.

'I won't promise you anything, Michelle.'

'I realise that. But even knowing she isn't forgotten helps. The last officer … Caldwell … He told me to forget. That was his answer. He told me some cases never got resolved. That they would never find out …' She choked back a sob.

It took a moment for her to recover, and Warlow held Gina back from speaking again, this time with a shake of his head.

Eventually, Michelle recovered enough to say, 'I'll get those details to you. It might be me who sends them for Chris, too. You can see what he's like, but he'll come around.'

'I appreciate that,' Warlow said.

Michelle ended the call.

They drove on until Warlow glanced over at a tight-lipped Gina. 'No comments? Rhys would have been jabbering away by now. Or at least eating some crisps. This silence is unnerving.'

'It's so horrible for them,' Gina voiced her thoughts. 'The relatives. And to imagine that one of ours was so … unsympathetic.'

'Yep. That was Kelvin Caldwell, alright.' He chuckled softly. 'The man had a talent for rubbing people up the wrong way. Even though he's dead, and you've only been on the team a couple of days, he's made you hate him already.'

'Rhys didn't like him.'

'There we are, then. That from a man with the agreeableness of a Labrador. And you know how agreeable they are.'

'I have to admit you'd have to do something pretty bad to get Cadi to not like you. Or Rhys, come to that.'

'And yet, Caldwell managed both.'

'I'm glad I never met him.'

'Amen to that. Now, Heather Messenger's ex-boyfriend, Wimbolt.'

'Wojak, sir,' she corrected him. 'Pitar Wojak. The address is just outside Hereford. Twenty minutes according to Google.'

Warlow grinned. 'I see you've adjusted to the team lexicon.'

'Have to, sir, otherwise I'd never understand a word Rhys says.'

'Right, give Mr Wojak another ring. No point us travelling all the way to Hereford if he's not there.'

So far, Gina's attempts at contacting the man had failed.

She failed again.

'So, what now, sir?'

'We head home with our tails between our legs. If needed we'll get someone from Brecon or Llandrindod station to pop over and do the needful.'

CHAPTER FOURTEEN

SAMANTHA COOMBS, mid-twenties, looked younger at a little over five feet tall and clothed in loose-fitting pants and sweatshirt in the current oversized vogue.

Gil often wondered if the fashion industry was run by a cabal of fairy folk who met once a year to decide which ridiculous clothing trend they might dangle in front of a gullible public *this* season. Chum the waters and then watch the ensuing feeding frenzy and hear the kerching of tills in response.

Samantha also wore a nose ring, albeit a subtle one, that glistened and made her look as if she constantly needed a quick nose wipe. But, despite her appearance, suggesting a feckless, fashion victim, not long out of teenage years, she turned out to be a personable young woman.

Gil and Jess met her in the living room of the house she shared with two other women overlooking the show grounds in Builth Wells.

'You never got the urge to move away, Samantha?' Gil asked.

She'd offered them water, but no tea, and the sergeant was doing his best to overcome his disappointment.

'I thought about it, but I have a boyfriend here, and Builth is cheap compared to other places. My work means I can more or less live where I want.'

'What is it you do, Samantha?' Jess asked.

'I'm a software engineer with Quindor. They're a London-based company, but I can work from home. From anywhere. Digital nomad, me. But my partner is local and works in farming.'

'Tough job.'

'The opposite of mine. He's a dairy engineer. Goes out to fix milking machines and all sorts of things. He does a lot of on-call, so he's busy. But I'm not a hermit. I went to Uni in Bristol.' She wrinkled a small nose. 'Didn't like it much. Too expensive, and I missed home.'

'What did you do there?' Jess asked.

'Maths and computer science.'

Gil's face registered his admiration. These were subjects that verged on the arcane as far as he was concerned. And, given what he knew of Samantha's domestic circumstances, her achievements were even more impressive.

'But you aren't here to ask me about my degree,' Samantha said. 'You're here because of those two people who were killed in the Cambrians.'

Jess seized on her perspicacity. 'Is it okay to talk about what happened to your dad?'

Samantha shrugged. 'Fine. I remember little about the time when it actually happened. I mean, I was five. I remember the fuss. I remember my mum being really upset. A lot of coming and going, the police, so many other people. Me and my brother spent a lot of time with my auntie. My mother didn't cope well. I don't blame her for that. The press … they were outside all the time. We couldn't go anywhere without them following us. It made my mother paranoid; I realise that now. But to us, it felt like she was just scared of everything. She stayed scared. Until it happened, she was bright and full of life. Afterwards, it was as if something had sucked all of that out of her.'

'She suffered from mental health issues afterwards, is that right?' Jess asked.

'She did. I had to grow up pretty quickly.' Samantha said this in a matter-of-fact way. 'My brother, though, he just didn't understand. It took him a while longer to work out why our mother had gone.'

'I understand she took her own life in the end?'

'When I was fifteen and Lloyd was fourteen. That was a dark period. But I got through it, whereas Lloyd struggled. After Mum died, we went to live with my aunt. She was my dad's sister and had two kids of her own, both younger than us. My aunt was … nice, but my uncle … He ended up being not so happy to have two more kids to look after. I left for Uni as soon as I was able. I'd promised Mum that I'd stick in school. I was good at maths. I'd got that from my dad. Lloyd left soon after that.'

'And what does he do now?'

'Lives in Welshpool. He's a delivery driver.'

'Do you see him?'

'Yes. Of course. And before you ask, no, he hasn't recovered, and he never will. He's bright. He could have done what I did, but what happened to my dad and then my mum, it soured him. Changed him. Now he's happy to drive vans and get drunk on a weekend with his mates.'

Gil waited for her to finish before speaking. 'Samantha, we're here for obvious reasons. This case will bring the press out in droves. Like hyenas to a kill. You need to be aware, and you need to warn your brother. And it'll mean us reopening your dad's case. We'll be asking questions again. Obviously, you were just a child, but I would say that if your mother, afterwards, ever mentioned anything that you think might be of use, please let us know.'

'What sort of thing?' Samantha looked mildly irked.

Gil smiled an apology. 'Anything. Sometimes, things occur to people, and they may even dismiss it as fanciful. But if anything comes to you, please contact us. Do you have a number for your brother?'

Samantha hesitated, her eyes fixed on Gil's and then shrugged. 'Maybe it would be better if he heard all this from you. Sometimes, he doesn't answer my calls or texts. He thinks I fuss too much.'

She gave them her brother's number. Gil thanked her, and he and Jess left her to it.

'It never becomes any easier to listen to that bloody story, does it?' Gil dialled Samantha's brother's number as they walked to the car.

'No, it does not,' Jess said. They both understood that Gil was referring to the stories of those left behind. The fallout.

When Gil's call was answered on the fourth ring, he put it on speaker. A brash voice came through against the background of a revving engine.

'Is that Bowen Metalwork? I'm going to get there as soon as I can, mate—'

'Lloyd, this isn't Bowen Metalwork. I'm Sergeant Gil Jones, Dyfed Powys police.'

'Police? Right …'

Both officers registered confusion in Lloyd's voice.

'We need a quick word, Lloyd. Any chance we could meet you?'

'I'm on a route here, and I'm late already.'

'It'll take five minutes. Where are you?'

'I'm on the way to Newbridge.'

'We're ten minutes away. You tell us, we can be there. Five minutes, I promise.'

———

LLOYD COOMBS' van might have been white once, but over time—and his clear unwillingness to bother cleaning off its layer of dirt—it had turned a dingy shade of grey.

Jess and Gil were already parked up on the side of the road. A turning off the A470 near a sawmill and a body shop; their designated meeting place. Mid-day had come and gone when the once-white van roared in and parked. The detectives got out, zipped coats up against the wind, and met Lloyd between the two vehicles.

He wore no uniform as such, though were van drivers

ever to form a cooperative, dark cargo pants, a baseball cap pulled firmly down under the hood of a hoodie, as well as several days stubble might well have come out top in a survey of preferred workwear.

Lloyd was thin and tired looking under the hat, which he did not remove when he greeted the officers. A long face and narrower features than his sister, but still no doubting the identical gene pool that spawned the two of them.

'Whassup?' he asked, walking over towards them with quick strides.

Gil made introductions and ran over their chat with his sister and their motivation for meeting with him.

'Yeah, old news,' Lloyd replied.

'You heard the press release?'

'Nah. Some bloke from the papers rang me and told me someone else had been shot. Twice yesterday and once today. Wants to speak to me about my dad.'

'Right, then we're too late. We wanted to see you and warn you it might happen.'

'Already has.' Lloyd was one of those people who never quite stopped moving. Touching his face, crossing his arms, fiddling with the strings of his hoodie. Seeing him now brought to mind the possibility of neurodiversity to Gil.

Like most people – or so he liked to think – Gil struggled with the term. Kids, who in his day were labelled naughty boys or girls, now had a whole raft of other labels attached to them to somehow excuse their behaviour.

Gil realised that for some, the diagnosis was needed and genuinely so, in order that help be sought and supplied. For others … not so much. A bit like the trend, these days, to label every little natural up and down of human existence as a mental health issue instead of a fact of sodding life. And as callous as that might sound, it did not change the mindset.

Lloyd's difficult childhood had brought him into contact with the police. Nothing serious. Raucous behaviour, some drunk and disorderliness when with a gang. From what they'd seen here, Gil suspected he probably couldn't help himself.

'You are under no obligations, Lloyd,' Jess said.

At this, Lloyd took off his cap, ruffled the flattened hair underneath before replacing the lid.

'But he's offering money, this bloke. Five-hundred smackers for a chat. I'm thinking, yeah, why not, if it's just a chat? I mean, I can't remember anything about it. I told him that, but he still wants to talk.'

And make things up afterwards, thought Gil, but held his peace.

'I mean, what happened happened. It's all there for everyone to see.' A brave attempt at dismissing the horror of his father's murder and his mother's suicide.

'You're not obliged to,' Jess repeated.

But Lloyd had made his mind up. 'You're here to talk about the same thing. But you don't have any cash. So, why not? I've said no photos, so …'

'There may be others,' Gil warned.

Lloyd shrugged. 'Well, it's all going to get stirred up again, isn't it? Might as well make a few readies. You got any clues about who did it this time?'

'This is all a part of that, Lloyd,' Jess said.

'Right.' Lloyd's smile dripped derision. 'Like I said, I'm on a schedule here. People are getting pissed off.' He half-turned before Gil called him back.

'Out of interest, which journalist called you?'

'Bloke called Lane.'

Gil exhaled a lungful of air through his nostrils.

'What we said to your sister is that if all this triggers anything in you, a memory, something your mother might have said that could have seemed unimportant then, we would want to know. Anything at all,' Jess said.

'I was four. All I remember is people being nice to me and my sis. And the fights in school when people made jokes about Robin Hood. And I know he didn't use a crossbow, but when you're a kid, that kind of logic doesn't work. But yeah, okay, if I get a flash of inspiration, I got your number on my caller's list now. I'll put a big blue tick next to it.'

A minute later, Lloyd roared away in his van, leaving the two officers in a cloud of exhaust.

'That thing needs a service,' Gil said.

'What do you make of that?' Jess walked back to the Golf.

'He's damaged goods,' Gil said. 'Just the kind of victim you don't want Lane anywhere near.'

'Yes, Lane. He's dropped off the radar since Hunt, hasn't he?'

'Wish he'd done everyone a favour and dropped off his perch.'

'Is he still threatening to write a book about Hunt?'

'I assume so.'

According to his statement, Lane had been drawn into the Hunt case at the isolated cottage known as Can Y Barcud, where events took a dark turn. Hunt locked Lane in the boot of his car and abducted Catrin Richards, later killing himself in a failed bombing attempt. It was pure luck—and Cadi's exceptional sense of smell—that led to Catrin's discovery, trapped in an underground nuclear observer corps shelter.

Thinking about all that sent a shiver down Gil's back. About how close they'd been to not ever finding Catrin. It had been the narrowest of shaves.

The hoped-for evidence they needed to build a case, one that Gil was convinced implicated Lane more than simply as a hapless stooge for Hunt, had never materialised. But Gil lived in hope. They said cream always rose to the surface, even curdled cream like Lane.

The analogy Gil preferred was that of a bloated corpse rising to the surface of a pond because of the accumulation of trapped, noxious gas. Of course, he needn't share that with Jess. But it would happen. Lane would slip up. And, for that, Gil was willing to play the long game.

Still, to think Lane would embroil himself voluntarily again in police business beggared belief. Yet, his motive could not have been plainer.

The Bowman case was one where the police had failed, and to have that glaring fact to reiterate in headlines was not an opportunity a miserable sod like Lane would ever pass up.

CHAPTER FIFTEEN

JESS SUGGESTED they skip vespers since Warlow and Gina's planned trip to Hereford had been cancelled. They had intended to interview Heather Messenger's ex-boyfriend to warn him about the incoming media attention and ask for any additional insights, but they couldn't reach him. Even so, they would be back far too late and with little to add.

On her way back to Ffau'r Blaidd, she decided to make a quick stop at Sherwood Forest. Before that, she had dropped Gil off at headquarters and briefed Rhys about their interview with Lloyd Coombs. She then made a detour to the old factory.

Jess had not expected to find Pauline Garston still there. But then, the opportunity of revisiting an old case with both the knowledge of hindsight and the extra ammunition that current forensics provided rarely arose. Pauline wanted to make the most of it.

'Don't you have a home to go to? Or someone waiting there for you?' Jess asked, grinning, when Pauline looked up at her arrival.

'I do, on both counts. But the someone is making supper tonight. The more I got into this, the more I started separating wheat from chaff to find anything that's still relevant. First of all, there was a guy who did some actual yomping for us. We used him to time how long it might take for someone to get from point A to point B.'

'But it's twenty years. Won't they be—'

'Before you say anything else, I've checked, and he's still alive and active in a rambler's group. Then, there are the farmers who use the place for grazing. Two of them are still around. And there's the crossbow guy. I double-checked. He knows more than most about the weapons. He was well-versed in his field, if I remember rightly, leaning more towards medieval reenactment than archery. Lives in Llandovery and still puts on chain mail. He'd just come back from some jamboree where they fight each other with wooden swords and say thee a lot. I think he's the grand poo-bah of the reenactment bods.'

'He could help now?'

'Oh, yes. I learned from him that in medieval times, they often used a hand crank to pull the drawstring back. That made firing a slow business. He's full of all that kind of thing. And, though he couldn't identify the bolt that was used, he knew someone who might and who did in the end.'

'Okay, can't do any harm. And he lives in Llandovery?'

'He does.'

'Evan will be driving back through there this evening. Might be worth him calling in.'

'And here are those copies of our last case review. It will save you some time. In fact, a lot of time. But of course, they came to no new conclusions, which is less than helpful. I've added names and contact numbers of the people just mentioned, too.'

Jess grinned. They'd lucked out here with Pauline. 'It all helps. Even the negatives.'

Pauline nodded and changed tack in an instant to became the ex-Deputy Constable again. 'How is the transfer working out?'

'You know about that?'

'Wales is a small country. Besides, we had a post open in North Wales when you applied for this one.'

'Yeah, but a bit too close to home for my liking. I needed distance. And so far, so good.'

'Nice to hear. Evan treating you well?'

'I don't have any grievances.' Jess searched Pauline's face for hidden meaning but found none.

'I keep telling Bleddyn Drinkwater how lucky he is having you.'

Jess thanked her and made the call to Warlow, who agreed it was a good idea to call in on the crossbow expert so as not to "waste the whole sodding trip" – his words. Knowing that Gina was in the car with him, she kept it purely business. Jess and Evan's relationship was never destined to be one filled with whispered innuendos or subtle double entendres. They were mature enough to skip the innuendo altogether and dive straight into direct entendres when the situation called for it.

Besides, she had Pauline Garston's words in her head as she drove down the curving road to Nevern. And they were enough to be going on with at the moment.

———

HUGO MILTON LIVED in a bit of a pile between the village of Myddfai and the market town of Llandovery.

They were well and truly back in Carmarthenshire now, as Gina directed Warlow along the winding roads to Milton House. It had a tumble-down gatehouse with rusting iron railings and a drive which needed the attention of a tree surgeon badly. The only thing that didn't need any TLC was a painted heraldic sign in blue, red, and gold centred on the rusting wrought-iron arch above the entrance. Someone kept the sign clean and polished, while completely ignoring every other aspect of necessary maintenance.

'What sort of place is this?' Gina asked.

Warlow emitted a low curse as encroaching branches whispered against the paintwork of the Jeep. Then he apologised and muttered, 'I'll put my money on someone eccentric.'

They rounded a bend into an overgrown courtyard, where

a beaten-up Land Rover sat, half in and half out of a garage, because the space where its front end should've been was full of unusual-looking metalwork. Unusual with regards to their presence in this day and age, at least. Shields, maces, halberds, spears and the rest, stacked haphazardly.

'Spoils of war,' Warlow said.

'What?' A note of alarm sounded in Gina's voice.

'He's a historical reenactment enthusiast.'

'Not real wars, then?'

'I think we would have been informed if he had declared war on Brecon.'

The house looked like something imagined by Poe. It hunkered rather than stood with gloomy vegetation on three sides and stained walls, dark with time and lichen.

The portico had faded tracery and the gable ends were steep. The stoned and mullioned windows had pointed arches.

The heavy-set man who opened the solid oak door wore a tunic of some coarse material that dropped to his mid thighs over leggings that looked, to Warlow's untrained eye, knitted. Thick calves ended in feet clad in felt slippers. At the top end, glinting deep-set eyes peered at them in amusement from a broad and weathered face with long grey hair and beard. He looked like he needed a tree feller more than a barber.

A smell akin to wet cardboard and damp dog met both officers from behind the man. Then again, it might simply be all eau de medievalist, judging by the cocktail menu of stains on the tunic, not to mention the occasional fleck of crumb in the beard.

'Mr Milton?' Gina asked.

'Ah, the King's guard. I have been expecting you. Come in.'

Warlow quickly realised the house should've been in a museum. Or rather, should be *the* museum. Medieval paraphernalia filled every available space with drawings, miniatures, and examples of weaponry, as per broken swords, axes, spears, and other … stuff.

Luckily, or not, depending on your viewpoint, Milton was

also a deep and booming talker. He offered a guided tour, even explaining away the accent that was clearly in no way local.

'Just me here, yes. In case you're wondering. We go back a long way on my pa's side. One of my lot did well in some battle, and we were ceded the land and title. The title is long gone as is the land which leaves me bugger all money to spend on the house. Dad insisted on me going off to school. I am an old Salopian, then Oxford, and ended up in the city for a few years with BND. Of course, we were still in Europe then, and so I got a few air miles under my belt. I escaped that because my heart is here. And this part of Wales is saturated with history, as I'm sure you're aware.'

Warlow was. But it took only five minutes to realise he was in the presence of a man with no filter when it came to his need to talk, bore, and stultify anyone who did not share his appetite for the past. When he finally came to asking if they would like refreshments, Warlow responded point-blank with a refusal and grasped the moment to speak.

'Do you listen to the radio at all, Mr Milton?'

'Please, it's Hugo.' He shook his head.

'TV?'

'Good God, no. I've tried, as much as possible, to recreate a medieval lifestyle. Such a simple time, one governed by strength of character, physicality, and a raw existence. Fealty and loyalty were—'

Warlow raised a hand. 'So, you won't be aware of the incident at Abergwesyn?'

'Pauline Garston mentioned something. But you know the Guard.' Milton inclined his head and put a finger over his lips.

Warlow indulged him. 'I do. So, let me tell you. Two people have been shot with crossbows. Two people in very similar fashion to the case you were involved in previously.'

Remarkably, Hugo, for a count of eight, was lost for words, but finally, he managed an incredulous, 'Surely not?'

'I'm afraid it's true,' Gina confirmed Warlow's statement.

'But ... good God, that's ... I'm genuinely flabbergasted.'

'From the arrows——'

'Bolts,' Hugo interjected.

'You were able to suggest a type of bow the last time?' Warlow asked.

'I was. That length of bolt would require a specific kind of bow. Of what was available, I was able to suggest which model of weapon might have been capable.'

'Do you own any?'

'I do not. My interest is in the history of weaponry, but I do possess some working replicas. I would give anything for an original. But I'd be pleased to show you.'

He took them through a couple of cluttered rooms where faded furniture took second place to open books and papers besides the odd rusty bit of weaponry, to another room with an open fire and a bay window desk, looking out over a view of open countryside, rolling down towards a vale.

Three crossbows took pride of place on two walls.

'On the left is a basic instrument with a cock-stirrup used for using your foot as counter pressure to pulling back the drawstring. Next to it is a bow with a windlass, a crank to pull the string back. It's big and sometimes needed two people to load. But much more pressure was needed as chain mail and armour got stronger. Modern crossbows still use a cock-stirrup and a cocking roll rope, which makes it much quicker. These you see here are reproductions, but the technology is the same. On average, a draw weight of 175 lbs and effective over about 200 metres at most. As mentioned, I'd be happy to help in any way I can.'

'Thank you,' Warlow said. 'We needed to make sure you will be available for a consultation.'

'Sounds a nasty business. Happy to help in any way I can.'

Fifteen long, silent minutes later, in the Jeep, Warlow began the much-needed conversation.

'Yes, I agree. It takes all sorts. And Hugo Milton is liquorice through and through.'

'I believe he truly would have preferred to be born five-hundred years ago, sir.'

'Why not? A time when life expectancy was probably

what, fifty-odd? I'd be dead. You'd have five children and probably would be dead, too. Rhys would likely be a general somewhere in Europe.'

Gina made a face. 'No antibiotics, no general anaesthetic, no doctors.'

'If you're only listing negatives, you're on shaky ground. There would not be any X, or TikTok, no YouTube challenges. There's three we wouldn't miss right from the off. But then there would also be body lice. Come to think of it, not much difference between the two in terms of bloody irritation.'

Gina smiled. 'Still, in a case like this, lucky he's around. Milton, I mean.'

Warlow nodded. 'Imagine how he must've felt when the Prince of Wales bought the Llwynywermod Estate.'

'Is that near here?'

'I'd say within a mile as the crow ducks and dives.'

'We ought to get Rhys up here, sir. He'd love all this.'

'Wouldn't he just. They'd get on like a hovel on fire. Speaking of the acting sergeant, why don't you give him a ring? Ask him to inform everyone that we will be starting early at HQ tomorrow. We'll give Sherwood Forest a miss until later.'

As she dialled her partner, Warlow pondered the fact that when he signed up for the job as a naïve twenty-one-year-old, he never imagined he'd be talking, in 2024, to a man dressed as Henry the VIII's uncle, asking about crossbows. By now, according to those ideals of the future he'd been promised as a child, there should be flying cars, colonies on the moons of Jupiter, world peace, and crimes solved by mutant savants before they even happened.

Thank you very much, Science lying Fiction.

Death by crossbow, though? He'd never read that on any page written by Nostradamus. He shook away the thought and turned up the radio.

CHAPTER SIXTEEN

THE HEADLINES that Jess read out over coffee early the next morning came as no surprise.

"Serial crossbow slayer stalks beauty spot."

A police spokesperson refused to rule out the possibility that the killer of two walkers in the remote hills near the Elan Valley reservoir complex in Mid-Wales could be the same killer who struck twenty years before. Nicknamed the Bowman, the murderer has escaped justice for almost a quarter of a century. Dyfed Powys police have urged walkers to be vigilant and not to venture out alone in the Cambrian Hills.

'Is refused to rule out the same as confirmed?' Warlow asked.

'To anyone reading this, I'd say yes, it is.' Jess was in a dressing gown, Warlow in pyjama bottoms and T-shirt, both reading from iPads. At Warlow's side, Cadi sat patiently, hoping for a crust. A hope that nine times out of ten did not go unnoticed. Her eyes flicked unerringly from the plate on the table to Warlow's face. As good as asking if he might spare a morsel of food for a starving animal. Even though she'd had a bowlful of food not ten minutes before.

Warlow, soft as ever when it came to the dog, snapped an inch of crust off and threw it in Cadi's direction. She caught the offering effortlessly, and the room filled with the disturbingly satisfying sound of a dog crushing toasted bread for seven seconds.

'This is only the beginning,' Jess said, watching the dog/man interaction with amusement.

She was, of course, referring to the press as a whole, and the obvious relish they'd have in stirring the conspiracy pot. Anything that might make the public clench their buttocks in fear.

A job they were very good at.

'I hope to God the Coombs boy sees some sense and doesn't let Lane get his fangs into him.' Warlow had listened to Jess describing her and Gil's chat with Lloyd with several prolonged shakes of his head.

'Gil fell short of offering to lend him a crucifix,' she quipped.

But Warlow couldn't even find it in himself to smile at Gil's long-running, semi-humorous thread implying that Geraint Lane was, in fact, a vampire. Though he was with him one hundred per cent on the bloodsucking.

Warlow's own encounters with various members of the press over time had convinced him that hyena, leech, sound-bite manipulating Canute, all had the potential to be as applicable as vampire.

During his time with the South Wales police, a journalist once arrived with a photographer and, in all seriousness, asked Warlow if he would pose holding a knife to illustrate the fatal blow delivered by a man they had arrested—someone who clearly suffered from a mental illness. The kind of sensationalist image reminiscent of 1960s pulp thriller covers or posters for old black-and-white films.

Warlow's response had brought him grief in the form of a reprimand from the higher ups, but also the immense satisfaction of seeing two idiots rushing out of the local nick under threat of violence.

Not a bloody clue, most of them.

Except for Lane. He was a canny, manipulative cove who most definitely had a clue. Several big, juicy ones. Lane enjoyed waving his knobbly anti-establishment stick whenever it was possible. That waving had almost got him killed by Hunt. Warlow hoped that one day, it might get him arrested.

'Right.' Warlow got up and gathered his and Jess's dishes and took them to the sink. 'This case will not sort itself out,' he muttered.

Cadi, realising that treats were now off the table, began nudging Jess's hand for a head rub. She got that, plus a smile from the lady in question. Warlow felt a thrill almost as big as the dog's in knowing that sometimes, that smile was for him.

He didn't always get a head rub, though.

———

Rhys, carefully applying the knowledge gleaned from Catrin's tutoring on organising the boards, did a more than passable job.

Now that they had Sherwood Forest up and running, other than a brief summary naming victims and dates from the Bowman case, the Job Centre and Gallery concentrated on the case at hand and the previous days' various interactions with relatives. Some of it could've been done by phone, of course, but these were all people touched by the death of loved ones. In Warlow's book, they all deserved personal contact and responded much better to it. The relatives needed to put faces to the names of the officers now tasked with digging into, and sometimes disrupting, their lives.

And so, tea already half-drunk from his Foxtrot, Foxtrot, Sierra mug, Warlow too studied the Job Centre with satisfaction. 'Everyone has seen today's headlines, I take it?'

'We have, sir,' Rhys said and added, 'I think the worst one was "Deathly Harrows".'

Warlow's eyes rolled.

'Please tell me that was the Guardian,' Gil said. 'Bloody ironic if they used a Rowling reference, though.'

'There's more to come.' Jess echoed Warlow's breakfast sentiment. 'Neither the initial investigation, nor the subsequent reviews established a link between Coombs and Messenger as victims.'

'None,' Gil agreed. 'And that's emphasised again in the summary document of the last review Pauline Garston provided.'

'Then that's our direction of attack. We need to establish the same lack of connection between Stuart and Nash. We can't afford to miss anything. Let's go around the room. Gina?'

'I'm chasing up Wojak again today, sir.' Their endeavoured visit to Messenger's ex-boyfriend had been unsuccessful. Disappointingly so because they'd been in the Herefordshire area, and the two birds-with-one-stone approach faltered.

'Pin him down for a video call. We're not going back up there now,' Warlow announced.

Rhys walked over to the map. 'CSI are continuing to search the crime scenes, extending out into the adjacent moorland.'

'We're not expecting to find much, are we?' Warlow muttered. 'How about traffic sightings?'

'Nothing so far.'

'Gil?'

'I'm chasing up Povey for any information on the bolt. We should get something soon.'

'Jess?'

'I met some angry people yesterday,' she said. 'Angry, blighted, and unhappy people.'

Warlow had deliberately left Jess until last. It was always worth the wait to hear her take. 'Like it or not, these cases are linked. Directly or indirectly. Somehow, we need to work out who is getting the most out of it.'

'That's an interesting way of putting it,' Warlow said.

'You mean, who is getting the biggest kick, ma'am?' Gina asked.

'Perhaps. Thrill of the chase, possibly? Some people can't resist it. I've seen it before. But it's possibly something else, too. Something we don't yet understand. Something we're not seeing at this moment.'

She was right. This case, more than any Warlow could think of, required them all to be on their game.

Gil's phone rang. He took it and looked up at the team with features arranged in almost comic disbelief as he slid a hand over the landline's mouthpiece and spoke one sentence.

'There's been another incident on the mountain.'

———

WARLOW WENT to meet with the rural crime unit up at the Elan Valley again. The second time in as many days he'd spent two hours in the Jeep. This time, he'd gone with Gil, leaving the others to their phones and screens.

The other side of police work.

This morning, March was doing its best to reassure everyone that spring was on its way after a dismal, wet winter. And, since it was by far and away the commonest national pastime, Gil waxed lyrical on the subject of climate.

'*Arglwydd Crist*, I remember I used to walk to school as a kid through snow. Actual snow. We'd slide on frozen stretches of standing water that were icy death traps in a sloping school-yard. We used to hope they wouldn't melt until after break so we could slide down the damned things at speed. I bet the teachers took bets on who'd be the first to break an arm. Usually, it was Shirley Mason. Permasnot in the left nostril, glasses like portholes. Some of the boys would lure her out onto the rink with a Sherbert Flying Saucer, and then we'd watch as she did all the ballet moves from Swan Lake arse backwards just to stay upright. And yes, I know it sounds cruel, but then ten-year-olds are not known for their compassion.'

'It's changed, the weather. No doubt about that.'

'I know we're talking nearly fifty years ago,' Gil said. 'But still. Now we've got rain, more rain, deluges, and then flooded roads from leaves clogging the drains.'

'I'm guessing you didn't pass the Met Office interview,' Warlow muttered.

'No. Something about not liking my delivery. There is no accounting for taste.'

With glorious timing that some people might consider suspiciously dramatic, a cloud emptied itself onto an adjacent hillside to leave a magnificent rainbow in its wake. All this as they crested one of the many hills this road traversed. The ride between Beulah and Llanwrtyd was best described as twisty.

'Always loved this run,' Gil said. 'Though not to be recommended with three under-eights in the car trying to read some books their grandmother thought might be a good way to distract them. We have made one or two vomit stops on this stretch.'

'Thank you for sharing,' Warlow said.

'Better get used to it, though. I can see us back and forth here if this case is anything like the last one. My guess is we'll need another staging post.'

'Yes. There is already talk of a task force.'

'You to lead?' Gil had one eyebrow cocked.

'I'm not holding my breath. And I don't like armies, you know that.'

'What's the alternative?'

'We're still in the golden period on this one. I'm going to do what I can to get an early answer.'

Gil undid his seat belt and then reinserted it.

'What was that for?' Warlow asked.

'Making sure I'm strapped in. I anticipate a bumpy ride.'

CHAPTER SEVENTEEN

CHRIS MESSENGER, like most idiots caught with their hand in the biscuit jar, decided on offence as the best form of defence.

'If I'm not under arrest, you have no right to keep me here.'

'Correct,' Warlow said. 'But, as Sergeant Thomas has already pointed out, there is someone in a sling not thirty yards away. One of my fellow officers is, at this moment, interviewing them to determine if, indeed, an offence has taken place. Until that fact has been established, you are not free to go. So, why don't we begin with you telling me why you are in this area. An area where a recent serious crime has been committed. One you are also linked to for all the wrong reasons.'

Warlow's words failed to sweeten Messenger's vinegary expression.

'Spare me the good cop crap.'

'You think I'm a good cop?'

Tomo snorted. 'I know a few people who have made that mistake.'

'You don't scare me. Either of you. Especially you, DCI wonder boy Warlow.'

'Scaring you isn't why I'm here. But understand this. Cooperation is our currency at this moment, and I dislike wasting time. We are conducting a murder investigation and as it stands, you're quids in on the information front. So, I suggest you spend some of that currency. In case this turns out to be a "your word against theirs" type of situation. Because, as it stands, it's their word and diddley squat from you at the moment. Only one way this can go.'

Warlow was not a man known for his patience, but he was happy to watch the inner battle being fought within Christopher Messenger's tortured brain.

Persist with his obnoxious innocent act or cooperate and hope Warlow might stretch to seeing things on his side of the looking glass.

Thankfully, Messenger's distorted form of semi-common sense prevailed.

'Guess what those bloody oiks were doing?' Messenger barked. 'Bloody TikTok. One of them had a toy fucking crossbow, and they were pretending to shoot an apple off someone's head. They were hoping I hadn't noticed. But they were wrong there. It went all quiet when I walked past. But I doubled back and caught them at it. Laughing and joking about it. And if you say it's a free country, you can piss right off.'

Warlow did not say that it was a free country. If anything, he felt a surge of sympathy for anyone being confronted by the fecklessness of today's Generation Z. But then, you couldn't go around thumping people at will.

'People can be … odd. Still, someone has been hurt here. So, let's start with why you were even up here in the first place, Chris, shall we?'

———

GIL INTRODUCED himself to the two young women and the man – he put them at no more than eighteen – or maybe younger. On Gil's scale of ageism, the bloke, therefore, was still a boy.

The girls, Rhiannon and Alicia, had their phones out ready for that text that just might change their lives, and therefore could not remain unlooked at for more than eight seconds. The companion, Lucien, took a more direct approach.

'Can we, like, press charges against that man?'

'Press charges? Where do you think we are, Yellowstone?'

'Isn't that what you do, though? Press charges?' Lucien was spoiling for a fight. And if Gil had found a paper bag nearby, he might have let him have a go at it just to see the paper bag win.

'If charges are to be pressed, it'll be us doing the pressing. First, we need to find out what happened.'

The girls exchanged glances, and it looked as if an unspoken decision passed between them who might be the spokesperson. Unfortunately, Lucien had other ideas.

'God, we were only filming. We had this sick idea for some content for our channel.'

Something in Gil's face made one girl realise he needed a bit of help.

'We post things online,' Alicia said.

'Why?' Gil asked, mainly because he'd always wanted to.

All three of the young people responded as if he'd just asked them to stand naked on an iceberg as it calved.

'It's what we do,' Lucien explained. 'This bloke comes past and goes nuts. Yelling and shouting. He grabbed the crossbow from Harry and when Harry tried to stop him, he went flying. I saw his hand bend back.' Lucien turned a disgusted face away and gagged.

'I'll talk to friend Harry in a minute,' Gil said. 'You realise someone was shot and killed up here?'

All three content makers let sheepish smiles creep over their faces.

'Obviously,' Lucien said.

'And you didn't think that someone might find you three mocking it up in a comedy way insensitive?'

'It was a toy crossbow,' Lucien said, or rather whined with an accompanying eye roll in his best explaining-it-to-a-boomer voice.

'But still in the same area where someone was killed by a crossbow bolt not two days ago?'

'That has nothing to do with us.' Lucien sounded aggrieved.

'Of course not. Yet, some people would think it was in very bad taste.'

'My God, whose side are you on?'

'The Law's,' Gil said. 'And that man that you think has no right to be triggered, and I'll say that again, triggered by your antics, is related to a victim that was killed in the same way a few years ago.'

Gil saw their faces change. The girls' hands dropped. Their phones suddenly not needed. Lucien, who was probably a mouth breather anyway, let his jaw drop open. Yet, it was he who managed to say in a shaky whisper, 'What?'

'Now,' Gil said. 'Stay here. And post nothing on your … channel,' he added heavy emphasis on the word, 'until I am back after speaking to your friend, Harry. Understand?'

Remarkably, that got three sets of nods.

————

AFTER HIS SISTER DIED, a much younger Chris Messenger found himself wild camping in the Cambrian Hills. Weekends mainly, once for a whole two weeks. He walked, watched, searched for some kind of clue. The area he visited was vast. And in all that time, no one bothered or challenged him when he set up his tent.

'I was engaged at the time. That went to the dogs. But I had no choice. I suppose I went a bit mad.'

Warlow had met other people who'd gone a bit doolally after someone close to them died. And there could be no answer to his question, but he asked it anyway. 'What were you trying to find?'

Messenger's expression, already haunted, took on an extra layer of horror. 'I've asked myself that a thousand times. There was no sense to it then and no sense to it now. Perhaps I was looking for the killer, perhaps for Heather. Like I say, I went off the rails. And now, after you lot called again, the madness came back.'

Warlow and Tomo stayed silent. They'd both heard stranger stories from people wracked by irrational convictions which were far more indefensible than this man's.

'When I saw those oiks up there with that bloody toy crossbow, I lost it. I took it off them. I may have broken it.'

'I counted eleven pieces,' Tomo said.

'The bugger fell and hurt his arm. That's it.'

Warlow ought to have pointed out how incredibly reckless Messenger had been to revisit a place harbouring so much horror and to interact with the youths.

Messenger lacked control. That was clear in every truculent glance he threw around the room in the Visitor Centre they'd purloined for the purpose of the interview, never settling on either of the officers. But Warlow threw him a bone. 'If there is anything concrete you feel the previous investigation failed to follow through on, I'd be glad to hear it.'

'Your lot were a shambles. Twice.' Another verbal jab from Messenger that Warlow let go because he suspected there was more than a grain of truth in it. 'They never found where the bolt came from. You read about all these bloody cases where technological advances and DNA get someone caught. Why haven't they done that? Why haven't they found who owned that bolt?'

Of course, a DNA check had been done on it several times. Nothing other than Heather Messenger's DNA had ever been found. Still, Warlow let Messenger have his head, but much of his ire had evaporated, and he was withdrawing into brooding truculence again. Now, his head hung forward, and the few words that he grudgingly spoke or delivered to the floor were in a changed tone as his belligerence finally ebbed away.

'When was the last time you were up here, Christopher?' Tomo asked.

'Last summer. I came up here for a week.'

'And how many times have you done that since you lost your sister?'

'Every year without fail. My partner … she's been great.'

'And you came alone?'

'Always. Did you know that the village, Abergwesyn, was a meeting point for three main drover's routes. Strata Florida in the north, Tregaron from the west, and up from Pembrokeshire in the southwest. Hard to believe people did that. Walked their animals across that land.'

The noises of a family with excited children walking through the reception filtered through the shut door, incongruous and brash.

'To answer your question, on the day it happened this time, I was at work. And next time, bring that detective constable. The good-looking one.'

Tomo's eyebrows shot up.

Warlow simply said, 'I will.'

———

HARRY, it transpired, appeared to be the brains of the outfit. At least, the one who had a girlfriend who could drive. It was he who'd suggested how much of a blast it might be to drive up to where the killings took place and shoot some … content. Harry also ended up paying the price. Arm in a sling, thanks to the centre's first-aid expert. He'd declined the offer of an ambulance.

'Can you move your hand?' Gil asked, with the dismissive certainty only the completely medically ignorant could muster.

Harry, probably only eight-and-a-half stone soaking wet, nodded.

'Wiggle your fingers?'

Harry nodded again.

Gil realised those answers told him nothing about the injury. 'We can still get an ambulance.'

Harry scowled. 'We have to make our way back. Alicia's dad would kill her if he knew she'd bunked off college. My mum definitely will. We had no idea this place was so far away.'

'Did you not look at a map?'

'Google directions, yeah.'

'So, not a map, then.'

Harry shrugged and another brief discussion about the merits of creating content out of other people's misery followed. To give him credit, Harry looked far more uncomfortable than Lucien did.

'Did the man hit you?' Gil asked.

'No,' Harry said. 'He, like, grabbed the crossbow. I grabbed it back. I put my arm out as I fell. I think it's a sprain.'

'Only an x-ray will give us the answer. And if you have sandwiches and a flask, you're welcome to bed down in A&E for the next twelve hours and get it seen to.'

Harry shook his head. 'No way. We've got to get back. I'll take some ibuprofen. If it doesn't get better, I'll go to my local hospital. I'm not going anywhere near one up here. Do they even have hospitals up here?'

'Yes. And running water. There's talk of electricity coming, too. Though we must have offended the railways because they decided to pass us by.'

It took a minute before Harry twigged that what he'd said might be construed as borderline racism. And that he was still in some sort of trouble and so better to tone it all down. 'I didn't mean—'

'Yes, you did. I'm sure the hospitals in wherever it is you are from are top drawer for wrist sprains. Now, I take it you are not planning on posting any of this nonsense? As I say, I'm no expert, but if Alicia's dad knew what was happening, he might take a dim view. And I'd most certainly want to follow up if anything appeared online. It's policy. And who knows what reaction you might get if the great mass of even-minded Instagram followers found out you were making fun of victims rels.' Gil let his words peter out and watched the panic flare in Harry's eyes.

'We didn't know … and we won't. I promise. I'm sorry that bloke was upset.'

'Hmm. That bloke is related to a person that died up here twenty years ago. But I'll inform him that you apologise. Your friend Lucien seems keen to make all this a six-part drama, though. The kind with bugger all action and lots of feels.'

'Lucien always wants to do that.'

'But social media can be an unpredictable creature, as we are both aware.'

'Look, I'm not posting anything. We won't.'

'You'll sort Lucien out, then?'

Harry nodded again. He looked very sorry for himself, and Gil experienced a rare note of sympathy when the injured boy said, 'I hope you catch whoever did this.'

'We will. If people stop distracting us.'

Harry winced and pondered for a moment before spoiling it all for Gil with a question of monstrous vacuousness. 'What's it like? Being shot by a crossbow bolt.'

Gil allowed a smile to play over his lips. One that contained a loss of all hope for the youth of today. 'That, Harry, is something neither you nor I want to find out the answer to. Believe you me.'

CHAPTER EIGHTEEN

MUCH LATER THAT DAY, after the two-hour journey back to Carmarthen, Warlow debriefed the team on his and Gil's damp squib visit back up to the Elan Valley.

'In a nutshell, the vigilante brother of one of the Bowman case victims, triggered by the recent murders, lost his rag over four idiots playing to the gallery. Not a happy bunny and has not been for twenty years. He is obsessed with our inability to solve his sister's murder and freely admits to being a little mad.'

'Add to that a gang of Instagrammers with not a firing neuron between them, who came for content and left with the "C" word ringing in their ears.' Gil began writing on the board.

'Not *the* "C" word, sarge?' Rhys asked with a note of mild alarm.

'No, not coincidence, or the vulgar word you are alluding to. This "C" word is the one that strikes fear into the hearts of anyone obsessed with S&M. And I don't mean the chain and whip variety. I mean Social and Media. For them, the "C" word is cancel.' He wrote it up and underlined it with a flourish.

'Are you charging Christopher Messenger?' Gina asked.

'We are not,' Gil replied. 'The four crossbow enthusiasts,

who incidentally don't know a drawstring from a fletch, do not want the escapade to become public knowledge.'

A bemused Gina required clarification. 'But I assumed they were going to upload content on Instagram or TikTok?'

'They were. But with no dates. If Messenger was charged, there'd need to be time and place. Bad news for the William Tell appreciation society idiots. Instead, we cautioned him, and he was happy to accept that.'

'Water off a duck's back,' Warlow muttered.

Much the same could be said about the Instagrammers. 'Guess what the injured party asked me?' Gil added a dramatic pause. 'Young Harry wanted to know what it would be like to be shot by a crossbow.'

Jess and Gina shared identical grimaces.

'No news from Povey regarding the bolt?' Warlow asked.

'None,' Rhys said.

The DCI glanced at his watch, disappointed to find that he still had not developed the ability to turn back or halt time. Four-thirty kept getting closer each time he looked. 'What a waste of a day,' he growled. 'And now I have a meeting with the Assistant Chief Constable and Superintendent Drinkwater. Any news on how Sandra Griffiths and Pauline Garston are getting on at Sherwood Forest?'

'Still sorting,' Jess said.

'At least that's something I can say we're working on. And we'll need another day or two to complete the task. Any other news?'

'Still awaiting calls with the new victim's partner's supervisor to confirm and establish her whereabouts,' Gina said.

'That's Amanda Beech?'

Gina nodded.

'What about Messenger's ex? The one in Hereford who's playing hard to get.'

'Nothing yet. He's acknowledged text messages. We're awaiting his callback.'

Another Warlow glance at his watch.

16.25.

Rhys noticed the glance. 'Into the lion's den, sir? Hakuna matata.'

'Not for me. I'll have the chicken bhuna,' Gil said.

Warlow got up from his seat. 'Tomorrow morning, 8.30 sharp, please. Judging by the quality of humour in those last two remarks, I'd give it half an hour and then call it a day.'

———

GIL TOOK Catrin Richards's call as he drove home on the fifteen-mile journey between Carmarthen and Llandeilo.

'Well, well. Feet up in front of *Loose Women* while Betsi is asleep, is it?'

'No, but she's just been fed, and my mother is doing the burping.'

'Ah, the burping. Much maligned skill. In some cultures, it remains a lifelong practice and is a sign of good health and a satisfying meal. Sit on any bus in Beijing or Keelung and you'd think you were in the frogs' chorus.'

'Long day, Gil?' Catrin's years of experience working with her fellow sergeant had made her an expert on his moods.

'Frustrating would best describe it.' He filled her in on his and Warlow's trot up the garden path with Christopher Messenger.

'Oh dear,' Catrin sympathised.

'Other, choicer, descriptors are available. But how are you and Betsi doing?'

'Well. She's up to twelve pounds now and meeting all her milestones.'

'*Mam fach*, twelve pounds? Hard to believe we all weighed that much once.'

'Harder in some instances than others.'

Gil took it on the chin but came back with the mildest of rejoinders to acknowledge her tetchiness. 'Getting enough sleep, Catrin?'

'Sleep … I remember that. You close your eyes and drift off and wake up eight hours later.'

'It gets better. Always does. Craig, okay?'

'Doing his bit. Fatherhood suits him. He now knows all the words to *Nellie the Elephant*, for example.'

'Britain's got talent,' Gil said. 'But not Craig.'

'Lovely to talk, Gil, but I have bottles to sterilise and get a wash on. The other reason I rang is to do with Napier.'

That took Gil by surprise, and his ears pricked up.

He'd watched the solicitor and the outbuilding he'd been in blown to smithereens in front of his eyes. Roger Hunt's promise to himself to punish Napier's supposed involvement in the illegal and salacious filming of guests at his Airbnb had culminated in a pipe bomb at an isolated cottage near Angle in Pembrokeshire. The memory remained starkly raw in Gil's mind.

'Don't tell me he's risen from the dead? If he has, they'll need a lot of superglues.'

'Funnily enough, in a way, he has. Not corporeally. More in a criminal fraud sense.'

Gil was now fully engaged. 'I'm listening. In fact, I'm pulling into the White Mill garage here to listen properly. Hang on.'

He manoeuvred the car to the side of the fuel and convenience store, in front of a lot selling four-by-fours. There were worse places to pull over. The Towy River snaked close to the A40 here, and the valley floor flood plain had few properties. Paxton's Tower, fully visible on the rising hills opposite, looked down as Catrin explained the reason for her call.

'Napier's death left a lot of his professional business unfinished. And he was the face of the business. An old-fashioned country solicitor's office. And though he had other people working with him, he'd been around the longest. He was trusted, handled finances and wills for lots of families and the *crachach*.'

Gil smiled at the use of the Welsh word.

Crachach. The petty gentry and cognoscenti found in all the little towns across the country. The kind of people who thought themselves better than everyone else by dint of position, education, or money.

'After he died,' Catrin continued, 'some people took their

business elsewhere. In fact, what we didn't know was that Napier had received, and sat on, several informal complaints about his handling of people's wills and estates. Quite a few relatives felt disgruntled. Some of his clients, especially people who died without many relatives at all, bequeathed him size-able sums. Anyway, I got a call today from someone in Financial Crimes to say they've been contacted by another firm of solicitors who believe they've uncovered evidence of embez-zlement.'

'I can't say I'm surprised. Rumours have been flying about for years. The Napiers lived high on the hog and liked to flaunt it.'

'Anyway, the reason I'm ringing you is to say that Financial Crimes are obtaining a warrant to access all of Napier's records.'

A small, tingling knot of excitement tightened somewhere in Gil's insides. 'That means we could have access?'

'Louise Sobell, the woman who spoke to me, had informa-tion about our unfinished business. She also confirmed that Napier's wife's legal team had been adopting stalling tactics.'

'By hinting at a civil action against Dyfed Powys for negli-gence over Napier being blown to kingdom come if we keep hassling for his records.' Gil knew all about it.

'Exactly that. Anyway, Louise is going to issue the warrant early next week for everything at his office and his home.'

'Napier's wife has had ten months to get rid of stuff.'

'But what you're looking for would not be anything to do with shady financial practices, right?'

Good question, that one, since he lacked precise knowl-edge of what he would be searching for. Something that might link Napier to one Royston Moyles and his use of the property known as Can y Barcud. A place where several serious crimes had already been committed.

Gil had nothing but his own nagging suspicions, and some thin threads of, so far, unexplained scribbled entries for guests at the Airbnb, referred to in diaries and calendars as "PP" and "VIP" and some thankfully non-explicit, but still intrusive photographs of young guests who'd stayed at the cottage.

One of which haunted Gil because of his similarity to a long-standing missing person's case. It had become a stone in his proverbial shoe.

But what Catrin was telling him now turned that stone into something much sharper.

'You still there, Gil?'

'I am.'

'Once I am better informed, I'll update you.'

'Much obliged. And if you ever want any help on child-rearing, I'm your man. They used to call me Spock.'

'After the bloke who wrote the baby books?'

'No, after the bloke with big ears and a bad haircut. The Lady Anwen always said I had a bit of alien in me, though which bit to this day she has not let on. I like to think it's my Plutonian knees.'

'Really?' Catrin's response was sandpaper dry, knowing there was more to come.

'Then again, I can't help wondering if it's more something to do with Uranus she might be referring to.'

Three seconds of silence followed before Catrin said, 'It's good to talk, Gil. I do miss the bants.'

'I appreciate the call. Regards to Craig, too, and the little one. Now, buoyed by your news, it's warp factor five to Llandeilo or I really will be in trouble since I am to pick up my granddaughter number one, Eleri, from football practice, and she does not take any prisoners on the timekeeping front. For an eight-year-old, she has a remarkably fierce temper and a tongue like razor wire. Last week, she called me an ancient marinade like the old man in the sea. Education has a lot to answer for, as does Sponge Bob.'

CHAPTER NINETEEN

'So, how long did you hold the barbarians at bay for, exactly?'

Jess asked the question as she and Warlow sat together in front of the TV later that evening. They were halfway through the 10pm news with the sound on low. Images from Eastern Europe, the Middle East, and the African Congo were gruesome enough without the explicit commentary.

Everywhere, the world seemed intent on tearing itself apart with conflict. You acknowledged the fact that existential battles were being fought on several fronts, with most of the populous sleepwalking into them all. Religion against religion, authoritarianism versus democracy, truth versus lies, with the opposition in each case developing new propaganda weapons as startlingly realistic AI. It made no difference which battle you fought. Skirmishes were beamed at every TV in every room in every country in the world and risked desensitising everyone to the horror.

Warlow couldn't solve the world's problems. But he could pick one he was aware he had a fighting chance of winning.

'I think Pauline Garston had a word with the chief constable. Drinkwater was all for handing over the baton, but the assistant chief constable was remarkably even-handed.'

They both knew what the task force might mean. Dragging personnel away from already busy schedules and jobs they had to do. It also meant that it was by no means certain that Warlow would continue to lead. There were superintendents galore in the wings itching to get their teeth into this one.

But with the Buccaneer's backing, he'd argued the need for all the previous information to be available, and Pauline Garston backed up the fact that they were still awaiting some evidence Tim Leach had somehow managed to not make available for the reviews.

Garston was aware of it only because of the closure of the Ammanford police station. In clearing it out, they'd found a few files marked for Leach's attention inside boxes of other files. But they had been pertinent to the Bowman. By then Leach had retired, and Garston was in post review and moved a few rungs up the ladder. She had to admit she had not bothered to look at them.

Yet, a requirement to examine them again now brought them to mind.

'We have another five days at most,' Warlow said. 'Four and a half for me because I've got a bloody checkup with Dr Emmerson in Swansea on Monday.'

Jess's face lit up. 'You could take Molly out for coffee. And less of the four-and-a-half days' crap, please. We won't collapse without you.'

He smiled an apology. Of course, they wouldn't collapse, and meeting Molly for coffee would be some compensation for the laugh-fest his consultations usually ended up being.

'I'll text. See if she is free, Monday pm, you said?'

'Lunchtime.' Warlow nodded and glanced at Cadi, stretched out near a radiator. The dog, one eye open, half listening to the conversation, caught his glance, and her tail thumped the floor softly.

'Time for a supper biscuit and a comfort break, miss?'

Cadi's tail thumped a bit louder.

'I swear, sometimes, I think you're talking to me,' Jess said.

'Join us. But Cadi does it outside on the cobbles, and it's

wonky out there tonight. They say we're in for a late cold spell.'

'No, thank you. I'll stick to the bathroom.'

'I thought you Northern girls were tough?'

Warlow got a gentle thump on the arm for that from one female in his life, and a cold nose on his hand from the other.

———

DESPITE THE FOLLOWING morning's early start, little or no new information could be added to the sparse database they already had. Warlow was hoping for connections. Something that might link the victims to each other. Some inkling why four people died.

Jess was right. There would be a link. However spurious it might seem. Not necessarily between victims even, but between the cases definitely. There were simply too many similarities for them not to be.

And so, dogged follow-up and diligence were their watchwords.

At 9:38, Gina finally took a call from Heather Messenger's ex-partner. He did not come across as someone who appreciated the messages sent to him by the officers recruited into the team from CID and who'd been tasked with contacting him until they got a reply. His call, taken via the generic number set up for ring backs, was patched through to Gina.

'Thanks for coming back to us, Mr Wojak.'

'I'm only doing this to stop you buggers hassling me.'

'We wanted to warn you—'

Wojak cut her off. 'Yeah, well, what happened happened. I've moved on. At least I've tried. I do not appreciate all this stuff being dragged out into the open again. I can tell you that.'

Gina had read the file. Wojak had been on the way to meet Heather Messenger when she'd been killed. He'd been questioned several times because of his inability to provide witnesses for where exactly he'd been when Heather and Coombs were killed. His assertion that he'd been in transit were backed up only by the odd text message. But the lack of motive and any physical evidence had finally cleared him.

'It might not be us doing the digging, Mr Wojak. The press—'

'Had a sodding field day at my expense when it happened. I've moved on. I have kids.'

'Our purpose for reaching out to you was to warn you of the likelihood that the press might want to stoke the fires again.'

'Jesus Christ. Can't you stop them?'

'No, we can't. They rightly would claim they were acting in the public interest.'

'So what? I'll be accused all over again?'

'No one is accusing you—'

'Because I'm not having it,' Wojak insisted. 'Anything you lot want to say to me or ask me needs to go through my solicitor. End of.'

Gina tried again, 'The reason for contacting you is to ask if there's anything at the time of the killing that you felt was—'

'I will not do your bloody job for you, for Christ's sake. I'll say it again. Please don't contact me again other than through my solicitor. I'll get him to give you his contact details. Who are you?'

'DC Mellings.'

Wojak ended the call, leaving Gina staring at the handpiece, listening to dead air.

———

THE ONE SLIGHT chink of light came from Povey.

'I have some info on the bolt. Not much, but I took the liberty of contacting Hugo Milton, the crossbow expert. I've got some questions for him regarding the new and old bolts.'

'Why don't we all meet at Sherwood Forest?' Warlow suggested.

'Lovely. I hear Nottingham can be very nice this time of year.'

'Unfortunately, the one I'm referring to is in an old factory in Johnstown.'

'You are no fun, Mr Warlow, did you know that?'

They met at 10:40. Warlow took Rhys, and they met Povey, Tannard, and Milton.

He had brought a working example of a crossbow with him. A replica of an old bow, but one with modern stringing. Rhys jumped at the opportunity of handling it when it was offered.

'Originally, this would've had a windlass crank to tension the drawstring,' Milton explained.

Rhys nodded, a strange light in his eye. Warlow understood immediately that the acting sergeant was all on board with all of this.

'That's the thing, isn't it? You needed little, or no, training to fire these. Whereas the longbow took years.'

'You are a student of history, sergeant.' Milton grinned, a flash of tobacco-stained teeth just visible through the beard.

'I know a bit. Wasn't every male child of a certain age expected to develop archery skills?' Rhys lifted the crossbow.

''Twas indeed the law,' Milton said. 'The Assize of Arms in 1252 required every able-bodied man practise archery. In 1363, it was made more obligatory and enforced on a Sunday. Whereas with the crossbow, once the string is tensioned on the stock, accuracy and speed of firing are the limiting factors, but training required is and was minimal. Richard the Lionheart met his end with a crossbow. So hated a weapon was it that the pope once banned it in 1139. The longbow, on the other hand, was basically your medium-range artillery.'

'May I?' Povey took the crossbow.

Tannard had printed images of bolts in her hand, and she held them up now.

'This one is identical to the bolt we found in Gerald Nash, and near the body of Kirsty Stuart.' Tannard pointed. 'If you look here, you can see markings. Not grooves as you'd expect to find in a fired bullet, but markings. The speed at which a bolt leaves the flight groove on the serving is approximately three hundred feet per second. It's likely these marks are made by imperfections in the groove as the bolt is drawn along its length during firing. What we can say is that the markings are the same in both bolts that were found.'

'The same bow fired both bolts, then?' Warlow asked.

'That would be our interpretation, yes,' Tannard said.

'The chances of these markings being the same in two bolts is minimal,' Povey added.

'Where are the bolts from?' Rhys asked.

Tannard pointed again to a blown-up image. 'The logo on the shaft here, where it attaches to the hunting tip, says Woodrow. It's a British company.'

'Ubiquitous I'm afraid,' Milton said. 'Easily obtained in speciality shops, and these days, of course, online.'

'Serial numbers?' Rhys asked.

'No. This is ordinance, don't forget,' Tannard replied.

'So, do we try to track sales in the last year?' Warlow knew how it sounded. The un-oiled creek of seized-up desperation.

'Can't do any harm, sir.' Rhys took the crossbow back and hefted it once more.

'This one is all wood, of course,' Milton said. 'Not like modern ones which are much lighter because of fibreglass, et cetera.'

'What about the bolts in the Bowman case?' Warlow asked.

'Bolt. There was only one found,' Povey said.

Tannard had other images. 'We've had a quick look through the archive. As you can see, this one looks well used, with many more markings from having been fired many times. Obviously, we only have a partial bolt from the first killings.'

Povey turned to Milton. 'You identified this as a bolt made abroad.'

Milton nodded. 'French manufacturer. That logo is DeSOL's. Mainly used abroad. I think they imported some for use in competitions. A few clubs. They were not for sale on the open marketplace at the time.'

Warlow studied the photographs and the blown-up logos. Slim picking indeed.

Pauline Garston appeared in his eyeline. Dressed in dark trousers and a white blouse, looking as if she'd never retired. She took in the little crowd and nodded to everyone, but then leaned in when she got to Warlow.

'I think we need a quiet word, Evan.'

Warlow followed her out into a storage area. He wanted to thank her for fighting his corner with the ACC and Drinkwater, though he still wasn't quite sure what she'd said. But before he could speak, the ex-DI in the Bowman case took a folder from her messenger bag.

'You need to see something.'

She opened the file and took out a plain see-through, perforated A4 slipcase. Inside was a printed letter, slightly awry, which meant it had been photocopied. 'This is a copy of Leach's lost files. I'm not sure how many times it's been handled, but I wanted to be safe. This was from the file.'

'The file supposedly lost in Ammanford with Leach's name on it?'

'That one, yes.'

Warlow accepted the A4 sheet. It was faded, but he could read the words. And, in so doing, felt the world pivot.

CHAPTER TWENTY

SOMETIMES, the difference between innocuous and incendiary turned on a windblown spark.

Such was the dilemma Tim Leach must have felt when he'd received the two letters Pauline Garston found in his files.

First, they were addressed to him at his home, not his work. He must have brought them to Ammanford, and the FYEO file he'd labelled with his own name and squirrelled them away without showing them to anyone. Especially not to his feisty, increasingly frustrated, junior colleague, DI Pauline Garston. He was well aware of what she might say. The same as what she said now.

'Crank letters,' she said. And with good reason.

The Bowman investigation dragged on for weeks and months, visceral and horrifying, with those involved becoming minor celebrities. But soon, those that could, the senior management, jumped ship on the press front once the turgid lack of progress in the case made them look ineffective. They happily dumped that burden, like everything else, on the man at the helm, Leach.

And how long does it take for a hero to fall from grace? There is more than one national figure who has the potential to answer that. About as long as it takes to send a salacious text to an impressionable young fan, or, God forbid, a photograph of something anatomical in all its mistakenly excited glory.

At least with Leach, his transformation from dogged detective to hopeless nonentity happened gradually. Perhaps that awareness had fuelled his reluctance to show these letters to colleagues, let alone the press. With the latter, he'd risk possibly offending the letter sender and cutting off lines of communication. As for the former, he risked, at the very least, a healthy scepticism, at worst, derision.

Everyone knew what could happen if you allowed your unconscious bias to guide the ship. History had its famously terrifying examples. False confessions, hoax recordings, with just enough information for the dangled carrot to manipulate and pull the strings. In the case of the Yorkshire Ripper, the dangling had meant Peter Sutcliffe was free to carry on whilst the police searched for a man with a Newcastle accent. That they'd all been hoodwinked by "Wearside Jack" beggared belief in retrospect. But the clever hoaxer had used information wrongly thought uncommon knowledge.

Hoaxers were clever buggers.

The first letter to Leach arrived five weeks after the murder. Machine printed and most likely written on a computer.

Dear Superintendent Leach,

I am writing with information about the killings in the Cambrian Mountains. What the papers are calling the Bowman. The man you want is Andrew Yardley. I know he's dead, but he and I were friends, and he spoke to me after killing those people at his house and after going up the mountains. He told me he got such a thrill killing the first time that he wanted that thrill again before he ended it all.

Yardley parked his van in the woods, then he took a tent and walked up the mountain to hide out. But when he saw the girl, Heather Messenger, he shot her. She was the first. Then he walked over the moor and waited until Phillip Coombs appeared. He did it that way so that he could double back to his tent. He said he couldn't take the bolt out of Messenger and thought he'd get caught because of that. Yardley got his equipment from France and brings it back on his lorry.

I wish you and your team success.

No signature and no initials

The second letter arrived five days later:

Dear Superintendent Leach,

In case you didn't get my last letter because the post is rubbish, I'm sending it again.

PS. Yardley is your man.

'How much of this could the author have got from press reports?' Warlow asked.

'A lot. There was speculation for weeks about who got shot first.'

'What about the bolt being left in?'

'That's a tricky one. We'll have to check back and see. That information could only have been obtained during the autopsy, but I can't recall when it became accessible to the press.'

'And the stuff about the bolt coming from France?'

Garston shrugged. 'Yardley drove long-distance lorries, that's true. But that was well known. And we'd been ringing suppliers by then, trying to find out where the bolt might have come from. So, not the press, but suppliers, yes. The letter writer could have got information that way.'

'Leach gets the letters and knows they risk being confined to the crank pile, despite one or two titbits. Suggestions that the letter writer possessed information. Something Leach believes only the killer would know.'

Pauline nods. 'Leach buys into it, and then does his utmost to reverse engineer Yardley as the suspect to find evidence to back it up. He made all of us try to squeeze Yardley through the neck of a bottle.'

'But you couldn't,' Warlow said. 'No matter how hard you all tried.'

Pauline Garston stared at Warlow like a flat earther being shown satellite photos of a round planet.

'It wasn't Yardley. He was considered, and we looked hard, but we found nothing at all. And the timeline was way too tight. His van was parked in the woods. Several people, walkers and cyclists, had noticed a van there for days before reporting it. Then we found him dead. Likely, he committed suicide just after the attacks in the Cambrians or around the same time. But once Leach was hooked on the idea, he found it impossible to let go. I remember it like it was yesterday. No matter how much we argued, he was convinced Yardley did it.' She shook her head. 'These letters are going to cause ripples.'

Warlow nodded. 'What bothers me is the other possibility here. That these did come from the actual killer with just enough detail to convince and confuse Leach.'

Pauline squeezed her eyes shut. Missed opportunities were the scars everyone involved in murder inquiries bore.

'If it's true, that's … despicable,' she said.

'Whoever killed Messenger and Coombs was very good at covering their tracks. Pauline, do you mind coming up to HQ with me? I will need to brief the team.'

THEY LEFT POVEY WITH MILTON. With Pauline Garston following, Warlow took Rhys, and the copied letters, back to the Incident Room.

They found Pauline a visitor's pass, but it took her twice as long to get to the Incident Room. Largely because of the hellos and handshakes she got from colleagues. When he heard she was in the building, Sion Buchannan came down to visit, followed shortly after by Drinkwater, "as it were".

But once all that was over and they were gathered in the Incident Room, Warlow got down to business and asked Pauline to recount everything she'd told him about the letters.

'So, he didn't want to show them to anyone in case they were labelled hoaxes?' Gina asked. 'Even though there are specific details that only the killer had knowledge of?'

'Or so Leach believed,' Gil said. 'It happens. I've seen SIOs get hung up on details that worm their way into their psyche.'

Truth and lies. Here they were again.

'We need to enter these as evidence and send the originals to Povey. See if we can get anything from them. Pauline has the FYEO file. I'd like to think Leach had the sense to keep the original letters relatively uncontaminated.'

Rhys made a note and then looked up with a pensive expression. 'Either the letter writer is correct, and Yardley did it—'

'He didn't,' Pauline countered. 'He'd had to have used a different crossbow and a different bolt compared to what he'd used when he murdered his neighbours.'

Rhys followed through with his thinking. 'Or the person who wrote the letter was the actual killer and tried to sway Superintendent Leach. Nudge him in the wrong direction.'

'That's about the gist of it, Rhys,' Warlow agreed. 'But there is the third option. That what's in those letters was common knowledge at the time. Don't forget the press feeding frenzy. As investigators, the murder team could not possibly have kept tabs on everything that had been written. It is possible that details about the bolt being left in and contacting French suppliers might have been leaked. All fodder for some mischievous arse to send in. Stir the pot to see how Leach reacted.'

'So, how do these help us?' Jess asked.

'In terms of getting us closer to whoever killed Stuart and Nash, not much. What it does tell us is that the Bowman, if he wrote those, is a devious bugger.'

'But it is progress of a sort, sir, isn't it?' Rhys asked, ever the optimist.

'More like five steps backwards, in my opinion,' Warlow muttered. 'Another unnecessary distraction. And, I suspect, exactly what the letter writer wanted when the bugger wrote them.'

CHAPTER TWENTY-ONE

ONE MAN'S meat was another man's salmonella, as an old editor of his was wont to say. And, as journalistic proverbs went, it just about summed up Lane's career. He searched for the edge in people, the corner of their life's carpet that, once lifted, revealed all the little creatures of the dark crawling about beneath.

His involvement as a coerced and blackmailed puppet of Roger Hunt's and, more specifically, his role in the abduction of Catrin Richards, orchestrated by Hunt, remained cloaked in well-crafted obfuscation. Partly because Lane was very good at that, and partly because there was a book in it somewhere.

In the statement he'd given to police, he'd told them nothing of how he'd been in fear of his life after Hunt confronted him, threatened him and, indirectly, his partner. That threat would manifest if Lane didn't cooperate. And there was no element of fiction in Lane's belief that the threat was real and would be carried out.

Hunt's descent into vengeful single mindedness oozed out of every pore. The leverage Hunt used—Lane's phone, taken from him during their first encounter, a so-called "mugging" at gunpoint—had been deeply existential. On that phone were incriminating photographs "obtained" as part of an in-depth investigation into paedophile vigilantism on the net. After Hunt had stolen his phone, Lane found himself in a rare moment of introspection. He wondered why, in the weeks following the vigilante investigation, he hadn't deleted all those photographs—especially since he had chosen not to store any of his photo library in the cloud.

But both the reflection and the answers he came up with were too uncomfortable to dwell on. Whether by accident or subconscious design, it remained a discussion he'd not yet been prepared to have with his own conscience.

Luckily for Lane, the phone and its memory card were now in the estuary mud under the River Towy, thrown there by Lane himself on its return to him by Hunt, after his part in orchestrating the abduction arrangements.

The truth, and that in itself was a very slippery eel in the Lane lexicon, remained concrete in terms of Lane's genuine fear of what Hunt was capable of. A truth borne out by the way the man had murdered two people and put another into a coma.

But, with Hunt's death, the only other source of the real truth about the situation evaporated. Lane took comfort in the idea that had the killer been aware of his true association with Napier and Moyles, the situation could have unfolded in a different manner.

But Lane's diligence in covering his tracks and with all three of them now dead, the gods, it seemed, were smiling down on him. Either that, or they were laughing their heads off at some dreadful revelation yet to come.

But Lane put all of that in a mental box on a tall shelf. So far, the gods had been kind. There was no reason for him to believe they would abandon him now.

The gambler's folly.

And, of course, the police had suspicions. Hunt had travelled by bicycle from his lair in mid-Wales. No doubt, the police would check CCTV and ANPR records for signs of Hunt's movements. But the meetings Hunt had set up with Lane always took place using bicycles to avoid triggering ANPR, and in locations off the beaten track. Lane had lived for months in fear of the police finding some link. Added to that, anxiety over his narrow escape from a worse fate at the hands of Hunt—whether physically or professionally—had affected him badly. He'd crawled away to lick his wounds while the thick dust settled.

Only now, after several months of lying low, Lane's reptilian confidence was slowly returning, and he was hungry again. Warlow's team had various names for the journalist. Unscrupulous, being the mildest. Vampire, blood sucker, hyena also featured.

But, if anyone asked Warlow, he would probably opt for Monitor Lizard. An animal that lies in wait for its prey, bites it, and then lets all the poison in its saliva slowly kill the victim. Lane was a slow poisoner.

A book about Hunt, seen from Lane's unique perspective, was in the second draft. And now that the Crossbow murders were creating headlines, he'd been approached by a couple of editors for anything he could get.

Lloyd Coombs became a very easy target. And, on the promise of a few hundred quid upfront and a lot more to follow, Lane arranged the meeting for that day at 10am. When Lloyd was on a break from his delivery job.

———

THE LAY-BY CONTAINED four parked vehicles besides the burger van dispensing breakfast to the lorry and van driver regulars when Lane pulled in. Lloyd had explained he drove a white Ford Transit. Lane would struggle to describe the vehicle that he saw parked up as white, but under the dust and dirt, it probably had been once.

Lane parked his Renault Captur and walked across to the van. The door opened, and Lane set eyes for the first time in person on the wiry young man he'd been talking to and texting.

'Geraint, is it?' Lloyd asked.

Lane did not hold out a hand, but acknowledged with a cheery, 'That's it. Lloyd, right?'

'Yeah.'

'Thanks for meeting me, Lloyd. Never been to this establishment before.'

'Oh, then you've missed out. Jim's sausage and chips in gravy is ace, I tell you.'

'I'll have to give it a go sometime,' Lane said. 'Tea?'

'I've just had one, but yeah, go on, two sugars.'

Lane approached the man standing in the burger van. A strong smell of grease and onions greeted him as he neared. The eponymous Jim looked to be mid-sixties, as wiry as Lloyd, but with a voice like a high-pitched winch in need of oiling.

'Two teas, please, both two sugars with milk.'

Jim let out a throaty, 'Coming up,' and delivered the beverages into paper cups from a silver teapot he kept topped up with hot water. The sugar followed via a crusted spoon he used to stir both. Lane got £2 change from a fiver.

Lloyd, standing in a patch of March sunshine, took the offered cup and then Lane sipped the brew.

The tannins nearly stripped a layer of skin from his mouth. He suspected if he painted Jim's tea on his skin, he'd save five days sunning himself on the Riviera.

'So, Lloyd. The crossbow thing. Must be a gut punch for you.'

'How do you mean?'

'If it's the bloke that killed your father, surely this should not be happening again.'

Lloyd frowned. 'What? Do you think that it's the same bloke?'

'Don't you?'

'The police don't.'

'Right, the police. Tell me, have they even apologised to you for not finding your dad's killer?'

'I was only a kid. I wouldn't know.'

Lane tilted his head. 'What about this time? They've spoken to you, haven't they?'

'Yeah.'

'Did they apologise?'

Lloyd's brows drew in. 'No. Well, sort of.'

Lane let this little barb of disquiet bed in and tweaked it a little to make sure Lloyd felt its presence. 'So, no formal apology. Then why did they contact you, do you think?'

Lloyd gulped a mouthful of tea. As he did, Lane let his eyes stray to the rubbish-strewn bushes at the edge of the lay-by, searching for a place to discard the brew.

'They wanted to warn me. About the press.' A wry smile crossed Lloyd's lips. 'About you, I expect. Oh, and to ask if there was anything I could remember that might be useful.'

'Is there?'

'I was just a kid.'

'Exactly.' Lane trowelled on the sympathy. 'Just a kid whose life was thrown into a blender and who has received no apology from the police for their ineptitude.'

Lloyd thought about the word, and Lane was glad to see it sink in.

'But they didn't kill my dad.'

'No, but they never found out who did, right? And now, they have the cheek …' Lane toyed with using temerity, but suspected he'd already pushed his luck with ineptitude. ' … the cheek to call for your help.'

That made Lloyd think. Slightly pouting lips were the giveaway. 'Well, if you put it like that.'

'I do. I put it very much like that. Lloyd, if ever a story needed to be told, this is it. I'd be the one to tell it. And since you're now in a unique position to ask the police questions, you can keep tabs on how well it's going. Between us, we can make sure there'll be no more mistakes.'

'Yeah …' Lloyd hesitated. 'I don't know, though.'

'There's money in it, Lloyd. People want to hear this stuff.'

The magic word did the trick. The widening of Lloyd's eyes told Lane three cherries had just come up.

'How much, like?'

'Depends on what we can sort out. A thousand for your story, but an extra two hundred for every bit of info you can get from the police.'

Still Lloyd prevaricated. But Lane had a cure for that.

'Think of it a bit like being a double agent. *Mission Impossible* stuff.'

As cultural references went, it was crude. But Lloyd was in his twenties. Films were his Encyclopaedia Britannica.

'Sounds good,' Lloyd said.

'Great.' Lane took out his phone. A current model iPhone to replace the one sitting at the bottom of the river. 'I'm going to record us.'

'But no photos, yeah?'

'I won't need to take pictures.' Even as Lane said this, and as a statement it was cleverly crafted, it brought to mind the stock images of the four-year-old fatherless child that would undoubtedly accompany anything the newspapers printed. A link back to the Bowman case. But no new photos. There'd be no need.

'Now, let's start at the beginning,' the journalist said. 'To when it all happened.'

'When I was four?'

'Why not? Kids' stories are always the best. Tugs at the heartstrings, you know.'

'A thousand quid, you said?'

Lane replied with a cheddary grin.

'Why don't you finish your tea in my car?' He pressed something on his keys, and the Captur's indicators blinked twice.

As Lloyd turned away, Lane deftly took three steps towards the shrubbery and emptied his tea into the ground, knowing that whatever greenery it touched would probably wither and die.

CHAPTER TWENTY-TWO

WARLOW HAD no option other than to run the new information about the letters found in Leach's file up the chain. Inevitably, it triggered another meeting with the powers that be. They held it in a conference room. That meant he did not need to go far. No coffees or pastries this time. Just bottles of water, and a nasty surprise.

Assistant Chief Constable Steven Reid, as always meticulously groomed, had no smiles for anyone today. Warlow had noticed that about the man previously. How easily the affected charm that must have worked on some, could give way to simmering desperation. Since his role was to deflect flak and fight fires, exuding an air of perpetually teetering on the edge of chaos hardly inspired confidence.

He flicked some lint off his dark sleeve as Warlow entered, hinting at the vanity underneath the subtle arrogance. Not that Warlow actively disliked the man, but neither did he consider him someone he'd want in his corner in a fight on the grounds that the bugger might have already placed a two-way bet.

Drinkwater opened proceedings, his bushy eyebrows like fuzzy caterpillars attempting a mating ritual on his forehead. Warlow swore he had even less hair on his thinning pate today than yesterday. 'Before we discuss the elephant in the room, any progress in the Stuart and Nash case, Evan?'

'We're running down the weaponry, specifically the type of bolt used and the bow that would be capable of firing it.'

The ACC looked even more miffed with the world than before. 'Aren't these things licensed?'

'No. It's unnecessary for ownership. It is illegal to fire a bow in a public place, though, sir.'

'Fat lot of bloody good that is.'

No one argued.

'What I want to know, and what the press will no doubt demand—' The ACC clearly had *his* elephant gun out, locked and loaded. '—is why these letters supposedly incriminating Yardley remained hidden for so long?' His gaze flicked accusingly from Buchannan to Drinkwater. They both in turn looked to Warlow for an answer.

'The simple answer is that Superintendent Leach secreted them away. He's in no state to provide us with a cogent reason now. But my best guess is that in a case like the Bowman's, you are always wary of armchair detectives.'

'But these letters name Yardley,' the ACC said almost petulantly.

To his credit, Buchannan weighed in, 'Tim Leach would have taken that on board. He spent significant time and resource trying to make Yardley fit but couldn't.'

'But, if he had exposed the letters, they might have initiated other lines of inquiry, surely?' Drinkwater said.

Other lines of inquiry, thought Warlow. They would unquestionably have sparked additional press speculation. In his own way, Tim Leach had done the right thing; look for corroborating evidence to see if he could make Yardley fit. His fault had been to get stuck in a groove and not be able to free himself from it.

'My feeling is that he felt it might cause further delays in the investigation, sir,' Warlow said.

'But the cat is out of the bag now. It means another look at the Bowman case in light of this information.' The ACC's words had an air of finality about them.

Warlow could've made it clear that Leach had spent an awful lot of time looking from this very angle already, even if he hadn't revealed his reasoning to everyone before. Trying to Photoshop Yardley into the frame yet again was doomed to failure. If Reid and Drinkwater decided to put him on this instead of letting him concentrate on the here and now … He glanced over at Buchannan, but his expression, fixed on a point three feet above the ACC's head, gave nothing away.

Studiously so.

'If I might suggest a way forward,' Drinkwater said. 'We need someone skilled in press relations to handle this and liaise. Someone who is also a seasoned investigator in her own right. That is why I asked Pamela to join us.'

Warlow turned to the fourth person in the room. Someone he'd wanted to ignore until that point because he'd not wanted to make eye contact.

Superintendent Pamela Goodey, aka Two-Shoes to all and sundry who'd had the misfortune of coming across her, allowed herself a self-deprecating smile that lasted all of four seconds before her lips slid back into steel trap mode.

The ACC considered this and, as so often was the case when it came to awkward situations demanding quick responses, misinterpreted change as progress and nodded.

Drinkwater continued, 'Pamela will work with Pauline Garston, who has generously volunteered her help as a consultant, and handle the press side of things with her usual tact, as it were.'

Jesus H Christ. Warlow almost said it out loud.

'Leaving Evan to continue with the Stuart and Nash case for now,' Buchannan filled in the blanks.

'We still retain the potential for a larger task force in the mix?' the ACC asked.

'We do,' Buchannan added. 'But with this unknown element to the Bowman case, handing it all over now might seem …' He pretended to search for a word.

'As if we were throwing in the towel before the bout had begun,' the ACC said, baring his teeth.

It was a solution of sorts. Even though it meant Warlow might have to, once again, work with Goodey, after a fashion.

Their track record in the cases they'd worked on together left a lot to be desired, from Warlow and the team's perspective at least. Goodey, he suspected, was so thick-skinned, she probably considered them all routine days at the office.

But then Typhoid Mary had thought herself a bloody excellent cook.

Goodey had been the cheerleader for two outsiders who had proven to be mavericks of the very worst kind. Kelvin Caldwell had been one of her protégés, and his involvement in organised crime was still the subject of glacially slow ongoing investigations. She'd then tried to shoehorn some talent in as a replacement for Gil, whom she considered well over the hill and on the slippery downward slope. That talent, one Detective Sergeant Hopper, proved to be an egotistical narcissist killer in his own right.

In terms of judging character, Goodey was lamentable. And yet, for all the wrong reasons, here she still was, having been moved sideways twice until the roundabout came full circle. It smacked of corporate chicanery. The kind where no one ever lost their jobs but simply took on a different role so that their stock options, or in this case, pensions, were not harmed.

Either that or her superiors simply needed to keep the wheel spinning until fate intervened and she either got a job on another Force or was struck by lightning.

Warlow prayed for thunder.

Goodey slid her bright, doll-like eyes over to Warlow. He hoped she was no telepathist.

'I am certain we can work together on this, Evan, to ensure the best outcome. Full disclosure on both our parts, and I will base myself at Johnstown to get out of your hair.'

Warlow nodded. He even found a smile from somewhere and hoped it didn't drip too much with gratitude instead of acknowledgement.

This was a first. Normally, she'd be sitting in his seat in the Incident Room waving a conductor's baton.

With a sudden flash of inspiration, he added some fuel to the fire. 'Good idea, ma'am. And of course, there is the possibility that DS Leach might have been sitting on some other evidence.'

Goodey's eyes narrowed in suspicion, but the ACC was on it like a grouper swallowing a sardine. 'Oh, God, there isn't, is there?'

Goodey stayed calm. 'Rest assured, I will be thorough. Tim Leach's files will be looked over. And as for the need for separation—' Her eyes softened in Warlow's direction as if acknowledging a point well played in the little power-tennis-match between them. '—there is a great deal of physical evidence, and it would only clutter things up to transfer all to HQ now.'

'Absolutely.' Warlow tried to be restrained while his brain did cartwheels at the thought of her being in another building in another part of town poring over Leach's detritus.

'Okay,' the ACC said. 'I don't wish to see Tim Leach hung out to dry on this, but we need a solid reason as to why these letters were not previously disclosed.'

'I am working on a strategy, sir,' Goodey said.

That seemed to satisfy him, though alarm bells were already ringing in Warlow's head.

Two-Shoes's strategies were, from previous knowledge, like landmines. Likely to blow up in your face if you stepped in the wrong direction. Still, the ACC had what he needed, he got up, and the meeting ended.

For a frozen moment, Warlow feared that Goodey might want to engage him in one of her famous "quiet words." Discussions that often left his skin cold and clammy. Or worse, chat and be pally as in "we're on the same team" kind of vibe. But she strode purposefully from the room, leaving Drinkwater to cosy up to the ACC as they both hurried out.

That left Warlow and Buchannan to wait until the room emptied.

'Best I could do, Evan,' the superintendent said.

'I'll make it work. And do I have you to thank for buying us some time on the Nash and Stuart case?'

'Bleddyn wanted to split up the team, put Jess on the cold case.'

Warlow nodded. 'Narrow escape, then. It's a bloody nest of vipers. The letter is a dead end.'

'Whatever happens, Pamela will see it as a win. You already have what you need from Pauline Garston, though?'

'I do. She's been great. Not sure what she'll make of—'

'I'll give her the heads up. She may even have had dealings with Pamela already due to the North Wales Force review. Meanwhile, you concentrate on Stuart and Nash.'

He must have read something in Warlow's face.

'I don't hear you cheering,' Buchannan added.

'The cases are linked.'

'The same perpetrator?'

'I doubt it, but I can't rule it out yet. Copycat perhaps. But we will find out.'

'It's a shoo-in. Now that you have Pamela to help.' Buchannan kept a straight face.

'The comedy store is looking for new acts. Unfortunately, Sion, you clearly are not in the running.'

———

HE BROKE the news to Jess first.

'Does that mean Sherwood Forest is off limits?'

'Let's just say that, territorially speaking, I'm going to need a visa. I did notice you getting on well with Pauline.'

'She knows some people I worked with in Manchester.' Jess held one eyebrow quirked. 'But, let me guess, you'd like me to keep chat lines open.'

'It'll seem less … underhand.'

'You're a devious man, Evan Warlow.'

'I'm a practical man, Jess Allanby. And we both know Superintendent Goodey cannot resist attempting to influence our investigation.'

'Have you read Pauline's review document in full?'

'Not yet.'

'You should. North Wales police were thorough. And

despite the absence of any fresh evidence to back the idea of Yardley's participation, they concluded that he would have been a viable candidate if there had not been a complete failure to uncover any indication of his presence at the location.'

'That must have eaten into Tim Leach.' Warlow shook his head. 'You can just see the TV documentary unearthing a yet unseen footage of Yardley's van with stock footage of someone with a rucksack climbing up the mountain. They'd make it up as they went along. If it had existed, Leach would have found it. Wishful thinking is not the same as hard evidence.'

'Is that what you're going to tell the team?'

'It is. Concentrate on what we know rather than what we don't for now. Let Goodey dig a hole for herself if she wants to. We stick with the facts.'

CHAPTER TWENTY-THREE

WHEN IT CAME TO INVESTIGATION, there could only be one approach. And it applied to all aspects of the case.

Identify

Interview

Corroborate

Eliminate.

Tactical and thorough and page 101 of the Criminal Investigation Handbook. But difficult when there were no suspects.

'Let's begin with Nash,' Warlow said. He'd gathered the team to brief them on the outcome of his meeting with the ACC. They listened with mute acceptance, as all good troops did when their generals made decisions. All except Gil, whose nebulous harrumph on hearing of Two-Shoes's involvement met with downward glances of disguised humour from Gina and Rhys and a wry smile from Jess. Warlow heard a muttered, 'Bloody Jack-in-the-box,' as a follow-up from the burly sergeant.

He knew exactly what Gil meant. No matter how tightly you closed the lid on her, Goodey could pop back up at any moment.

'Still nothing but the much-loved retired GP, sir,' Gina said by way of an answer to the posed question. 'Not so much as a parking ticket on his record. No disgruntled relative who assumed he was a Shipman. No drug addict harbouring a grudge over not being issued a prescription. And, the GMC have confirmed that he was not a subject of any complaints channelled through them. Squeaky clean and straight as a die.'

'What about the girl?' Warlow asked.

'Kirsty Stuart's partner has thrown up one tiny wrinkle. She is an activist.'

'Not another one,' Gil growled.

'She's been arrested on charges of causing a public nuisance and breaching the Public Order Act as part of the Planet SpOil protests in Bristol last year. She got six months and served two.'

'She's one of the walking dead?' Gil asked. His term for the members of Planet SpOil, whose favoured tactic of go-slow traffic disruption had alienated the public so much, needed no explanation.

'She is,' Jess explained. 'She sat down on the M32 as a coach load of rugby supporters on the way to Bristol Bears game arrived. Her tactic of throwing green paint at anyone who tried to move her backfired when some of the stuff got into a little girl's eye. She ended up in the Bristol Eye Hospital. No permanent damage. Still, Amanda Beech narrowly avoided an assault charge.'

'And we have some fiery text exchanges between Stuart and Beech that morning.'

'Okay. So, worth a chat, then,' Warlow confirmed.

'Are we thinking she fell out with Stuart and took revenge?' Rhys asked.

'We're exploring all avenues at this stage,' Jess explained. 'But it still leaves us with any potential spillover from the original case to consider.'

Warlow did his best to diminish the scowl that threatened. He knew he'd have to share his thinking and findings with Two-Shoes, as well as being more careful about where he put his investigative feet for fear of treading on toes. But until then, they'd barrel ahead on all fronts.

'What are you suggesting?' Warlow pressed Jess for an answer.

'I'm wondering if the original perpetrator enjoyed the hoo-ha of the first case so much he wants more of it.'

'After twenty-odd years?' Rhys both looked and sounded highly sceptical.

'Perhaps he's been unable to indulge himself?' Gina suggested.

'Like being in a coma or something?'

Gil raised one very bushy eyebrow. 'You are definitely watching far too much rubbish TV, Rhys.'

'Prison?' Gina suggested.

'Possibly,' Jess said. 'We've all seen that before. Well-adjusted prisoner out on licence and early release turns recidivist as soon as the prison gates close behind him. It's a stretch, but stranger things.'

'We should look at people even remotely linked to the Bowman case, who were subsequently jailed shortly afterwards.' Warlow spoke, Rhys wrote up the action for posting.

'Then there is Christopher Messenger, brother of the first victim. A loose cannon if ever there was one,' Jess said.

'But he had an alibi for the Stuart and Nash deaths, didn't he?' Gil asked.

'Work,' Gina said. 'But as yet not corroborated.'

'And finally, we have Messenger's reluctant ex, Mr Wojak,' Gina said. 'I've chased up his explanation for where he was that day, and I'd hardly say it's watertight.'

'He's the one who doesn't want a fuss because he's "moved on," right?' Warlow recalled previous discussions about Wojak. 'Maybe we ought to get him in for a formal chat. Through his solicitor, of course. Might bring him down a notch or two. "Moving on" as an excuse for non-cooperation makes me … antsy. Besides, if I was in a relationship with a person who'd lost someone from a violent act, what kind of human being would I be to object to my partner getting some closure?'

No one argued. It seemed uncharitable, and possessive, and not quite right.

'Should we speak to the new partner, then?' Gil asked.

Warlow grinned. 'Can't do any harm.'

Four posted-up names had now appeared on the Job Centre.

Chris Messenger with both a red and a green star attached to the name to show some crossover between the green, the Bowman case—and the red, showing most recent attacks.

Heather Messenger's ex and his partner only had green stars. And now, Stuart's partner, Beech, had a red star indicating their involvement only with the Stuart/Nash murders.

It looked complicated, but it wasn't.

'I'm loving the traffic light system there, Rhys,' Jess said.

'They were the only two colours left in the box.'

'What if you're colour-blind?' Gina asked. 'I have a cousin who has red-green colour blindness.'

'She's right,' Gil said. 'Your system falls apart where the hue-diverse are concerned.'

'That's not a proper term,' Jess said.

'I beg to differ,' Gil replied. 'Huw Diverse was one of the best wing forwards we had in the rugby team I played for as a boy. Diverse was not his real name but fitted with his colour deficit and the fact that he only knew the first two stanzas of *Calon Lan*, one of my favourite hymns and a bus staple on the home journey from an away game.'

Gina snickered. 'How does that work?'

'*Dau* is two in the mother tongue – Dau-verse, see. Two verses. Rugby club humour is not known for its intellectual sophistication, but in this instance worked on multiple levels. Anyway, old Huw managed okay on the rugby field except on murky wet days, the like of which we unfortunately see all too often on weekends here in West Wales. On those days, the line between ground and horizon might blur a little. Big problem for Huw with the red/green blindness, especially if the opposition played in red. Big time lack of contrast. He tackled his own teammates on more than one occasion. Bit of a liability but fearless in the ruck. Never settled in the team, though. Always had one eye on a better one a few miles up the valley. That was old Huw; the grass was always greener. Though that would be a bit rich in Huw's case, because how the hell would he know?'

Rhys let out a wheezy hoot at that.

'Mind you,' Gil continued, 'we had some fun serving him gooseberries instead of tomatoes. You may think it's cruel. We thought it was the height of entertainment. And we could have used limes, but we weren't barbarians.'

'Talking of entertainment,' Jess said.

Warlow glanced at his watch. 'Is it that time already?'

'It is, sir. Are we all going?'

'We are,' Warlow said.

Gina perked up. 'I could stay if you like?'

'No. We all need to see this,' Warlow insisted. 'As unpleasant as I suspect it is going to be.'

———

MILTON HAD SET up in the supply yard behind Sherwood Forest on a weed-strewn, concrete parking area. He wore poorly fitting jeans cinched well below his ample belly, and a leather waistcoat over his faded shirt.

Highly inappropriate for a cold March day; there'd been reports of snow overnight up north. But then, Milton had not struck Warlow as a man troubled too much by the weather. He'd pushed a pair of goggles up over his forehead and, in his left hand, carried a crossbow. Not one of his medieval reconstructions, but a modern-looking weapon with a camouflage print over most of its surface. Clutched in the fingers of his left hand were some bolts. The same size and colour and bearing the lethal tips that had caused all the damage to Stuart and Nash.

Povey, Tannard, and Goodey all stood behind Milton as Warlow and the team walked around the side of the building.

'What have we missed?' Warlow called out.

'Nothing. We waited.' A grinning Milton pulled his goggles down to cover his eyes.

They positioned themselves near Goodey and Povey and

watched as Milton utilised some black nylon cocking ropes to pull back the string of the weapon. He placed the bolt in the channel, keeping the instrument parallel to the ground, stepped forward, and, with a broad stance, pointed forward.

The target hung from a steel rig, dangling by nylon rope from a crosspiece, pink flesh glistening in the March daylight. A sizeable chunk of pig, three times the size of what you might put in as a Sunday roast. Next to it hung a second target of roughly the same size and shape. Only this one had been draped in what looked like a coat. Ten yards behind the target stood the back brick wall of the factory.

'Is this really necessary?' Gina's expression oozed distaste.

Goodey answered her with an almost imperceptible upward tilt of her chin. 'My idea. It will give us some approximation of the penetrating power of these bolts. Mr Milton agrees.'

'Ah, okay,' Gina said, flushing.

'I'm twenty-five yards back,' Milton said.

He lifted the bow, placed the stock into his shoulder, peered through a modern-looking telescopic sight, and fired. They all heard the string release and watched the carcass lifting alarmingly, causing the supporting rig to clatter and bounce as the bolt hit, followed by a tinny screech as the projectile, having gone right through porcine flesh and bone, hit the bricks of the building, rocketed up, and fell to earth a yard from the wall.

'Bloody hell,' Rhys said.

'The second carcass is identical but is covered with the same layers as worn by Gerald Nash.' Milton spoke the words as he loaded the bow and repeated the exercise. This time, the carcass lifted as previously, but there was no clatter of steel head against the brick wall. Instead, the arrow stayed protruding from the coat-covered flesh. Four inches of it, not including the flight, showing.

Tannard stepped forward. 'As you can see, the coat absorbs some of the bolt's energy and slows it down.'

'So, you're saying Nash's clothing prevented the bolt from going through and through?' Goodey asked. 'And might also have caused the retention of the bolt pieces in the Coombs case twenty years ago?'

'Different bolt and perhaps a different crossbow, but that's my opinion, yes,' Tannard explained. 'Mr Milton agrees.'

'We need to take all that into account,' Povey said. 'Since the injury was through and through in Stuart's case, we can assume it was done from closer range.'

'Nash was shot in the back,' Rhys said. 'He might've been unaware of the killer's approach.'

'Would you like to repeat the exercise?' Milton's voice came to them across the car park.

'No, that would not be necessary,' Goodey replied. 'I think we have enough to assume the killer underestimated the power of the bolt in both Coombs and Nash's cases.'

'If the aim was to recover the bolts in the first place,' Warlow said.

Goodey's raised eyebrows posed the unspoken question.

Warlow obliged. 'We're assuming the killer, in both instances, did not want us to know he used a crossbow. I'm not so certain that was the case.'

But Two-Shoes seemed to lose interest in Warlow's theorising. She turned back to Milton. 'Once again, we are indebted to you for your expertise, Mr Milton.'

'You got some identical bolts to those used on Stuart and Nash, I see,' Jess said.

'I have contacts in archery clubs through my reenactment hat. And the hunting heads were purchased easily enough online by your colleagues.' He nodded at Tannard.

Something about all of that triggered an itch in the inside of Warlow's skull. But he was given no time to scratch it, not then, because the words he dreaded followed, uttered calmly by Two-Shoes. 'Could we have a quiet word, Evan?'

CHAPTER TWENTY-FOUR

As Warlow disappeared around the side of the factory, pointedly refusing to look back at the grinning faces of his colleagues, Rhys walked over to Milton, who was collecting the spent bolts.

'Incredibly powerful these things, aren't they?'

'King killers,' Milton said.

'Pardon?'

'Pierre Basile is the boy from Limousine credited with killing Richard the Lionheart at the siege of Chalus-Chabron in 1199. Shot in the shoulder by a crossbow bolt after having removed some of his chain mail. As so often was the case, the wound was not fatal but turned gangrenous. He died an undoubtedly unpleasant death a few weeks later. He showed mercy to the boy, but later reports are that Pierre was flayed for his act.'

'Bloody hell.' Rhys grimaced.

But Milton looked amused. 'It would have been a raw existence.'

'And you do battles and stuff?'

'Reenactments, yes,' Milton said.

'What was it like, then, a battle?'

'Arrows and bolts could be a slow death. They tried to remove them, but into the wound with the arrow tip would go dirt or a filthy piece of your clothing. Bandages would be ripped cloths on the battlefield, covered in mud and dirt or horse manure. There are reports of arrows sometimes dipped in faeces.'

'And no antibiotics?'

'Other than honey or Verdigris or turpentine.'

'Bloody hell,' Rhys repeated the oath with feeling.

A shout from Gil drew his attention. He turned and raised a hand. 'I have to go. But this stuff is fascinating.'

'You ought to come to one of our reenactments. Get a taste of what it was really like. You'd make a wonderful lancer.'

'Nant versus Crymych seconds in the cup is close enough for me.' Rhys grinned.

Gil and Gina were waiting for him when he joined them.

'We're off back up to HQ,' Gil said.

'What was all that about?' Gina pointed towards a whistling Milton.

'Just medieval warfare chat. He knows a lot about it.'

Gina shuddered. 'My question is, why?'

'You can't deny history, Gina,' Rhys said.

'No, but who wants to be in it? Empire, repression, dictatorships, murder, come on.' Gina sounded animated.

'Absolutely.' Gil said this with a glint in his eye. 'Thank the Lordy that's in the past. *Do svidaniya* to all that, I say.'

Gina rolled her eyes. 'Okay, I know there are some places in the world that aren't … perfect. Quite a lot of places, actually, but still. And I mean, shooting bolts into pigs' carcasses? Ugh.'

Jess joined the three of them. 'Right, can't say I enjoyed that, but it was educational.'

'Horrible,' Gina said.

'Unfortunately, horrible is in our job description,' Jess observed.

She sent them all back to HQ to carry on and waited for Warlow in the Jeep. He emerged from the factory half an hour later looking like a dental patient post a filling without anaesthetic.

'Well?' Jess asked as Warlow drove out of the industrial complex.

'I had to fill her in,' Warlow said.

'Like a ditch?'

'I wish.'

'Were the theatrics with Milton really all her idea?'

'They were. Makes her feel like she's doing something.'

'And what are *we* doing?' Jess asked.

'Not much. Hardly any point for vespers today. We've learned nothing new this afternoon, apart from how to skewer a shoulder of pork from twenty-five yards. I'll let the troops go early. Tomorrow, I'm going back up to the Elan Valley with Gina. Get the lie of the land.' He looked out at the darkening grey day. 'It'll be cold.'

'I'll text her to make sure she has walking boots and thermals. She did not enjoy the show today.'

'No, I'm not surprised. But I'll make it up to her tomorrow with hours of sparkling repartee in the car.'

'You taking someone else as well, then?' Jess kept a straight face.

'Hilarious, DI Allanby.'

———

WHEN THEY RETURNED to the Incident Room, the expressions on the faces of the three team members who had gone ahead immediately conveyed to Warlow that something was amiss. A break in the case? But his optimism was trampled under the weight of one word.

'Lane,' Gil said.

Gina had her screen open on an article that had appeared on the Mirror's website.

The headline was classically lurid and derogatory.

Police incompetence threatens to prolong the hunt for crossbow killer.

In what can only be described as a cascade of failures, the Dyfed Powys-led investigation into this chilling case has left the public with more questions than answers.

A stark reminder of the tragedy was plastered across the pages: an old photograph featuring the first two victims – Coombs and Messenger, and more recent snaps of Stuart and Nash. Adding to the heartbreak were stock images of the two young Coombs children, innocents caught in the wake of this brutality.

As efforts to track down Stuart and Nash's assailant gain momentum, police have turned to the unsolved Bowman killings to see if they can shed new light on a previously stagnant investigation.

The eerie parallels between the method of murder – a deadly crossbow bolt again in the cases of Stuart and Nash, and the unfortunate Bowman victims Phillip Coombs and Heather Messenger – have prompted detectives to revisit the archives. Superintendent Pamela Goodey, relocating all the evidence of the Bowman case to an abandoned factory in Johnstown, Carmarthen, now leads a thorough re-evaluation of how the initial case was mishandled.

'Was this leaked?' Warlow asked.

Shrugs all around.

Superintendent Goodey was quick to make the most of what they knew. 'As always,' she explained, 'we must learn from our mistakes, leaving no stone unturned.'

In response to inquiries regarding apologies to the offspring of the late Phillip Coombs, Goodey stated, 'I understand that the unresolved questions surrounding the Bowman killings have caused much pain, and for that, I can only offer my sincerest apologies.'

But for Lloyd Coombs, who was just four years old when his father, Phillip Coombs, was murdered, the situation opens old wounds. The murder left him and his sister without paternal guidance. Their mother's subsequent mental health struggles culminated tragically, leaving them under the care of their aunt and uncle.

'You forget,' Lloyd said, 'I can't conjure up my dad's face from memory. Sure, there are photos and such, but he's not etched in my mind, you know? And now, there'll be more children and grandchildren who won't even have that.'

His words ring true. The anguish of the Coombs family has resurfaced in a monstrous and sickening way, and Lloyd Coombs firmly believes that there's a sinister connection at play.

'It's plain as day,' he asserted. 'If the police had done a proper job years ago, those two lives wouldn't have been snuffed out today.'

Warlow stopped there. 'No mention of the Yardley letters?'

'Not yet,' Gil said. 'They're releasing that information today.'

'I can't wait to see what Lane will have to say about that.'

Goodey had explained the timeline of releasing information to Warlow during their tête-à-tête. His eyes were still on the screen. 'Is it worth reading the rest?'

'There is another paragraph on the Coombs kids, but the rest is all about the rubbish policing reviews. The population is at risk of further attacks, etc. The usual rhetoric.' Gil arched his back in a stretch.

'I don't suppose he mentioned Hunt?'

'Course he did,' Jess snorted. 'And plugged the book to come.'

The book in which Catrin Richards would feature. Great.

'He makes out that Lloyd Coombs is an angry man,' Gina said. 'That's how I read it.'

'That's how he wants you to read it,' Warlow muttered. On that depressing note, he called a halt to proceedings and asked them all to come in early the next day.

There were no dissenters.

———

WARLOW AND JESS drove home in separate cars. As usual, Warlow took a slight detour to pick up Cadi from her sitters. After the usual effusive greeting, he thanked the Dawes, and man and dog arrived home to find Jess already changed into jeans and sweatshirt, preparing to heat up some leftovers.

He watched with a smile as woman and dog reacquainted themselves, then idly picked up some letters from the kitchen work surface addressed to him. The usual circulars went straight into the bin, and it would have been a full house were it not for the one manila envelope with his name and address typed on it.

He took it with him as he walked towards the bedroom. 'I'm going to get out of this suit,' he called out.

No one answered. Jess and Cadi were still having a moment.

And so, tie off and shirt buttons undone, Warlow sat on the bed and ripped open the envelope. Inside was a single sheet of A4 with typed words on un-headed white paper.

———

Dear Mr Warlow,

You may, by now, have come across some letters I wrote to Detective Superintendent Leach during his investigation into what the press call the 'Bowman' killings. Then Yardley confessed his crime to me, but alas, Superintendent Leach could not convince others.

I was hurt by that. And it gives me no pleasure now to be proved right.

Warlow paused, feeling his brows bunch. What the hell was all this?

Yardley has returned to kill again. Yes, I know his body has been burnt to ashes, but his tortured soul has surely come back to the place that condemned him. Though I think Yardley was not himself when he did those things. Something else was in him. That something may have waited twenty years, but he will come back again, mark my words. Did you notice the killings took place near burial mounds? Something haunts those hills. Something that searches for willing vessels to carry out the acts it requires.

Where now is open moor, there once were sacred groves.

Think on that DCI Warlow. There is more to come.

Unsigned.

PS. In the public interest, I am sending copies to news outlets. They will receive it tomorrow. Only fair you get a first look.

Warlow, now aware that this would need to go in as evidence, got hold of his phone and took some photos. When he had not come out of the bedroom for ten minutes, Jess appeared in the doorway.

'You okay?'

Without speaking, Warlow pointed to the single sheet on the bed. He showed her the images on his phone.

'Oh, God,' Jess groaned. 'They're already coming out of the woodwork.'

'Are they?' Warlow's response made Jess look up.

'Surely, you don't think this is … anything?'

'Goodey hasn't released the information on the letters to the press yet. We would have heard if she had.'

Jess's frown deepened as she tried to follow Warlow's train of thought. 'So …'

'Whoever wrote this references those letters. I think it's the same person. We'll get Povey on it. She'll be able to tell us if it's the same sentence structure, use of words, etc. But I think it is.'

'But it's BS.' Jess's cynical smile was questioning.

'Of course, it is. But it's BS with insight.' Warlow found his briefcase and took out an evidence bag, slid on some gloves, refolded the letter and put it back into its envelope.

'But … something haunts those hills?' Jess persisted with her scathing tone.

Warlow, though, remained troubled. 'Whoever wrote this mentions sacred groves. Druidic stuff. And no one knows anything about that lot.'

'But—'

'BS, yes, I know. But it'll send the press into a frenzy.'

'Is that what it's about?'

Warlow sighed. 'Who the hell knows? I don't. In fact, I know nothing at all about this case the longer it goes on.' He heard the anger rising in his voice.

Jess's hand on his arm was a welcome touch. 'How do they know where you live?'

'Not difficult these days via the Interweb.'

'Should we be worried?'

'Might not even be him.'

Jess sighed. 'Come and have some supper and a glass of restorative grape juice.'

'Is it the Primitivo from the weekend?'

Jess grinned. 'Two glasses left.'

Warlow let his head fall forward. 'You had me at grape juice.'

CHAPTER TWENTY-FIVE

WARLOW SLEPT BADLY. When he opened his eyes and glanced at the digital clock, 05.10 glared back at him, bright against the darkness of the room, with no chink of dawn yet at the window.

He lay there for ten minutes and then got up, doing his best not to disturb the sleeping form at his side. He stood for a moment, letting his eyes adjust to the darkness, noting even in the thin light from the clock that Jess had one bare leg outside the duvet. For a second, he toyed with flicking on the light to get a better look.

Jess had good legs. In fact, she had *great* legs.

Warlow smiled. He was still getting accustomed to this. After years of never expecting to wake up next to anyone ever again, here he stood, contemplating becoming a bloody peeping Tom.

If he told her, she'd laugh and say he should have put on the light. That thought brought an entire catalogue of other ideas to his head.

'*Down boy*,' he thought-whispered. '*There is a time and a place.*'

Downstairs, Cadi did her best to knock over magazines left on chairs with her tail as she waddled about, snorting with her toy bear Arthur in her jaws.

Warlow dressed, put on a headband light, opened the back door, and breathed in the frosty morning air.

Only a few days remained until the spring equinox. But clearly, no one had sent West Wales the memo.

He took the dog up along the lanes this morning; lanes graveyard-quiet and traffic-free at this time of the morning. He could have taken the river to the estuary and thrown the dog a ball, but this was not one of his long walks. This was a can't-sleep-and-need-to-clear-my-head walk.

Half an hour later, they were back. He gave the dog a chew to keep her occupied and then looked at his phone and the letter he'd taken the photograph of once again.

Povey would run this through some expert or some algorithm, and she would tell him if this had been written by the same person who wrote the Leach letters. The act of sending copies to the press had malicious intentions. Whoever wrote these, and if they were the same person, involving the press added an extra twist of the knife.

Warlow could feel the unpleasant tingle that was a harbinger of another meeting with Drinkwater and the ACC.

He made tea and sat, cogitating. At 06:35, his phone chirped. An answer to the WhatsApp text he'd sent out. Warlow opened his laptop and made the FaceTime call to his sons. Tom, in London, was up already to prepare for his commute to Northwick Park Hospital in Harrow. And Alun, in Western Australia, where the time stood at 14.35.

'Morning,' Warlow said.

'Hi, Dad,' Tom called back, holding a piece of marmite covered toast between thumb and forefinger.

'*Tadcu*!' The urgent greeting that came through from Perth was from Leo, Warlow's grandson, who stuck his grinning face up close to the iPad camera they were using. 'Lego!'

A small plastic figure in a typical stylised shape veered in and out of focus.

'Come back to the sofa, Leo. Let *Tadcu* see everyone.' Reba Warlow, Leo's mother, pulled the child away to reveal herself, tanned, in shorts, on the sofa. Leo squirmed, then moved away, making a noise like a train and rushing off. Reba smiled in apology and said, 'How are you, Evan?'

'Well. How's Eva?'

'Okay. Alun is looking in on her. She's been a bit sniffly. We've given her some Calpol. Leo had a cold a couple of days ago.'

'Ah, the joys of having a toddler, or as I like to call them, mobile Petri dishes.'

Reba replied with a sanguine smile and waved to Alun as he entered the room.

'Hi, Dad.'

Warlow liked to make these calls early and neither of his children minded. At this time, Alun was usually around, and Tom was on the way to work. But it had been a couple of weeks since they'd all spoken because of Tom's late skiing holiday and Alun's work commitments. They were due a catch-up.

'I've been reading about those crossbow killings, Dad,' Tom said. 'You're not involved, are you?'

'I am,' Warlow said.

'Oh, God.' Reba winced. 'It all sounds so horrible.'

He should not have been surprised to hear that it had reached Western Australia. It was making news everywhere. But his boys were the children of a police officer, and they knew better than to pry. Besides, this morning, he had a different agenda.

As yet, he had not told the boys about Jess. At least not about him and Jess. Tom had already met her and Molly over the summer when he and Jodie had visited.

But, as far as the boys were concerned, she and Molly were still lodgers. But Warlow, having given it a fair shake of the stick, now felt that they ought to know about ... developments.

'How is Jodie, Tom?' Warlow asked.

Tom's partner worked as a nurse. Sometimes, their shifts clashed.

'She's fine. In the shower.'

'Oh, excellent,' Warlow said with no good reason. He was procrastinating. 'Busy day at work, Tom?'

'Always busy, Dad.'

'How about you, Al? Same old?'

'Yeah. Sorry, you're missing Eva. But she's been grizzly. Best we let her sleep it off.'

'Of course. Actually, I wanted to speak to you both, anyway.'

'About what?' Alun looked intrigued as he slid into the seat next to Reba.

'Something personal.'

'Not your HIV, is it?' Tom asked.

'No … not directly. It's just that—'

He got no further. Behind him, a tousle-haired Jess walked into the room in her above-the-knee nightie, arms and shoulders bare, with slitted eyes blinking against the living room light.

'Evan, have you seen my black bra?'

As frozen moments went, it was a minus thirty with wind-chill classic.

Warlow turned to look at her. She, meanwhile, groggy from just getting up, took in the laptop, and the faces staring back at her as she stood behind Warlow's chair. A coy smile spread slowly over her lips, and her eyes opened a lot wider. She raised her hand and called out, 'Morning!'

Tom, the Joker, asked, 'Well, Dad, do tell? Where is Jess's bra?'

Warlow, looking at Jess, said, 'I think I saw it in the bathroom. I picked it up and hooked it on the back of the door.'

'Thank you,' Jess said brightly, pivoted, and left the room.

Warlow turned back to face the boys and Reba. Broad smiles could be seen on all three of their faces.

'Is that what you wanted to tell us, Dad?' Tom asked. 'That you're wearing bras?'

'Only on weekends,' Warlow said automatically, realising at the same moment he was spending too much time with Gil.

Reba laughed at that, but Tom and Alun remained expectant.

'Nothing to do with bras,' Warlow said, 'but all to do with the woman who wears them.'

'You and Jess?' Reba sat forward with a squeal. 'Yes!'

She raised a fist and turned to her husband. 'That's $20 you owe me.'

'You've been running a book?' Warlow's expression took on a pained surprise.

'Of course, we have,' Alun said. 'I said deffo by the summer. Reebs said after Molly went to Uni.'

'Me and Jodie suspected it had been going on a for a while.' Tom grinned.

Warlow could only shake his head. 'Am I that bloody transparent?'

'We had hoped you would open your eyes,' Tom said. 'She's great, Dad.'

'Well, next time, I promise we … that's Jess and I … will be prepared. Dressed and … prepared. Tom's met Jess, but you two haven't … other than to say hello.'

'I'm looking forward to it. Another Northern lass in the fold,' Reba said. 'Something about us, you know.'

He was at the point of coming back with a blistering retort when Leo reappeared, and any more sensible conversation got lost in a discussion about a kangaroo they'd passed on the road that morning.

———

LATER, as Warlow poured his first coffee, Jess strode into the kitchen, dressed for work even though it was a Saturday, as if nothing had happened.

'You found your bra, then?' Warlow asked.

'Yes, thank you.' She gave him an exaggerated smile.

'Pretty good way to demonstrate our … arrangement,' Warlow said, cringing at his own words.

'Glad I could be of help.' Jess, smelling wonderful, came and stood next to Warlow and placed a cup under the coffee machine's espresso nozzle.

Warlow listened as the beans ground and the black liquid

trickled into her pre-warmed cup. Without taking her eyes off the process, Jess spoke.

'I have two questions. First, why haven't you told them before, and second, does the … arrangement meet with their approval?'

Warlow took his cup back to the breakfast table. 'As for the first question, I wanted to be sure that you … that we …' He sighed. 'I hadn't told them because I needed to be sure. That you were sure. As for meeting with their approval …' Warlow picked up his phone. 'Several text messages of congratulations. They're all delighted, and the boys have emphasised how I am punching well above my weight.'

'Well, that's obvious,' Jess said, lifting the coffee to her lips, the muscles under her eyes bunching.

He was about to come back with a pithy remark when both his and Jess's phones buzzed at once.

Two hours earlier, just before Warlow took Cadi into the frosty morning, maybe even as he contemplated Jess's bare leg, a figure dressed in a hooded and dark coat crossed the road towards the little cul-de-sac where Creddal's Metals Factory, aka Sherwood Forest, nestled.

The streets were lit, but at this hour, nothing moved. No doubt there'd be CCTV cameras somewhere. But the figure walked quickly and with quiet determination, obscuring any features that might have been picked up on camera with a scarf tied over their face and a shapeless knee-length padded coat.

In their hand, they held a canister of the type some people carried in their cars, full of spare fuel.

The factory lacked police presence. Why would there be? They were using it as a repository. No crimes had been committed there.

Not yet.

Moving swiftly, the figure slid out of the CCTV coverage of the neighbouring property.

Steel shutters guarded the main vehicle entrance into the building, but a separate wooden door led to the reception area. The figure undid the canister's cap and poured the contents along the base of the door where there was a gap big enough to also accommodate a few thin sheets of newspaper.

Then the door was doused.

A match flared, and the paper, still damp, ignited in flames that spread quickly across the reception area floor, following the trail of petrol, and soon engulfed a wooden desk.

The figure walked calmly away while flames flickered through the reception area window.

———

WITHIN FIVE MINUTES of receiving the call, Jess and Warlow had already begun their journey to Carmarthen, where fire-fighters were battling an arson attack.

CHAPTER TWENTY-SIX

THEY'D CORDONED off the access road to the factory. Warlow parked in a small U-shaped block which housed an engineering works and a double-glazing company. Jess pulled up next to him in her Golf.

They walked through the array of parked vehicles to where a group of forlorn-looking people stood, well back from where the actual business of putting out the fire was taking place at the hands of tan-and-yellow-clad firefighters in their Xenon kit.

The fire was out, though two big red engines stood in the space in front of Sherwood Forest. Thin wisps of smoke drifted up from the reception area, but on the whole, the place remained structurally intact.

As Warlow walked under the police tape and nodded to the Uniform guarding the way, he noted that the Great and the Good had been summoned. It looked as if the feared meeting with Drinkwater and the ACC was going to be an alfresco affair on this chilly morning.

'Evan,' Drinkwater said. 'Bit of a mess.'

Warlow noted the fire officers still milling around like ants. 'Much damage?'

Goodey answered, her body stiff in the cold despite a

heavy, black-padded coat that made her look twice her normal size. 'From the fire, no. But from water, yes.'

Pools of the stuff lay on the tarmac in front of the building.

'And definitely arson, we think?'

Drinkwater sent him a glum glare. 'The fire investigator says so. Petrol under the door.' He nodded towards the blackened reception area and the ACC talking to a man with a red helmet.

'How long before we gain access?'

'Hours,' Goodey said.

'Anybody see anything?'

'We're canvassing. Not many people about this early. We need to check for CCTV.' Goodey's lips barely moved when she spoke.

'Is there much point in me hanging on, then?' Warlow asked.

She didn't answer immediately. Instead, she brought up an image on her phone and showed him and Jess a photograph of the inside of Sherwood Forest, taken, she explained, by the fire investigator.

Again, everything looked in place, though there was a significant blackening of the walls near the reception area. However, the water dripping off the tables and pooling on the floor told a different story of another kind of damage.

'Sprinkler system?' Jess asked.

Goodey nodded.

It would take days, if not weeks, for things to dry out, and even then, it was likely that some of the paper-bound evidence might be totally useless. Warlow felt heat rise in his cheeks. Not only for the damage he was looking at, but for the fact that Goodey might want to revert to the Incident Room now.

'I'm going to see what is salvageable later. We need to move it somewhere.'

'Right,' he said. 'I'm going to be up at the reservoir.'

She didn't ask why. Small mercies.

———

GINA, thirty years and some younger than Warlow, wasn't even out of breath as they crested another grass-covered hillock south of the Elan reservoir. The scene where Gerald Nash had been found was still marked by fluttering blue and white police tape. The Tyvek evidence tent had long gone, but the tape still marked the area.

Warlow wondered how much of a deterrent fluttering tape might be for the morbidly curious and said as much to Gina.

'Anyone could cross that tape for a selfie,' he muttered.

Gina frowned. 'Why? Why would anyone want to take a photo of the actual murder site?'

'Likes? Social media can be a very dark place. It takes all sorts, Gina.'

Warlow held his phone up, showing an OS map of the area.

'Are we looking for anything in particular, sir?'

A brisk and bitter wind was blowing down from the north. Gina clapped her gloved hands together for warmth.

Warlow turned to the DC. She wore a windproof jacket, a bobble hat, and gloves, with blonde hair peeking out from beneath the hat around her ears.

She'd been quiet on the way up, pensive and polite, and not remotely enthusiastic. Now, out in the open, this was a different woman.

Warlow had already explained to her about the letter he'd received from someone purporting to have accepted Yardley's confession for the first murders. Jess would have done the same for Gil and Rhys.

'There were hints at burial sites in that letter. I wanted to see how close the crime scenes were to those sites in reality.'

They both looked around at the vast and open moor and the miles of nothing around them. A light dusting of snow had fallen overnight, covering the ground in this barren patch. The wind had blown some of it away, exposing the foliage beneath. In other areas, the snow had settled, building up against the stone outcrops that occasionally appeared.

'Thing is, sir, there are loads of Iron Age remnants up here. I've talked to Rhys about it.'

Warlow laughed softly. 'Sorry I missed that conversation.'

Gina smiled, her lips not quite able to show all her teeth because they were sluggish from the cold. 'He says we don't know the half of it.'

'No. We don't. And the reference in the letter is vague. I can see Bwlch y Ddau Faen marked here, but that's a few miles away.' Two Stones Pass in English referenced an even more remote spot at a boundary between two *cantrefs*, a reference to a patch of land containing a hundred hamlets or dwellings at one time.

'Hard to believe anyone really lived up here, isn't it, sir?'

'Different climate then. I read somewhere it was a temperate rainforest. There's still some of that in the Elan Valley.'

'Was that what whoever wrote the letter meant by sacred groves?'

Warlow grimaced. 'That's the thing. It's got the both of us wondering, hasn't it?'

'So, why are we here, sir?'

Warlow shook his head. 'To get a feeling.'

'And what's that, sir?'

'You tell me. What's the overwhelming sensation you get here, Gina?'

The young DC looked around again. 'Its remoteness?'

Warlow nodded. 'People walk these hills to get away, to be one with nature and all that ... stuff. I can buy into that. We've all done it. But imagine if you met someone up here. Someone with malice in their hearts. Where is there to run to? Sometimes, the wide-open spaces can be worse than being locked in a box.'

Gina looked about her and then stared at Warlow. 'You could always run, sir.'

'You could. But how far? And what if someone was shooting at you with a crossbow?'

Gina shuddered. 'Is that the motive behind the killer's choice of this place?'

Warlow shrugged. 'If we knew the answer to that, we'd be halfway to catching the sod. There's an element of romanticism in that letter, though, don't you think?'

'Hardly, sir.'

'What, sacred groves? If the rewilders had their way, we'd be planting a million trees up here. Some people call this a desert. But sheep live in this desert and farmers earn a living from that.'

'Do you believe this is related to the environment? The killings?'

'There's a hint of it in the link to Stuart and her partner. We need to follow that up. But can we rationalise an act of murderous wantonness with that? Yes, the environment gets people agitated. On the one hand, we have the enviro-zealots, and there are few more zealous, ready to vilify the Welsh-speaking farmers that have been here for years for their denuding slash and burn tactics, certain that they need to "educate" the heathen and long live the Green Empire. On the other hand, you have families who've lived and worked here for generations, and they dislike being told what to do.'

'But—'

'And, before you say anything else, I suspect that what I've just said is all smoke and mirrors. In my opinion, the letter writer just wants to put one great big wellie in the muddy bottom of the pond to watch the silt billow up. Or light a fire in a factory and watch the smoke obscure the view.'

'This case, sir, it's so … complicated.' Gina looked genuinely bemused.

'It is, and it isn't. It is to us now, but it won't be when we find the answers.'

'Will we, sir?'

'Oh, we will.'

A fresh gust of wind sliced through both officers, and they turned their backs as it threatened to push them across the face of the slope they stood on.

'Are we going further on, sir?'

'We are going back to the Visitor Centre for a cup of hot tea, Gina.'

'Thank God.'

'But, before we do, I want to hear what you will tell the team when they ask you what we learned from driving two hours north to get here.'

Gina shivered. 'That it's cold and barren up here.'

'Yes. And?'

'And, that if you were trying to find someone, you'd have no chance because it's so big.'

'And?'

'If you did find someone and meant to do them harm, then … there is nowhere to hide.'

'Excellent. Write that down in your notes when we get back to civilisation.'

Back in the warmth of the Visitor Centre and with their teas half-drunk, Warlow took a call from Jess.

'How's the repartee?'

'We've abandoned that for English breakfast tea. What news on the fire?'

'Two-Shoes has found somewhere for the Bowman evidence to dry out. She's got some industrial dehumidifiers on the go and the good news is that it's in a smaller factory unit, but still in Johnstown.'

Warlow grinned. 'Right, for that you can stay at mine tonight.'

'I might take you up on that. And, CCTV has shown us someone walking towards the factory carrying a petrol can. Covered up, of course, but not exactly being furtive about it. Little chance of identifying from the CCTV, though.'

'Oh, you wicked woman. Give with one hand and take away with the other.'

Jess ignored him. 'But we also have one interesting little development. Lloyd Coombs's van was spotted in Carmarthen last night. We're searching for that, too.'

'Coombs?'

'I know. We're tracking him down and bringing him in for questioning. How are you doing up there?'

'All done. Gina is about thawed out, so we'll be heading back soon.'

'With a bit of luck, we'll have Coombs here by the time you arrive.'

Warlow ended the call to find Gina looking at him in amusement.

'You and DI Allanby make a good pairing, sir.'

'You make us sound like a Cabernet Sauvignon and a sirloin steak. Which one am I?'

'The steak.'

'Meaty and delicious?'

'I was thinking more … rare, sir. Crusty on the outside but tender when cut.'

Warlow gave her a wry smile. 'Oh, very good, Detective Constable. I see you fitting in very well.'

'Was it good news, though, sir? About the fire?'

'I'll tell you in the car on the long drive back to HQ.' He slid his coat off the back of the chair as he stood up. 'Now, if this was Rhys, I'd need to ask if he wanted to stock up on snacks and use the toilet.'

'No need, sir. This tea will see me through. But a loo stop would not go amiss.'

'Right, meet me in the car after the comfort break.'

CHAPTER TWENTY-SEVEN

FINDING COOMBS PROVED SURPRISINGLY DIFFICULT, and it wasn't until Sunday morning that a response vehicle pulled him over while he was driving his van. Upon seeing the blue lights behind him, he called his sister, who urged him to remain silent until a solicitor could be contacted, in case the police wanted to question him

They did.

Jess and Rhys did the honours in the interview room on a quiet Sunday afternoon. Weekends meant nothing in a case like this. Warlow, Gina, and Gil observed from a monitor as Lloyd fidgeted in his seat.

'So, let me get this straight, Mr Coombs,' Jess, reasonableness personified, asked. 'You had a meeting and wisely decided not to drive home after consuming alcohol. Instead, you slept in the van.'

'That's it. For most of yesterday, yeah,' Lloyd said, his fingers fluttering over the paper cup of coffee they provided for him. 'I had a few too many jars, so I stayed put. Safer that way.'

Jess took his point and peeled it apart. 'It is an offence to be drunk in charge of a vehicle. And if you had your keys with you in the van, even if you were asleep, you're still liable.'

'Wha'?' Lloyd asked, his face distorting in disbelief. 'How?'

'Asleep or not, it's possible for you to have woken up and driven off, while still above the limit.'

'But I didn't,' Lloyd said.

'No, you did not,' Jess agreed. 'And if that is true, it is at least in your favour.'

'Why were you in town, Lloyd?' Rhys posed the question.

'Meeting someone.'

'Anyone we know?'

'Bloke called Lane. There's a Spoons by Marks & Spencer. Bought me a slap-up supper, and we had a few pints.'

'Geraint Lane?' Rhys's smile bordered on the sour.

'Yeah, that's him.'

'Then we do know him.'

'Yeah, well, like he pays me to talk. So, I talk.'

'Have you read what he writes?' Jess asked.

'Nah, I don't read much.'

The solicitor sitting next to Coombs cleared his throat. 'Is this in any way relevant?'

Jess let her gaze drift across to the balding man with his scruffy tie.

He pretended to stare back but struggled, as most people did, when confronted with a Jess Allanby glare. But she put him out of his misery. 'No, not directly.' Then she turned back to the antsy Lloyd. 'And you were in the car all night?'

'Yep.'

'Parked where?'

'Right. Someone said that there was a spot near the river wall, just off one of the roundabouts. Some kind of recovery service down there. Quiet night all in all.'

'At no point did you leave the vehicle, walk across to the industrial estate in Johnstown?'

'No. Why would I do that?'

'To take it out on the police for not finding your father's killer,' Rhys said.

'Take revenge?'

'Come on, Lloyd, it's on all the news channels. A fire in the factory being used to store records.'

Lloyd, his mouth turned down at the corners in total bewilderment, shook his head very slowly. 'I got no idea what you're talking about, mate.'

'You carry spare petrol in your van, Lloyd?' Jess asked.

'Yeah. I can't afford to get stranded. My patch, where I deliver, it's in the wilds.'

'When was the last time you filled up that can?'

'About a month ago. For the can anyway.'

'If we look in your van and find a petrol can, it'll be full?'

'Yeah. Should be.'

'Okay, then,' Rhys said.

───

IT WAS FULL, Gil explained to Warlow in the observation room. 'Of course, he might have more than one and got rid of the can he used, but so far, his story holds water.'

Warlow massaged the skin above his eyebrows with the thumb and middle finger of his left hand. 'He's cooperating with the van?'

'He let us search it. We found the can. That's about it.'

They all turned as the door opened and a Uniform stuck her head in. 'Mr Warlow, there's someone in reception asking to speak to you, sir.'

'Who?'

'A Samantha Coombs, sir.'

The big sister.

Warlow nodded. 'Okay, tell her I'll be along in a few minutes.'

───

AS BEFORE, Samantha Coombs looked in control. She sat opposite Warlow and Gina. Not in an interview room, because this wasn't an interview, but a room in the police station that functioned next to headquarters. They'd found a space to have a chat, but Warlow got the impression that she was interviewing them.

'Lloyd's van is in the car park, so it's clear that he's here.'

'He is.'

'Can I ask why he's here?'

'We needed to ask him some questions. That's all.'

Samantha's expression gave nothing away. 'The fire? It's all over the news.'

Of course, it bloody was.

Gina gave her the stock answer. 'We're not able to share that inform—'

Samantha didn't wait for Gina to finish. 'My brother is a lot of things, but he's not an arsonist. And he isn't a killer.'

'Were you aware that he spent the evening in town and slept in his van on Friday night then disappeared for a whole day?' Gina asked.

'No, but I'm not his keeper.'

'Yet, here you are,' Warlow said.

She smiled. A shadow of the real thing, but the rest of her face hardened. 'It's difficult for most people to understand what happened to us. After my father died, my mother didn't cope. Not at all. We lived with her, and she kept the busy-bodies away, but that's about it.'

'You've already explained all that,' Gina said.

Samantha nodded, but the bright challenge in her eyes didn't fade. 'What I left unexplained are the promises I made to my mother. That she made me make. Like always looking after Lloyd, and …' For a second, Samantha's control wavered, but it reasserted itself just as quickly. 'What I'm doing here is keeping my promises.'

Warlow had read the file on the Coombs family. It echoed what Samantha had said, but there were blanks that required no effort to fill in. 'You stayed with your aunt and uncle for two years after your mother died but left as soon as you could.'

Again, Samantha regarded him coolly before answering, 'I was five when my dad died. He was a history teacher. He made me a wooden castle to play in and shields and wooden swords for me and Lloyd. I was almost sixteen when my mother passed. I had to leave Lloyd with … *them*, for a while, until he was old enough to leave, too. That was hard for him. Until I managed to organise something for both of us.'

'Was it difficult living with your aunt?'

'I'll give you the answer I gave everyone else. Including the social services who kept telling us how lucky we were to have someone take us in. Lucky …' A contemptuous smile flickered over her lips as she repeated the word. 'My aunt … did what she could. My uncle treated us like aliens. Not quite the Harry Potter cupboard under the stairs stuff, but close. Don't forget, I was almost sixteen.'

Warlow felt the hair on his neck prickle.

Gina leaned in. 'Are you saying he abused you?'

'He would have. But he had a daughter. Younger than me. Let's just say he made sure he was always upstairs when I got out of the shower. I made sure never to be at home with him alone. His daughter, Alys, she's my cousin. Not close, but close enough. She was his princess, and I know he never touched her.'

'But you?'

The little smile hardened into a thin slash. 'He never touched me, but he made sure I saw when he touched himself.'

'What about Lloyd?'

'He never pretended that he liked Lloyd and made that obvious. He never hit him, but psychologically, he might as well have. We struck a deal. Unspoken, but … if I let him get his kicks, he'd leave us alone.'

'You still have the option to request us to investigate this, you realise that,' Gina said.

Samantha nodded. Everyone around the table knew well that there were precedents. Abusers could no longer rely on time as a shield. But Samantha shook her head. 'He was careful. It would be my word against his. Besides, my aunt … she is unaware of it. That's the trouble. And she tried hard with us. If I accuse him, it ruins her life and her daughter's too.'

Her bright eyes appeared to be focused on something that

lay beyond the reach of both Warlow and Gina. Images from the past, perhaps. Warlow, for one, was glad he wasn't seeing them.

Samantha stared directly at Gina. 'But it's okay. I have it all up here in a locked box.' She tapped her head. 'And the world turns, doesn't it?'

Warlow filed that away. Once again, Samantha impressed him. Gil might call her a bit rum. But then, she had every reason to be.

'Do you see your uncle and aunt at all now?' he asked.

'No. My aunt calls, but I don't answer. He never does. My mother left us a little money. It helped get me through college and set up Lloyd with a rental deposit. He earns enough to pay his rent. That's why the journalist's money seems so good to him. If you think he had anything to do with this fire, you're wrong.'

'Lane, the journalist he's speaking to, he won't help matters. If anything, it'll only get Lloyd fired up,' Warlow said.

Another smile from Samantha, this one sceptical. 'From what I've read, he seems to be getting to the heart of the matter.'

'From what I've read—' Warlow chose his repeated words carefully. '—he's stoking the fire. Winding your brother up with hearsay. It wouldn't take a genius to see Lloyd getting angry.'

'About you lot not being able to do your job, you mean?'

She was feisty, this one.

'Yes, exactly that.'

'So, you've charged him, then?' Samantha's question already had an answer, and she knew it.

'No. We do not have enough evidence to do that.'

'Right, so, you've finished with him?'

'Not quite.'

'Then I'll wait.' She got up, but Warlow called to her.

'You can wait in here if you like. Would you like some tea?'

'I'd like to get out of here with my brother. It's a long drive back home.'

Right on all counts. Warlow had a stiff back from four hours in the car to prove it.

'I'll see what I can do about that.'

———

THE DCI GATHERED the troops in the Incident Room, letting Lloyd Coombs and his sister cool their jets.

'Anyone spoken to Lane yet?'

'Not yet,' Gil said. 'Besides, all he can do is tell us where Lloyd was earlier that evening.'

'Still needs to be done,' Warlow said.

'Let me do it,' Jess volunteered. 'I have some garlic in my desk drawer.'

'Stick to the phone, you'll be okay,' Warlow said. 'But, if his story pans out, I don't think we can keep Lloyd Coombs. Besides, we need to look at all the other likely candidates.'

He wandered over to the list of names they had up.

Chris Messenger.

Amanda Beech

Wojak or partner.

They'd all need contacting.

'We have Stuart's partner coming in tomorrow, sir.'

'Okay, that's a start. Gil, can you contact Chris Messenger?'

'Love to,' Gil said. 'Especially now that Povey's established that the letter sent to you was posted in rural Herefordshire at some outlying post box.'

'Really?' Warlow asked.

'Village post box. No CCTV. One collection a day.'

'Right. Let's get to it. Tomorrow's Monday, and the press are going to get copies of the letter sent to me. I think the ACC wants to get out in front of it with a press conference first thing.'

'You involved in that, sir?' Gina asked.

Warlow grinned. 'Unfortunately, I have a hospital appointment and a meeting with my social media advisor.'

Gil nodded. 'Give our regards to Molly when you see her.'

CHAPTER TWENTY-EIGHT

THE CASE, already big news, had become a headliner by Monday.

Warlow had gone in early, but still listened to Jess explain to the others the joys of her telephone conversation with Lane, who had, for once, been remarkably cooperative. He hadn't even asked Jess why she wanted him to confirm the evening meeting with Lloyd Coombs. Jess's alarm was raised when he'd been polite. But she already knew Lane would undoubtedly have already been primed by Lloyd.

After that, it had simply been a question of everyone getting on with their jobs. Jess was waiting for Amanda Beech to come in for a voluntary chat. Gina had spoken to Wojak's partner, Heather Messenger's reluctant and solicitor'd-up ex, and Gil had gone directly to visit Chris Messenger at his work.

'Surprise visits. Always the best kind. *Fel llwynog*,' Gil had said. Like a fox.

———

AMANDA BEECH, hair short, makeup-free apart from some eyeliner, like most people sitting opposite a police officer in an interview room, looked discomfited. It was just the two of them, Jess and her. Though this was a chat, and she'd come in of her own volition, the circumstances that brought both officer and interviewee to this point were hardly auspicious. No point pretending otherwise.

'Thanks for coming in, Amanda,' Jess said.

Beech wore cargo pants and a jacket over a black T-shirt. Her reply came as a brisk nod.

'You told us you were working from home the morning Kirsty was killed?'

Jess could've chosen different phrasing, but she needed to get to the core.

A muscle under Amanda's left eye flickered. 'I was working from home.'

'We've accessed Kirsty's phone records. In truth, her phone is in our possession. And thank you for giving us passwords. Saves an awful lot of time.'

Another nod, this time brisker.

'There'd been some exchanges between you that morning,' Jess continued.

Amanda's lips quivered, and she turned her face up to look on the ceiling at something that wasn't truly there. 'It was nothing. Just … stupid banter.'

Jess glanced down at the printed transcripts. '"Be careful out there. They know you're up to no good. They're sensitive. They'll feel your negative energy."'

'Just banter,' Amanda whispered.

Jess waited.

'A little in-joke.'

Jess waited a little longer.

Eventually, Amanda looked up. 'It's no secret that we sometimes had animated discussions about her role with Redoubt Energy. And however you perceive it, windmills are a blight.'

'They'll know you're up to no good?' Jess repeated.

Amanda responded with an eye roll. 'You won't understand.'

'Try me,' Jess said.

'Kirsty and I were partners. She liked to think of herself

as bisexual. She'd had boyfriends before. Me, I'm more pansexual, and I've sometimes identified as ecosexual.'

Jess was genuinely inquisitive. 'That's not one I have stumbled across.'

'Where you consider nature a sensual partner. Lover Earth.'

'As opposed to Mother Earth?'

'Exactly. What Redoubt Energy is considering is a form of abuse bordering on the sexual. Digging up. Inserting.'

Jess had been making notes. Now she stopped and put down the pen. 'They'll know you're up to no good refers to the Earth?'

'The land. The planet. The ecosystem.' Tears had sprung to Amanda's eyes. 'Kirsty was aware of my feelings. And what she was doing ... it had become a bone of contention. My message ... I wanted to remind her.'

Jess paused for a beat before speaking, loading that beat with her incredulity. 'You can understand how this appears.'

Amanda wiped a tear from a cheek. 'I loved Kirsty. I love the Earth. Surely, you can see how much of a dilemma that was, can't you?'

Jess didn't comment.

People held various beliefs throughout the centuries. That the Earth was made six thousand years ago. Psychic surgery had the potential to cure cancer. Or that tobacco was a sacred herb that, if it was blown up the backside, would cure just about anything. It was a free world, and unless you lived north of the border, belief was not an arrestable offence.

Not yet.

Jess was not there to pass judgement.

'Talk me through the rest of these ... messages.' She slid the transcript over the desk towards Beech.

———

IT APPEARED that Warlow's afternoon clinic appointment might have been considered as late morning at 12.05 since the am clinic was still ongoing. The consultant looking after his HIV, Sonia Emmerson, was always direct and always liked to give him extra time if needed.

'*Ddim yn pilo wyau,*' as Gil would say. As a literal translation it hit the nail in the head, meaning that she didn't bother peeling eggs. Warlow liked that no-frills approach.

'All good,' Emmerson said, when Warlow finally got to see her. 'CD4 normal once again and no viral load.'

'Still want me to pop the pill, though?'

'I do. We could try without, but why risk it? You're having no side effects from the anti-retrovirals?'

Warlow shrugged. 'Do they make you a bit cranky?'

'No, that's simply a combination of your naturally ebullient personality and the job you're in.'

Warlow had asked for that. He grinned. 'None taken.'

'So, we'll see you in six months.' Emmerson did the ritualistic closing of the notes that signalled the consultation was over.

But for once, Warlow did not leap out of his chair. The sterile room with its posters and trays covered with blue paper dressing towels appeared to possess a magnetic effect.

'I wanted to ask you something.'

Emmerson sat back.

'I, uh … I have a partner now. We sleep together. She is of the opinion that I don't need to use a condom in this situation.'

'Is she trying to get pregnant?'

'Good God, no.' Warlow chewed over that idea and promptly spat it out. 'She's mid-forties.'

'That means less and less as the century progresses.' Emmerson's matter-of-fact delivery spoke volumes.

'So, her getting tested—'

'For what?'

'HIV.'

Emmerson nodded. 'Does she want a test?'

Warlow remembered the conversation he'd had with Jess about this. 'No. It's me that's asking.'

'Do you believe you can compel her to get tested?'

'No. Not a chance.'

Emmerson gave nothing away in her expression, but it was obvious to the two of them that Warlow was attempting to paddle upstream against the current. 'Right. Do you want me to give you a copy of the studies on unprotected sex between partners where one partner has HIV and no detectable viral load?'

'No. But remind me.'

'No cases of HIV transmission recorded.'

Warlow nodded.

Emmerson cocked her head. 'You've been honest with your partner?'

'About the HIV? Yes, of course.'

'And she still wants to do things … her way?'

'She does.'

'Good, I'm pleased for you. I believed you were beyond help.'

'You and a lot of others.'

'I was talking psychologically.'

At least she hadn't said psychiatrically.

Emmerson trod on Warlow's silence with another question. 'If your partner – does he or she possess a name?'

'She. Jess.'

'If Jess wants to talk anything through, ask her to give Jenny a ring.'

Jenny was a no-nonsense nurse practitioner who'd initially called him monthly for check-ins. Over time, their communication became less frequent, occurring about every four months. Now, these calls mainly served to remind him to get a blood test before his clinic appointments. 'Okay. But she won't.'

'Sounds like someone who knows her own mind.'

'Oh, yes. She does that, alright.'

'Someone to keep you on the straight and narrow, then?'

'She's a police officer, too.'

'Great. Then you have lots to talk about besides your HIV.'

Warlow huffed out a laugh. He liked Emmerson.

———

GINA AND RHYS used the SIO office to make a call to Bea
Trent, the enigmatic Mr Wojak's partner.

'Thanks for agreeing to speak with us, Miss Trent,' Gina
said when the call connected.

'It's Bea.'

On speaker, Rhys made introductions. 'I'm Detective
Sergeant Harries, and I'm here with Detective Constable
Gina Mellings, Bea.'

'We've spoken already,' Bea said.

'That's right, and we appreciate this,' Gina confirmed.

'Just so you know, Pitar knows I'm speaking with you.'

'Right,' Rhys said, trying not to sound too surprised.

'I told him he was being a stubborn idiot, but it's like
having a conversation with a breeze block. Pitar is a bit …
contrary.'

'How long have you known each other?'

'We've been partners for fifteen years.'

'Has he discussed the events around Heather Messenger's
death with you at all?'

'What do you think? Over the years, as the case was
reviewed and resurfaced in the newspapers, we talked about
it, alright. At the time, it greatly affected him in a bad way. A
very bad way.'

'Is that why he won't talk about it now?'

'He is a stubborn man.'

Rhys threw Gina a look. 'I have to ask you one question.
Can you tell us where he was Friday night and early Saturday
morning?'

'End of the school week. We did what we always do: fish
and chips and a couple of glasses of wine. Look, Pitar may
come across as uncooperative, but it affected him badly like I
say. The police interviewed him eight times because he
couldn't account for all his movements.'

Rhys and Gina had both read the files. Wojak had been
on the way to meet with Heather Messenger when the fatal
attack took place in 2001.

'He hates the press. They've already been on to him to find out how he feels. I could tell them. He bloody hates it all.'

Hates it all.

'So, can you confirm you were with Mr Wojak on Friday night?'

'We've got kids, sergeant. I teach. Pitar goes to five-a-side. He's too old, but he's stubborn, as I think I've already said. He came back about half-eight. We had a late fish supper and watched the news for half an hour at ten and then we went to bed. He was still next to me when I got up the following morning, if that's what you want to know. Is this about the fire?'

Another exchanged glance between Gina and Rhys. 'What time did you get up?'

'I'm up at seven. So is Pitar. Kids have football on Saturday morning, and me and Pitar do a big shop.'

'Is there any way that you could convince him to come in and have a chat with us?'

'I think he's told you he only wants to be contacted via his solicitor. He doesn't want this case to turn into another nightmare. Not for him and not for us.'

'That's understandable,' Gina said.

A bell clanged in the background.

'Right, that's break over. I've got to get back to work. I teach, and that's the bell. You can contact me anytime, but Pitar will only speak to you through his solicitor.'

When the call ended, Gina looked disappointed. 'It's her word, I suppose.'

Rhys shook his head. 'Sounds like Wojak wants to be as far away from this as he can.'

'Still …'

'No, the Wolf will be happy with that. Identify, interview, corroborate, and eliminate.'

Gina smiled. 'Thank you, sergeant.'

'Any time.' Rhys grinned.

CHAPTER TWENTY-NINE

WARLOW HAD PROMISED to pick Molly up at 1pm. Since Singleton Hospital in Swansea was at the right end of town and next door to the university campus, he was in the car and on the way when the 1pm bulletin came on Radio 4. The soundbite was bad enough.

'Police hunting for the killers of two people murdered by crossbow on a remote mountain in West Wales today revealed some startling new evidence. At a press conference, a spokesperson told journalists that a letter addressed to one of the investigators may have been sent by the killer.'

The statement was explored further in the news magazine programme that followed. A presenter took up the baton.

'Dyfed Powys Police today admitted that the chief investigator of the notorious Bowman case, where two people were murdered by crossbow twenty years before, had received letters hinting at the killer's identity. They also said they had received a letter that was "highly likely" in their own words, to have come from the same source in relation to the two recent murders that took place in the same location. This marks a bizarre turn in what has already become a notorious case. I spoke to a local journalist who has been following events in Carmarthenshire. Geraint Lane has interviewed several people caught up in this extraordinary and harrowing investigation.

'Geraint, what do you make of these new revelations? Letters

suggesting a potential rite? An arson attack on a records repository? I mean, what on earth is going on?'

'Jesus Christ,' Warlow muttered. 'Bloody Lane again.'

'Good afternoon, Martha. And that is a great question, by the way. One I suspect the police here are asking themselves.'

'Is that your general feeling? Are they aware of who is behind all of this and what is going on?'

'Hard as it might be to believe, given the amount of time and resource DPP has thrown at this case—'

'DPP?'

'Dyfed Powys Police. They've spent thousands of man hours, but they seem as clueless about this fresh case as they were with the old case.'

'Is the thinking, then, that both cases are definitely linked?'

'It's been difficult to get any coherent information from DPP. And now, with the revelations surrounding the letters, written by someone who clearly has knowledge that only the perpetrator could have, the failure of detectives to capitalise on this evidence only worsens the situation.'

'I understand you've been in contact with the son of one victim from the Bowman case? I should explain to listeners that the case was given this rather grizzly name because the victims were shot with crossbow bolts. Is that correct?'

'That's right. DPP released details of these letters, which initially implicated a man called Yardley, who also shot and killed his neighbours with a crossbow. Yardley committed suicide twenty years ago, shortly after the murder of Phillip Coombs and Heather Messenger. During the initial investigation, however, the DPP was unable to discover any compelling forensic evidence of Yardley's involvement. But his name is mentioned again in the new letter.'

'Yes, we've seen copies of this letter in which there are hints at some kind of ritual. Can you explain that?'

'Only that the area in which the murders took place, both twenty years ago and last week, are very close to Iron and Bronze Age burial sites. As well as possibly being linked to Druidic practices.'

Warlow listened, his jaw tight. The gawkers would be firing up their vehicles now on the way to have a gander.

'And what about the investigation into the new killings of Kirsty Stewart and Gerald Nash?'

'That, of course, is opening up all kinds of old wounds.'

'For you to pour salt into,' Warlow muttered.

'And have you received any information on whether police are making any progress at all with that?'

'My guess is that they'll bring in outside help because it's clear they need it. I suspect this is way beyond their own staff's pay grades.'

Warlow flicked the radio off. He did not want to hear anymore, though he suspected there would be more.

The ACC would want a rebuttal. Two-Shoes, the media doyen, must have decided to come clean on the letters. He'd ask her, though he'd probably get more sense from one of Gil's granddaughters. Because at least they knew their arses from their elbows and could name them in two bloody languages.

Molly had texted to say she'd be in front of the Costcutter to the left of the main entrance on the Uni campus. He spotted her as she waved, bundled up in trainers, jeans, a puffer jacket, and a stripey hat covering her dark hair.

'Wotcha,' she said as she opened the door.

'Oh, been mingling with the cockney brethren I see.'

'Okay. *Shwmae*, Evan.'

'Now you're talking my kind of language. Where to, milady?'

'There's a place in the uplands that's quite nice. Coffee is great and they do homemade savouries and cakes.'

'Sounds good.'

It took him five minutes to drive in and find a parking spot. They weren't far from Cwmdonkin Park. This was Dylan Thomas's country, Swansea's most famous son.

The café looked unprepossessing. A shop front, some wire chairs, and metal tables outside, all unoccupied on this cold day.

Molly found a corner table in the place called Hot Kettle, and he let her order two flat whites, carrot cake, and a ham and cheese croissant to share. The place was buzzing but bucked the franchise trend enough to still offer service by way of drinks and food delivered to a numbered table.

When it arrived, Warlow savoured his coffee and squeezed his eyes shut in something approaching ecstasy. There'd been a very pretty leaf pattern in the froth, but sometimes that could mean style over substance. Not the case in the Hot Kettle. The coffee had a nutty edge, no bitterness and a lingering flavour of faint liquorice.

'Good brew,' Warlow murmured.

'See, told you.' Molly cut a chunk of croissant with a knife. She was about to pop it into her mouth when she froze as some memory triggered a moment of horror.

'OMG, Evan, how was your appointment? I totally forgot.'

'Flying colours,' he said and cut off his own chunk of croissant, leaving a decimated battalion of flaky pastry crumbs dead on the plate. The corpses, he suspected, would be removed by index finger if Molly's previous culinary approach to croissants was anything to go by. 'How's this term been?'

'It's good. More than good. I've made some good mates, and the course is really interesting.'

'Not been radicalised yet, then?'

'Think I will be?' As always, her response was half a challenge and half a tease.

Warlow simply raised an eyebrow.

'There are a lot of shouty people around,' Molly said, dropping her voice. 'You can't walk down the corridor without a pamphlet being stuck in your hand. If it isn't the Middle East, it's TERF wars or abolishing cars. Trouble is, you're not allowed to be neutral. If you're not for, then you must be against. I hate that kind of binary attitude.'

Warlow chuckled.

'But I will survive. Most people just want to go with the flow. Say yes to everything and wear a badge, even though they don't feel it. Makes for a simple life. Not so sure about outside in the real world, though. Mostly, I do not engage.'

Wise words indeed.

'Speaking of the real world,' Molly continued. 'Mum says you two might go on holiday?'

'Did she?'

'Yes. And I don't mean back to that shepherd's hut where

you two finally played doctor and nurse. I mean a proper one. Now that you've plucked up the courage to tell Alun and Tom you're sharing a bed with a divorcee.'

Warlow's mouth had dropped open. Not an unusual occurrence in Molly's presence. 'Didn't take long to make the Allanby news bulletin.'

'Reba has reached out on Instagram.'

'Thank God we've got around to discussing social media. Gil would've been so disappointed if we hadn't.'

'And how are Gil and the rest of the team?'

'Fighting a good fight against incredible odds.'

Molly's face became suddenly serious, and she stopped chewing. 'Oh God, I heard about those letters on the radio today. That journalist … ugh.'

Warlow sat back, once again disarmed by Molly. 'You're a student. What the hell are you doing listening to radio four?'

'I have quirks.' She shrugged. 'That was Lane, right?'

That made Warlow smile. She was indeed Jess's daughter. 'Yes. Public enemy number one.'

'He was horrible. Even his voice got on my nerves. But this case … Is someone really writing letters?' Molly was studying criminology and psychology, and she was one of Warlow's favourite people. So, his normal steel shutter approach to discussing anything case-related to anyone outside the team did not apply here.

'Yes, someone sent a letter to me.'

'Oh, my God. He or she?'

'Hard to tell. As is what endgame they're aiming for, other than to enjoy the chaos they're creating.'

Molly tilted her head. 'Perverting the course of justice. Like John Humble in the Yorkshire Ripper case. Good old Wearside Jack. He enjoyed the notoriety, didn't he?'

'Oh, you've done your homework. And this is a perversion, no doubt about that. But Humble was a bored troublemaker. This person … not so sure.'

'There are cases of misplaced guilt as well, though. The paradox of self-disclosure. Some people genuinely even believe they know the truth.'

'I see those lectures are paying off.' Warlow sipped his coffee. 'I'll bear all that in mind.'

'Alright, no need to be snarky.' Molly had a shorter fuse than her mother.

'No, I mean it. The author could be delusional. That's one aspect we have not considered.'

She smiled at that, after searching his face for any sign of a patronising glint.

Conversation drifted into lighter things. Croissants and carrot cake were eaten. Crumbs digitally removed from the plate.

Half an hour later, they were back in the car.

'Lectures today?'

'One at three.'

'I can tell your mum all is good?'

'Ye-ah.'

Warlow picked up on the lilt and threw her a glance.

'It's nothing,' Molly said. 'But, because you're always telling me to be "hypervigilant"—' She made rabbit ears in the air around the word. '—one of my girlfriends said a bloke was asking after me last week.'

Molly was approaching nineteen, had her mother's great bone structure, and most males with a pulse would look at least five times, let alone twice when she walked into the room. And this was a university, with slightly less than half of its attendees maxing out on testosterone levels.

'Yes, I know what you're thinking and, of course, there is that. But this was in a club in town. I wasn't there, but it was a student night.'

'Could it be someone you know from old?'

'Possibly, but he was late twenties.'

'Okay.'

'Look, say nothing to Mum. It's probably someone I met before or a friend of a friend sort of thing.'

'But you'll be careful.'

'I will.'

Nothing more was said because nothing needed to be. They'd talked about this. About the fact that Molly's dad,

Rick Allanby, had run-ins with organised crime in Manchester and had been extracted from undercover after threats were made to him and his family.

One reason Jess and Molly had moved in with Warlow had been a need, after a warning from Greater Manchester Police, for hypervigilance. It was a word that they batted between them, these days almost jokingly.

That status had been de-escalated, but you never knew. Warlow was quietly grateful for Rick Allanby's catalogue of indiscretions, as it had brought Jess and Molly into his life.

But crime gangs were anything but forgiving. And vendettas were not purely the purview of mafias or convenient tropes that only existed in films.

Criminals could be unforgiving bastards.

———

WARLOW DROPPED Molly back in front of Costcutter on the university campus, waved, and went back out to the seafront road. Instead of turning left back to the city, he turned right, back up past the hospital, heading north to hit the M4 at junction 47. This took him on the road between Singleton Hospital and the university playing fields. He'd noticed the archery targets as he'd driven in that morning.

On a whim, he turned into the grounds and parked up near someone who looked like they might be a groundskeeper. The shovel and wheelbarrow were the giveaway. Warlow flashed his warrant card.

'You have archery targets here, I see?'

'Yep.'

'Is there a club?'

'Yes, there is. Twice a month. They book a slot. To make sure the area is clear, you know.'

'Crossbows?'

The groundskeeper blinked as two and two made four in his head. 'These are just kids.'

'Who looks after the equipment?'

'There's a lecturer who runs things. Do you need his name?'

Warlow looked at where the archery targets were, well away in the top corner of a field. 'No. But mind if I take a look up there?'

'No, feel free. The next club meeting isn't until next week.'

Warlow thanked him and walked off, leaving the slightly bemused man to watch the police officer tunelessly whistling as he went.

CHAPTER THIRTY

WARLOW GOT BACK from Swansea to find tea ready and the Human Tissue for Transplant box open for business.

'Is this what you do when I'm not here?' he asked, noting the fresh brew gently steaming in mugs.

Jess handed him his Foxtrot Foxtrot Sierra mug with a chin down, eyes-up look. She had her back to the room and said quietly, 'Molly texted. She says thanks for the coffee and cake.'

'Don't forget the croissant,' Warlow said. 'She's on good form.'

'How about you?'

'Don't need another MOT for six months.'

Jess's smile in response had a soupçon of relief in it and her heartfelt, 'Great,' gave Warlow sudden pause.

'You don't need to worry about me,' he replied quickly.

'Someone has to.' Jess's words came across as surprisingly tender, and his usual bluff response, which was to be flippant, foundered as she turned away to address the gaggle of extras that had accumulated over the last two days.

Staff had been co-opted. There were half a dozen Uniforms and secretaries now as part of the investigative team.

'Listen up,' Jess said. 'By now, unless you live in a cave—'

'Or a nuclear bunker,' Rhys said. A phrase that earned him looks of horror and disbelief from Gina and Warlow.

'—you know that the press are in a feeding frenzy, having been informed of the letters and the case. I hardly need to say it, but what goes on in this room stays in this room. We have press officers and senior officers handling the fallout. What we need to do is concentrate on the investigation.'

Warlow could not have put it better himself. In fact, he probably would have put it much worse with his usual jaundiced eye. Unlike Jess, who knew exactly what note to strike.

'I think now might be a good time to catch-up with progress.' She glanced at Warlow, who nodded, before she turned back. 'Gina?'

'Rhys … Sergeant Harries, and I spoke briefly to Bea Trent, Pitar Wojak's partner. The man himself, as you know, has been reluctant to engage with us, ma'am.'

'Was he ever seriously in the frame the first time around?' Warlow asked.

Rhys angled his head to denote doubt. 'No, but he was a blip on our radar. His partner tells us he's psychologically scarred still from the Bowman case. But she confirms his alibi for the night of the arson attack.'

He walked up to the Job Centre and put a date next to Wojak's name, and then put a red line through it.

'Thank you,' Jess said. 'My discussions with Kirsty Stuart's partner, Amanda Beech, confirmed that there'd been some conflict between them. Verbal jousting that continued as an exchange of texts between them the morning of the killing.'

She went on to explain about ecosexual identity and Beech's Lover Earth philosophy. To be fair, no one laughed or commented. The old DEI training was obviously paying off.

'We've also contacted Beech's company, who confirmed she was on calls with her team leader that morning. We can effectively eliminate her.'

'Gil not here?' Warlow asked, glancing around.

'He's on the way to Chris Messenger,' Rhys said. 'Though I think that will not be as easy as he thought. Apparently, Messenger is out on-site visits.'

Warlow pushed off from the desk he was on.

'I come bearing gifts.' He picked up a Sainsbury's plastic bag which looked half empty. He reached inside and took out three long sticks. Except that they were not sticks. One was longer than the other two, which were thicker and shorter. All three were fletched, and all three had narrow, metal, almost blunt, tips.

'For reasons that we do not need to go into, I was near the university sports ground in Swansea today, and they have an archery range. I took a walk around. There is a hedge behind, and in that hedge, I recovered these three projectiles. The longest clearly is from a bow, the other two are crossbow bolts. None of these have the hunting tips. These are what they call field tips for target shooting, not the broadhead we've seen used in our case. But the bolts have the same manufacturer's mark as on the bolts found at the Nash and Stuart scenes.'

'What's the significance, sir?' Gina asked.

'I'm not entirely sure, except that I found these after fifteen minutes of looking. We probably ought to ask Milton about them. Someone give Povey a ring and ask if he's around today.'

Rhys did the needful while Warlow drank his tea and partook of a custard cream, un-dunked. Too many eyes watching and hoping for structural collapse.

Rhys finished his call. 'Looks like Milton is not present today, sir. And Povey says we'll be lucky to get hold of him. He often switches off his phone and picks up texts only late in the afternoon.'

'Hmm.' Warlow bit into his biscuit. 'Where is Gil now?'

'Got as far as Brecon, but I think he's aborting the road trip, sir. Messenger is in the middle of Herefordshire somewhere and on the move.'

'Okay. Then let me call him.'

Warlow retreated to the SIO office, took some snaps of the projectiles he'd found after laying them out on the desk, and sent them over the ether to Gil. The sergeant rang back immediately.

'What's all this, Evan?'

'Stuff I picked up on an archery range. Lost in a hedge behind the targets, it looks like.'

'Someone needs to go to Specsavers, then.'

'The bolts look like the ones found at the scene. Milton is not around today, and he's not answering his phone.'

'Probably out building a moat,' Gil said.

'Well, you're close to his place if you're coming back from Brecon. Fancy calling in? It's not far from Llandovery.'

'Fine. It would save this from being a totally wasted journey. I should have contacted Messenger before I left, but I wanted to turn up unannounced, like a dose of … flu.'

Warlow was pleased that he'd used flu as the exemplar and not a more colourful disease. 'Milton won't mind you calling, I'm sure. He's enthusiastic, to say the least.'

'Consider it done. And you? How was your appointment?'

'Not for the scrap heap just yet,' Warlow said.

'Damn, that's another bet I've lost to Rhys.'

'Let me know how you get on,' Warlow said with admirable restraint.

———

GIL PUNCHED the address Warlow texted through into his sat nav. He turned up the radio, which, until a few minutes back, had been in a dead zone. For some gremlin-based reason, the radio crackled back into life on a different channel. This one a Welsh language channel. Within seconds, Gil was belting out the chorus of *Yn Yma O Hyd* – *We're Still Here* – folk singer Dafydd Iwan's ode to the tribulations and resilience of Welsh culture and language over the years. A proper spine-tingling anthem that was a defiant railing against the threat – originally military, later cultural – posed by the country's much bigger English neighbours.

These days, as much as anything, used as a psychological tool by Welsh soccer – and sometimes rugby – fans at international matches.

Gil enjoyed the singsong, though his politics were for his own consumption. He avoided discussion other than with people he could trust, like Warlow, much like one might avoid religion or Assisted Dying. Trigger-happy he was not.

His job meant he needed to be neutral on many things. At least project an openness, as much as his conscience allowed. But he had little time for populism and the nationalists who put identity before the economics of survival. What he craved, like most parents, for his own children and grandchildren, was a safe place to live, where endeavour, kindness, the law, and common sense prevailed and were rewarded in a democratic meritocracy.

He'd thought he actually lived in a place like that once. But he made no apology about hoping that one day, everyone would wake up from the spell that had been cast over the last dozen years. Yet, the country, if not the world, seemed full of strident, self-absorbed people in a constant state of anger about the rest of the world refusing to see things their way, and never mind science, truth, and history, which, through no fault of their own, were most definitely on the twenty-first century's naughty step.

When he was in optimistic mode, he hoped one day there'd be a reckoning.

When pessimism overwhelmed him, he saw himself being burnt at the stake for heresy.

Warlow had been right when he used the Addams Family vibe as a description for Milton's house. The chilly March afternoon had become still and grey, though there was plenty of light left.

He drove through the iron arch and crawled up the curving driveway to pull up next to a seen-better-days Land Rover.

'At least you're home, Mr Milton,' he said to himself.

Gil got out and walked to the oak door, lifted the knocker three times, and waited. He took in the same lichen-stained stone and rusting iron hinges that Warlow noted on his visit.

Nothing happened after three knocks.

Gil tried the door again.

He was about to try for a third time when a sudden movement caught his eye. He turned and stepped back to look at the side of the house.

Those two movements probably saved his life.

Something struck the back of his left shoulder before his gaze locked on.

The blow spun him around with such force that he pivoted and fell, knocking his head against the stone of the portico. The world brightened, then dimmed as his head exploded with pain. Then, and only then, did he feel a worse pain in his shoulder.

Stunned, Gil looked up to the corner of the building, but there was no one there.

He tried to move but froze as a wave of excruciating pain shot through his back. He stopped moving and gingerly reached over.

There was something protruding from behind his shoulder blade.

Out of the corner of his eye, he saw a black shaft fletched orange at the end.

A bolt.

'Shit,' Gil uttered, and found enough adrenaline to crawl back into the shelter of the portico, manoeuvre his other shoulder against the door, and rest his head. Not knowing what else to do, he banged his skull on the door and yelled.

'Anyone there? Anyone?'

His breath became ragged as fear and pain gripped him in equal measure, praying that no one was going to appear at the edge of the portico with a crossbow aimed at his heart.

He heard a shuffling from behind him. No, from inside the house, followed by bolts shifting, and then the door opened.

There was Milton. But not the Milton, he knew. This was a pale, shaking Milton, with what looked like a tea towel wrapped around his leg.

A tea towel scarlet with blood.

Milton glared out at the courtyard with terrified eyes, reached for Gil, grabbed his collar, and dragged him in.

Gil winced but kept quiet, helping as much as he could by

bicycling with his feet. Then he was inside, and Milton slammed the door shut before bolting it.

'What's going on?' Gil croaked.

'Someone is out there. Someone shot me, and by the looks of it, by Christ, they shot you.'

'Have you called—'

'I dropped my phone. I was on the way back to the house from the garden. I don't have a landline.'

'Use mine.' Gil groaned with effort, and a wave of nausea washed over him as he reached for his inside pocket, the movement of his shoulder a fresh agony. But his fingers locked on the oblong, and he held the phone up. 'You call. I'm going to pass out. Passcode is 9996.'

The last thing Gil saw was Milton's stubby, shaky fingers punching in numbers and holding the phone up to his ear.

CHAPTER THIRTY-ONE

BY THE TIME Warlow got to the hospital, they'd already taken Gil to the operating theatre. The DCI knew the A&E sister well enough to get the brief rundown on his colleague's injuries.

'It looked like the bolt hit his scapula from the back. There's an obvious comminuted fracture, looks like the scapula split.'

Warlow was lost for words. Another bloody bolt? He didn't much like what the sister said next, either.

'The orthopods said the bolt hit at an angle. Your sergeant was lucky because it was headed straight for the big vessels around the heart. Those big bones have come in useful at last.'

He'd need to research the meaning of comminuted. Something not good, no doubt. In his experience, medical jargon seldom was. And he'd be the first to admit that his knowledge of anatomy, as for most non-medical people, remained a vague imaginarium of tubes and organs occupying the space inside a person's frame. If he needed ever to point out where his stomach or his liver was, he might get the side right, but the position was horribly wrong.

He took a little comfort from hearing the bolt had not reached its intended target.

They kept Milton in A&E for treatment. Fortunately, his wound was only superficial. A deep furrow was opened up on his thigh by the bolt, which needed to be cleaned and stitched.

He, similar to Gil, had a fortunate escape.

Warlow found Milton recovering on a trolley in a curtained cubicle while they attempted to find him a bed. He'd complained of some chest pain, probably an anxiety attack, so the doctors wanted to be sure and insisted on monitoring him overnight.

He wore a blue-patterned gown, stretched over his ample abdomen, with sheets covering his lower half. But he was sitting up with leads running up under his gown and over his neck to a beeping monitor next to him.

'Can you talk?' Warlow asked.

'Yes. All a lot of fuss over nothing, if you ask me.' Milton waved vaguely at the leads and the ECG.

'They know what they're doing,' Warlow said.

'How's your colleague?'

'In surgery. Fractured scapula, whatever that means. We're awaiting reports.'

Milton winced. 'It's lucky that a field bolt was used. At least, I'm assuming it was.'

'Why do you say that?'

'If it was a broadhead, I would have lost half of my leg. And the same applies for your sergeant. It would have cleaved straight through his scapula.'

'What happened, exactly?'

Milton ran through the events. How he'd been outside, pottering about. A cracking twig in the woods to the side of the garage drew his attention. When he stepped out to look, he'd seen nothing until. 'Out of the blue, I heard a bow's trigger click and suddenly, I got this pain in my leg. Only a glancing blow, but it felt like somebody was slashing me with a knife. When I looked down, I saw blood. I had absolutely no clue what was going on. I hobbled back to the kitchen through the back door. Obviously, I'd been shot, but there'd been no gunfire. So, I assumed it must have been an arrow or a bolt. I tied a tea towel around my leg and realised I'd lost my phone.'

Milton shook his head at a regretful decision. 'I abandoned the landline two years ago, and I must have dropped my mobile outside.'

'Did you see anyone or anything at all?'

'Nothing. Except for that cracking branch, there'd been nothing.'

'What about Gil?'

'I'd been back in the kitchen for maybe five minutes. I didn't hear a car, because I was too preoccupied with my leg, I suppose. But then there was this knocking. I'm ashamed to say I didn't answer immediately. I thought it could be whoever shot me, so I stayed in the kitchen, but he shouted, and I heard him moaning. I went to the front door. He was half collapsed with a bolt stuck in his shoulder. I dragged him inside and called for help.'

Warlow's pulse thrummed in his ear. 'You saw no one?'

'No. Whoever shot us must have crept up on me, and when Sergeant Jones arrived …' Milton winced as he shifted in the bed to get comfortable.

'None of this makes any bloody sense,' Warlow said. 'Why is someone targeting you?'

'Are they worried I might find something?' Milton asked. 'Is it true that someone attacked the storage facility as well?'

'They did. What are they scared of?'

Warlow got no answer.

The curtain shifted behind him, and Jess appeared. 'Gil's out of theatre. Fractured scapula, but no other major injury.'

Warlow put his hands on his hips, turned away, and sucked in air. He'd been through too many of these bloody moments. With Jess, with Rhys, and now Gil.

'You okay?' Jess put a hand on his arm.

Warlow looked down at her hand. 'I suppose there's no way of seeing Gil now?'

'He'll be out of it for a while,' Jess said. 'But I hung about outside the theatre to talk to the surgeon. He seemed upbeat.'

'Glad someone is,' Warlow grumbled, and then turned

back to Milton. 'We'll need a formal statement, Mr Milton. Try to remember everything, even the minor details. But as of now, your house is a crime scene.'

'It's a good thing that they're keeping me in. Never rains, but it pours, eh?' Milton's smile had a bitter edge to it.

———

THOUGH NO MURDER had taken place, and Rhys voiced his thanks to the gods for that, there might as well have been for all the attention Milton's property was receiving.

'God,' Gina said, as they parked up in the job Ford Focus. 'It's mad here.'

They'd been directed to a spot just inside the gates by a Uniform in a Hi-Vis jacket acting as a marshall. They reached the courtyard on foot and took in the vehicles all around the perimeter.

Povey's team took measures to cordon off the centre and the garage area. Milton's Land Rover was also relocated out of the way.

'It's what happens when one of our own is a victim,' Rhys said with an air of grim satisfaction.

Tannard waved as they stood looking around. She wore her snowsuit, as did all the technicians moving about carefully in the courtyard. The front door of the house stood open and more snowmen were moving about inside. Rhys saw flashes as photographers captured evidence.

'I can't let you in yet,' Tannard said. 'But put some over-shoes on, and we'll go around back.'

'Was this where Gil was shot?' Gina asked.

'From what he could tell the paramedics, and what Milton said, he was knocking on the door when he was hit from behind. Just inside the portico.' She pointed toward the door. 'Which means the shooter was somewhere in that direction.' She held her palm open and vertical, then shifted it toward the edge of the house and the garage, still overflowing with half-repaired medieval weapons.

Tannard led them to a tent where they put on some overshoes and then took them around the far side of the house to the rear. The back door stood open here as well, and a cordoned-off path leading around to the garage blocked off access that way.

'If you want to step into the garden,' Tannard suggested.

Gina and Rhys followed her. From that vantage point, they could look in through the open back door into the kitchen, now lit by arc lights. Tannard pointed to the marked path from the back door around the house.

'This is the path Milton took after he was shot. There are blood spatters just inside the back door. Looks like the shooter stayed on the eastern side of the property.'

'Have you found anything useful on the grounds?' Rhys asked.

'Not yet. Obviously, we're looking for footprints and anything else that might have been left, but so far, nothing.'

'CCTV?' Gina asked, but with hope more than expectation.

Tannard's smile was almost pitying. 'Mr Milton is a medievalist. So, no. There is no CCTV.'

'Access to the woods? What about that?' Rhys asked.

'The copse on this property slopes into the valley below. Anyone could get in. There is a fence, but it's forty metres away and easily climbable.'

'Nothing concrete I can tell DCI Warlow?' Rhys tried not to sound forlorn but failed.

'Early days, Sergeant,' Tannard said. 'Early days.'

CHAPTER THIRTY-TWO

IT WAS WELL after 7pm in the Incident Room, and no one had left for home. The team was one down, but no one was complaining.

Warlow stood in front of the Gallery and the Job Centre, looking for a domino to push over. 'We need to account for movements.'

'For who exactly, sir?' Rhys asked.

'Everyone on this board. Start with Christopher Messenger. He was the man who Gil was going to surprise, correct?'

'Gil said Messenger had gone out on a site visit.'

Warlow turned to Rhys. A lesser officer might have wilted under that fierce glare, but the acting sergeant, like everyone in that room, Uniforms included, shared the same steely determination that had spread quietly from one officer to the other since hearing about the attack on Gil.

Jess took up a marker pen and found an empty patch of whiteboard. 'Besides Messenger, several people have been down to us over the last couple of days to give statements or answer questions and could've been travelling back to Mid-Wales. That puts them all in the frame. I'll speak to Amanda Beech.'

She wrote Beech's name up and her own initials next to it.

'Samantha and Lloyd Coombs were here too,' Gina said.

Jess wrote Gina's name next to Samantha's and Rhys's next to Lloyd Coombs. She hesitated then but added Wojak's name. 'No one has actually spoken to him yet.'

'He needs to be questioned now. If it means dragging him and his solicitor in, fine. Let's do that,' Warlow said.

'That's unlikely to happen tonight, sir,' Rhys said.

'All the more reason to start the ball rolling. He won't like it, but we are way beyond that now.' Warlow's gaze drifted across to the image of Milton's house. 'Nothing from Tannard?'

Rhys replied, 'She says they're almost finished there. They've found another crossbow bolt similar to the one that hit Gil. They're checking it, but it's possible it may be the one that struck Milton.'

It was evidence, but only time would tell if it would help. Meanwhile, the killer who'd attacked one of their own remained at large.

Rhys's phone made a noise like a submarine's echo sounder. He glanced at the screen.

'That's one of the Uniforms at the hospital. Gil is awake, and his wife is with him.'

'Right. I'll go.' Warlow turned to Jess for approval. 'No one else needs to come now. You've all got things to do.'

'Hopefully by the time you get back, we'll have some answers,' she said.

———

WHATEVER DRUGS GIL had received for pain relief, they seemed to be working very well. Perhaps, judging by the vapid grin on his face, a bit too well.

They'd put him in a side room, not because of security or that they felt he was at risk of further attack, but to stop the hyenas from sneaking in. And for hyenas, read the press. Both police and the hospital authorities knew that a photograph, even one from a phone, could earn the sneaky snapper a small fortune.

Warlow could see it in his mind's eye. Gil, in pain, one

arm and his head in bandages. An image of the fallen hero. Just what the bloodsuckers liked.

Except that was not the image that greeted Warlow as he pushed open the door.

Gil was sitting up, left arm in a neat sling, looking a little pale, but otherwise intact. A drip snaked from a plastic bottle on a stand into a bandage on his right arm. The plastic bottle contained clear fluid, nothing claret-coloured. Anwen, Gil's wife, sat next to her husband wearing a wan smile.

'How are you feeling?' Warlow stood at the bottom of the bed, his expression anxious.

'Like the treble twenty on a dartboard.' Gil grinned. 'Only glad the bugger didn't finish with the bull's-eye.'

Anwen, several Tupperware boxes open on her lap and on the coverlet, sent Warlow a faux grin. 'We've had lots of darts references. And before you ask, the drip is for intravenous antibiotics.'

'Fancy a sarnie, Evan. She's brought in some coronation chicken. The queen of sandwiches, and on seeded bread. Guaranteed to get you going, that bread. We know how to live in the Jones's household. *Mynufferni*.'

Despite the circumstances, Warlow grinned, too. 'So, surgery went well?'

He glanced at Anwen for the sensible answer.

'The bolt is out. The scapula broke into four pieces with minimal displacement. They don't repair them surgically, so the surgeon said—'

Warlow held up his hand. 'Scapula? Now, that's the big triangular bone in the shoulder?'

'That's the one. Bit like an upside-down sail. Anyway, treatment is a sling and physio.'

Gil worked on his coronation chicken sandwich with a smirk on his face. 'Scapula. Maybe we ought to go to Castle Scapula and speak to Count Scapula. Bone up on vampires.' He chortled at his own pun, not caring that the masticated coronation chicken in his mouth became disconcertingly visible.

Warlow's smile oozed amusement and disgust in equal measure.

'He's been like this since coming back from the theatre.' Anwen sighed. 'Do they still use laughing gas, I wonder?'

'I don't believe so,' Warlow said.

'Well, whatever it is they've given him, it's very … effective.' Anwen tagged on another sigh.

Warlow tried one last time and turned again to Gil. 'You realise you almost died?'

'Die diddley eye die died?' Gil said.

'Exactly,' Warlow said. 'Die diddley eye die died.'

'You hum it, I'll play it,' Gil said, pretending to bow a fiddle which, with one arm in a sling, looked very odd. But Gil was full of it, his nonsense almost infectious.

Warlow took in a breath. 'Oy, Yehudi, can you concentrate for a minute?'

'Yehudi Menuhin. Never genuine, was Menuhin. Always on the fiddle.' Gil giggled at his own joke.

'Gil, concentrate.'

'Concentrate? Of course. I'm a concentrate pianist. See me tinkle the ivories. Not on the ivories, that would be very rude and an offence. And anyway, Seeme Tinkle used to bowl for Surrey. Evil googly he had.' Gil laughed again, his time helpless with mirth at his own words.

'He's all over the place,' Anwen said.

'As the bishop said to the shark,' Gil added breathlessly. A quip that brought another bout of Muttley wheezing that passed as Gil laughter.

Warlow tried not to smile, but damn the man, it was entertaining.

'Gil.' Warlow tried raising his voice, which drew a sharp stare from the sergeant, but no lessening of the mirth. 'Can you tell me anything about the shooter?'

'I can William Tell you bugger all.' Gil giggled and picked up a Tupperware box. 'Sandwich?'

'Did you see anything?'

'I saw my life flash before me. Dirty bugger.'

'You're wasting your time, Evan. He's as high as a kite.'

'Yeah.' Warlow nodded. 'Still, it's good to see him ... happy.'

Warlow stepped to the side and offered his hand.

Gil put the sandwich down, looked at the appendage, and said, 'I don't care if you're Ginger bloody Rogers, I am not dancing with you.'

Warlow sighed again. 'I think I prefer the moody cynic.'

'Ever met his brother, R cynic?'

'I'm beginning to wish I had,' Anwen muttered.

Warlow took a step back and sent her a sympathetic look. 'If and when he reaches the shores of sensible and he tells us something useful, give me a ring?'

'You might wait a long time. I've been waiting for years.'

'But I'm glad to see he is okay.'

Anwen fussed with the sandwiches and fished out a serviette which she used to dab her face. 'I'm getting a bit too old for all of this.'

Warlow frowned and moved back to kneel next to her.

'He's made of old boots, you know that.' He put his hand on her shoulder.

She reached up and squeezed it, her eyes still moist. 'Any idea who did this, Evan?'

'I'd be lying if I said yes.'

'It's such a horrible case. Four people are dead, and now ...'

Could've been five, Warlow thought, but sensibly put the brakes on the sentence before it reached his voice box.

'Anwen,' Gil said, with mock sharpness.

'Yes, Gil?'

'That man is a police officer. Put him down now.'

'I know that. Shut up and eat your sandwich.'

'Coronation chicken. Food of the gods, or is it dogs?'

Anwen picked up two Tupperware boxes. 'There are rounds of salmon sandwiches in here and a dozen Welsh cakes in the other box. Your lot must be starving.'

Warlow didn't even consider objecting. Anwen had been in this game for a long time as the partner of a police officer. She knew they'd all be hungry back at the Incident Room.

'Thanks,' Warlow said. 'Much appreciated.'

'Did I tell you about the latecomers at the police officer's ball, Anwen?'

'Yes, many times.'

Gil ignored her. 'Mr and Mrs Disorderly and their son Duncan ...'

'I think I need to leave now,' Warlow said.

' ... Mr and Mrs All Cars and their son Colin ...'

Gil was on an opiate roll.

Anwen tried to ignore him. 'Take care, Evan. Thanks for coming. He appreciates it, though you'd never tell.'

'Mr and Mrs Cuff and their daughter, Ann ...'

Warlow, too tired to say much more, looked at the sergeant and shook his head. 'Thanks for the food and look after him. He's a treasure.'

Anwen responded with a Gil-ism of her own, 'As in should be buried on a desert island?'

Warlow grinned. That one definitely had its source in the Gil archive.

Gil ploughed on, 'Mr and Mrs O'fcrime and their daughter, Sienna ...'

'Keep in touch,' Warlow said.

The last thing he heard Gil say as he exited was. 'Mr and Mrs Ningall and their daughter Eve ...'

God, the man was incorrigible. But Warlow was smiling as he walked out of the door.

———

HE RANG Jess as soon as he got outside.

'And?' she asked.

'He's fine. High as a bloody kite on whatever they've given him for pain. Think Gil, only with ADHD and attempting stand-up.'

'That's ...' Jess failed to find the word and settled for. 'Poor Anwen.'

'What about things your end?'

'Ah, right. I've been told to tell you as soon as you rang

that the ACC is calling an urgent meeting, and you need to be there.'

Silence.

'You still there, Evan?'

'Unfortunately, yes, I am.'

'Buchannan said that Drinkwater had told him to think of it like a COBRA meeting. All essential personnel.'

'More nest of bloody vipers than cobra, I'd say. Oh, God.'

'No, just you.'

'Don't you start with the funnies. I've just had a wheel-barrow load from Gil, but he has an excuse.'

'No, you're right,' Jess said. 'You'll need all your good humour to get through the next few hours.'

CHAPTER THIRTY-THREE

20:15. To Warlow, it felt like Groundhog Day. Somewhere around two-thirds of the way through the film, where Bill Murray was heading downhill towards his low point.

Earlier on, Rhys had suggested Daniel in the lion's den. This time, though, Warlow found himself in there alone, and without the tamer. Sion Buchannan had been in meetings with the commissioner all day. And the evening dinner in Cardiff that followed required his presence. While the superintendent tucked into *filet mignon*, Warlow was left in the room feeling very much like a goat tethered to a tree.

The ACC still wore his uniform, as did Drinkwater and Goodey. This time, however, there were other faces in the room. Another couple of superintendents from across the patch. The Force area was divvied up into Basic Command Units, and each of those had its own command structure.

Gil would have been horrified. Warlow heard the sergeant's voice in his head.

'If all the bloody pilots are here, who's flying the plane?'

Good question.

Reeves, the ACC cleared his throat. There was no coffee or tea on offer this evening. Catering staff had long gone home. But Reeves had found a bottle of water from somewhere, and he drank from this now without a glass.

'Thank you all for coming. We are in an unprecedented situation, and after today's events, we should, at the very least, hold a strategy meeting.'

Drinkwater's florid complexion looked stoke-primed this evening, and he spoke next. 'The press are having a field day at our expense. Two more people attacked, including one of our own officers. And, Evan, do we really have no idea who was behind all this?'

'Has it even been twenty-four hours since we last met, sir?' Warlow said. It wasn't meant as an excuse. Just stating a fact.

Reeves bristled. 'Twenty-four hours of no progress. It can't go on. We appreciate your efforts, Evan, but I'm changing the direction of this … debacle. As of now, Pamela Goodey will supervise both aspects of this investigation. Reviewing the Bowman case and the most recent murders.'

Goodey, one of her best professional smiles pasted on her lips, nodded in appreciation. It made her look like a ventrilo-quist's dummy who'd won the lottery.

'Once we finish the recovery of usable evidence from the fire at the factory, I will run things from the Incident Room here, at HQ.' Goodey made the pronouncement, looked around at the faces and settled on Warlow's. 'I've asked DCI Braeburn from Aberystwyth to be my deputy, along with you, of course, Evan. We need more boots on the ground. He will join the team tomorrow.'

'What are your thoughts, Pamela?' Reeves sounded pathetically desperate.

Warlow sat back. This should be good.

'Considering the letter received by Evan, and the clear link between whoever wrote that and the cold case, I've contacted someone from Cardiff. An expert in ancient history. She will visit the scenes to give us her opinion on the likelihood that there is any quasi-religious element that might be significant.'

Christ, thought Warlow. *It'll be a psychic next.*

'I see,' the ACC said. Clearly, he was as surprised as everyone else. Unfortunately, his tone did not contain anywhere near enough scepticism for Warlow's liking.

'Whoever wrote those letters has inside information,' Goodey added.

The ACC sent Warlow a desperate glance. 'Evan? Your thoughts?'

'My honest opinion? This letter writer is going to be laughing like a drain when he or she sees people running around, trying to add credence to what he's written. Credence to his ...' Bullshit sprang to mind, but he tried to stay professional. ' ... machinations.'

'You don't buy into the Druidic reference?' Drinkwater asked.

'I do not.'

Two-Shoes sat up a little straighter on hearing Warlow's remarks. She was not one to forgive sleights easily. One of her many little foibles. There was a coldness in what she said next that did not surprise Warlow in the slightest. 'And what line of investigation are you taking, Evan?'

'The team is contacting all those we interviewed. Every one of them could have been in transit near to where the attacks on Milton and Gil took place. Don't get me wrong, I'm not dismissing the letters out of hand. They are important. If I might be candid, ma'am?'

'Feel free,' Two-Shoes said.

'We risk giving too much weight to the letters. Whoever is writing them is attempting to do the same again; distracting us by suggesting something bizarre that gets everyone agitated. Yardley was never a viable person of interest. But those letters and the letter writer got under Tim Leach's skin, so we need to be very careful.'

'What if it is the killer, though?' Drinkwater said.

'There's a good chance it is,' Warlow admitted. 'And they know exactly what they're doing. It's legerdemain.'

Drinkwater frowned, and Warlow put him out of his misery.

'Deception, sir. Trickery.'

Two-Shoes gave nothing away. 'Interesting theory, Evan.' But she parked any further comment and opted for stating the obvious instead of a petty power play. 'Bring those people in tomorrow.'

'Some of them will come in tomorrow, ma'am. Those that can't, will be visited.'

'Of course.' Two-Shoes nodded sagely. 'Boxes need to be ticked. But then we also need to be thinking outside of those boxes, don't we, Evan?'

Reeves hadn't finished. 'Can we also please warn everyone involved to be careful with the press? Otherwise, there will be consequences.'

He looked more flushed than usual this evening.

Warlow felt obliged to answer. 'My team is always careful about the press, and by press, I mean Geraint Lane. But he is getting fed by Lloyd Coombs. And he's confident, like any fox let into the henhouse. Half of what he writes about is fabrication. I have no control over that.'

'Please have a word with all personnel, regardless. In addition, I think we need to meet every day from now on. I need to keep a handle on this.'

'Think of these like COBRA meetings, as it were,' Drinkwater said.

The ACC didn't quite wince but took no notice as he finished up. 'Now, we all have homes to get to. Let's hope the next time we meet, we'll have some answers.'

He stood. But Warlow remained seated and raised his hand up.

'Yes, Evan? I'm sure what you have to say is relevant, but could you keep it brief?'

'I only wanted to update everyone in this room on Gil's status.'

Warlow saw the ACC visibly wilt, caught out in a callous omission.

Drinkwater mumbled, 'Surgery, isn't it?'

'He's been out of surgery for a good couple of hours. The bolt hit his scapula and fractured it, but he didn't suffer any further internal injury. He's in a sling, and it's unlikely he'll need more surgery.'

'That's good news,' the ACC said. 'I will visit him tomorrow.'

'That means he'll be out of commission for some time, then?' Though her tone was neutral, Warlow knew full well that Two-Shoes was no fan of Gil's, and he heard the schadenfreude tinkle in her question.

'I'm sure he'll bounce back, ma'am.'

'Excellent,' the ACC said. But his eyes were now on the door as he gathered up his papers.

Warlow got up, too, keen to make as quick an escape as he could. But he never made it as again, the fateful words he'd been dreading reached him through the shuffling of papers and scraping of chairs.

'Could we have a quick word, Evan, before you rush off?'

He turned. Two-Shoes had not risen from her chair.

Warlow dredged up a rictus grin and stood while people shuffled past him.

'Of course, ma'am,' he said. He didn't sit in the end but stood like an errant schoolboy in front of her.

'Thank you for your input on the letters. I'll take all of that onboard.'

'Pleasure, ma'am.'

'And I am truly sorry about Sergeant Jones's ordeal. Rehabilitation from these types of injuries can be drawn out, can they not?'

'Wouldn't know, ma'am, I've never been shot in the shoulder by a crossbow bolt.' It sounded sharp but bounced off Two-Shoes's leather skin.

'No. Few people have. Still, it will give Sergeant Jones an opportunity to review his situation. There could be compensation involved. Injured in the line of duty and all that. And when he comes back, he'll need an occupational health assessment. Sometimes, these things have a silver lining.'

'Are you suggesting Gil should consider retirement, ma'am?'

'That would be entirely up to Sergeant Jones. But, as I say, he might have limited capabilities. And that job in Evidential Retention is still there if he wants it.'

'I'm sure he'll be delighted to know that offer is still on the table as he lies on his sickbed, ma'am.'

This was not the first time Two-Shoes had tried to prod Gil towards a different, less demanding job. Warlow knew what Gil's response would be too.

The slightest narrowing of Two-Shoes's eyes was the one sign indicating she might consider Warlow's answer in any way sardonic.

'Sometimes, the universe sends us a message, Evan.'

'In the shape of a crossbow bolt, ma'am?'

'Perhaps. But as of now, any decisions made going forward ought to come via me.'

'Absolutely, ma'am.'

'Good. Always best to be on the same page,' she said.

Warlow left the room. He waited until he was outside before he let out a muffled scream. This wasn't a case of him feeling rebuffed or emasculated, though he had to admit he was a little miffed, but things were moving far too quickly for his liking.

He didn't like Goodey because she had her own agenda and paraded her ambition on a bloody great standard that she carried on her high horse. Drinkwater was not quite as bad, but they were both climbers and didn't mind whose head or hands they stepped on as they scrambled up the ladder.

And, of course, Warlow risked being labelled a misogynist for even mentioning that she might hold an agenda, but she'd made some regrettable choices in her career. Choices which somehow ended up being swept under the magic carpet of this brave new world.

'Christ, Warlow,' he muttered to himself as these thoughts squirmed around like some blind worm in his brain. 'Bang, bang, Maxwell's cancel hammer is poised above your bloody head.'

But people had suffered because of decisions both Two-Shoes and Drinkwater had made. Catrin Richards had almost died as a result of one of their bright ideas, and yet the two of them had wriggled out from underneath that one, too. Miraculously unscathed in the reshuffle.

Warlow wasn't fully able to blame them for Gil being a victim. Not yet. But, at times, he had the impression that he and the team were nothing more than cannon fodder, waiting for Drinkwater or Two-Shoes's whistle to send them over the top of the trench.

But this investigation was in its early days. Plenty of time for more mayhem yet.

He rang Jess from the Jeep.

'Is there any skin left on your back?' she asked as an opening gambit.

'Please tell me you've opened a bottle, and it's breathing?'

'I've opened a bottle, and it's breathing.'

'Did I ever tell you are one of my favourite females?'

'No, but I live in hope.'

Warlow snorted. 'Two-Shoes just threw out the idea that Gil took a bolt in the back as a message from the gods to either consider early retirement or take the job supervising disposal of evidential detritus from old cases.'

'She probably considered that a kindness.'

'Like a lioness chewing on the hind leg of a still-alive wildebeest is a kindness you mean?' Warlow waited a beat and then added, 'She is also now officially in charge on the investigation.'

Jess went quiet and then said, 'She's calling in rein-forcements?'

'All the King's men.'

Jess sighed. 'We might need a bit of a holiday after this.'

'Shepherd's hut?'

Jess's turn to laugh. 'What is it with you and confined spaces?'

'Do I need to draw a diagram?'

'No, I think I get the picture.'

CHAPTER THIRTY-FOUR

SLEEP HAD NOT COME EASILY to Warlow again that night. What kept him awake had little to do with the posturing and manoeuvring at work that he couldn't control. What truly haunted him were thoughts of how lucky Gil was to have thick bones.

They'd joke about his armour plating in the days and weeks to come, no doubt. But during the dark watches of the night, Warlow's imagination conjured up a multitude of other scenarios. Ones where Gil turned just six inches more, and the bolt entered from the side, penetrating his ribs and shredding his aorta and pulmonary vessels.

Or where Gil, ducking, felt the bolt snaking through his neck and shattering his spine, or going right through one eye, a la Harold at Hastings.

Warlow read once that the worst thing you could do was put on a light and read something in bed when insomnia called. Better you got up and moved to another room. Keep the bedroom for sleep and other activities of a more stimulating nature. Activities which had only returned to Warlow's world over the last few months, having taken a pre-Jess unpaid leave of absence spanning several years.

So, at 2.15, he'd sneaked into Molly's empty room so as not to disturb Jess, to sit on the chair with a book. Something distracting and different. He still hadn't fully completed the entire Steven King oeuvre, and so Duma Key, with its slow build-up of suspense and its haunted, loner protagonist, cursed by destiny to be alone, had sufficient emotional connections for Warlow to stay engaged until distraction permitted weariness to resurface.

He returned to his bed at 3.45 with thoughts of a Florida beach and the gentle movement of shells on the tide to lull him into another couple of hours of rest.

———

JESS HAD a bowl of yoghurt and muesli on the go at breakfast, while Warlow stuck to his coffee-only regimen.

'Thought I'd drop in on Gil first thing,' he said. 'See if he's landed safely after being in orbit.'

'Tell him I'll be in at lunchtime. If he needs anything, text me.'

'You'll be at the end of the queue for delivering alms. What with Anwen and his daughters.'

'I'll be at alms's length, then?'

'Oh, early morning puns. Is that your attempt at cheering me up?'

'Is it working?'

'It'll do for now, thank you.'

Warlow dropped Cadi off at the sitter and, while Jess drove directly to HQ to rally the troops, he took the eastern bypass to skirt Carmarthen town and headed for the hospital.

———

GIL WORE earphones when Warlow stepped into the room. The sergeant had his eyes locked on the window and the view beyond towards the houses of the adjacent village of Abergwili.

'Anything interesting?' Warlow asked.

Gil pulled the earphones off. 'One of the girls brought these in. I'm listening to the news. So naturally, I'm checking out the locks on the windows to prepare for chucking myself out if I listen for more than ten minutes.'

'Yeah, it's dire. You should listen to some music instead.'

'Not in the mood.'

Gil did look pale and certainly nowhere near as full of fun as the previous evening.

'Remember me calling in last night?'

'No. But the Lady Anwen tells me this morning that I was in excellent form.'

'You were, in a Pythonesque kind of way. You know, in a, "he's a very naughty boy" kind of way.'

Gil wrinkled his nose. 'Sorry.'

'Do not apologise. It was better than what was on TV. Mind you, watching a slug crawl up a cabbage leaf is often more enthralling than TV these days. How are you this morning?'

'Stiff and sore. And before you ask, no, I saw bugger all. Maybe a vague outline, but well hidden. If I saw anything, it or they were melding with the trees behind. And for no more than half a second before that bloody bolt hit me.'

'Well, you've poked the hornets' nest at HQ, so thanks for that. The ACC has blown the task force summoning horn and put Two-Shoes at the helm. Braeburn's been crowbarred in, and I'm to do as I am told.'

'That'll be a first, then. You're on the bench?'

Warlow shrugged.

'But Two-Shoes? Christ, I'd be interested in knowing the details of the contract she signed with Beelzebub.' Gil winced, but this time the discomfort was emotional.

'Know any good physios for when you get out? She'll be gunning for you.'

'There's Jack Bevan, ex-physio for the Scarlets. He's still knocking about. Has a place near Catrin and Craig in Tumble.'

'Okay, well, she'll insist on an occupational health assessment.'

Gil read the subtext. 'Don't tell me she's pushing the retention of evidence gig again?'

'It's there if he wants it.' Warlow made his eyes big and his expression stony.

'Christ, that's scary. As if she was in the room. Right, well, thank her for that and tell her I'll think about it.'

'Really?'

'Yes.' Gil waited for three seconds. 'There, thought about it. And the answer is still a big fat no. Besides, I have got unfinished business, as you know.'

Warlow knew. The Napier and Moyles case cast a long shadow, and Gil wanted to bring all that into the light. Warlow harboured no doubt that he would also be successful. Given time.

'Good,' Warlow said and stayed with Gil for the best part of an hour.

———

AFTER HE LEFT, a text from Goodey told him she'd be in the Incident Room by 10.30 and would need to be brought up to speed along with Superintendent Braeburn. Warlow drove back to HQ with his mind on Gil and luck and a job that got you very little thanks.

When Povey rang, it took him a minute to get his mind in gear.

'Bad time?' she asked, sensing he was a little distracted.

'No. I've just been to visit Gil.'

'Is he okay?'

'Not bad, considering.'

'That's good news. And what a relief. Can you pull over? I'm up in Aberystwyth at a suicide. Jo is on this call too. But she wants to send you something to look at. Better we continue with a face to face. Do you have an iPad or a laptop with you?'

'I do.'

Jo Tannard's voice came through. 'I'm sending the image via email. You need to see it while we speak.'

Warlow tried to work out what it was they were not telling him here. 'Can't it wait until I'm in the office?'

'It could,' Povey said, 'but we thought you'd want to hear it first in private.'

Without prying eyes and ears was how he read that.

'Okay.' He'd taken the quicker, direct route to HQ on the dual carriageway, and now as he approached a roundabout, he turned into the parking area outside the Bishop's Palace and fished out the iPad.

Tannard's email contained two attachments. Two-line drawings labelled as "Milton Property." But this was incomplete. Only three walls of the property were drawn, displaying the back and the front with doors to the kitchen and hall, and the garage and grounds labelled. There were several lines in red added and one dotted red line that stretched from the garage to the front door. The second, solid red, from the back door into the garden beyond.

His phone rang again, and he accepted the group video from Povey. Both her and Tannard's faces appeared.

'What am I looking at here?' Warlow asked.

Tannard spoke. 'These are ballistic estimations based on what Gil could tell us, as well as Milton's statement. If you look at A1.'

Warlow looked at the first image and the red line from garage to front door. 'I see it. Roughly in line with what Gil has told me. His brief glimpse caught sight of somebody moving at the side of the garage in foliage and then he was hit in the shoulder.'

'Right. But it's B1 we wanted to discuss with you,' Tannard said.

He picked up something in her voice that he couldn't quite place. These two highly qualified scientists dealt with horror every day. But something was disturbing Tannard's normal millpond delivery.

'Milton told us he was shot in the garden, between house and garage. It would make sense if the shooter targeted him first and then Gil showed up.'

Warlow envisaged the scenario.

'The broken red line in diagram B1 is the shot in line with where we think the shooter was when he shot Sergeant Jones.

If he was roughly in the same place, then the bolt that struck Mr Milton and grazed his thigh, even if it was deflected, should have ended up somewhere in the area shown to the east of the house.'

Warlow nodded. It made sense.

'But we found the bolt south of the property. It is the only other bolt we found, and it has blood on it, matched by typing to Milton's blood. We'd need to check DNA, and we will. But it seems obvious. And if we track its flight, given that it had hit and stuck in a willow tree, and the angle at which it struck, the flight trace—the unbroken red line—leads directly through the back door.'

Warlow frowned. 'Hang on, that makes no sense at all. Could it not have been deflected?'

'Yes, but it would have needed a massive deflection.'

Warlow frowned. 'Okay. How else might this bolt have struck the tree at that angle?'

'The most obvious way,' Povey said, 'is if the bolt was released from either inside the back door, or just outside the door.'

'What does that mean?' Warlow demanded. 'That the shooter was in the house? Milton wouldn't have got that wrong, surely?'

Neither CSI officer spoke.

Warlow looked at their faces. 'Wait, there's something else, isn't there?'

Tannard looked most uncomfortable now. 'We found no blood between the garage and the back door. But there was spotting on the threshold. And in my opinion, spray direction indicates one trajectory only.'

'I'm listening.' Warlow breathed out the words.

'It looks like the bolt was shot from inside the house, struck Milton and carried on through the garden.'

'But he mentioned nothing about the shooter being in the house, or at the back door—'

Suddenly, it clicked for Warlow. What Tannard and Povey had concluded.

'We've double-checked everything,' Tannard said.

Of course, they had.

'I need to talk to Goodey about this.' Warlow started the Jeep's engine but paused long enough before putting it into gear to say, 'Bloody good work, you two.'

But neither of them looked thrilled. Because they, like Warlow, understood the consequences.

CHAPTER THIRTY-FIVE

LLOYD COOMBS SAT in his van in the car park at Dyfed Powys police HQ, waiting for his sister. When another request for him to attend again had come the night before, his first instinct had been to tell them to piss off. He'd lost two days' work already, and the people who paid him were getting very, very cheesed off. He rang his sister, Sam, and she immediately told him he had to go and that she would go with him. They'd had lunch in a pub yesterday in Builth, with several witnesses, before travelling home. Important for establishing an alibi for the police.

She used the word alibi easily. Like she knew what she was talking about. But then, she always did. She said it was likely to do with that copper who'd been shot with a crossbow, but she couldn't be sure. Still, the prospect of another drive to Carmarthen, even though he spent his life in his van, held little attraction.

What swung it for him was a chat with Lane. He'd told the journalist that he'd been contacted yet again, but the journo's reaction had been much like his sister's. He ought to go, Lane said. And there'd be a decent wedge for him if he found out something that Lane could use.

The promise of money. Always a sweetener.

So, at 10:20 that Tuesday morning, Lloyd reached for his

fags, glad the day was dry, got out of his van, and lit up for a cheeky ciggy in the fresh air of Dyfed Powys HQ car park.

———

BY THE TIME Warlow got to HQ, he'd decided that grabbing a bull by the horns, even though it might involve being gored and impaled, sometimes was the best strategy. And, as he noted Superintendent Goodey exiting her black Audi Q3 just as he pulled up, he decided that luck, fate, happenstances, could not be denied.

Warlow got out quickly and called after her, 'Pamela?'

She turned expectantly, but he noted immediately the way her brows dropped a centimetre on seeing him.

'Evan,' she said as he approached. 'On time for once.'

There she was. The Goodey he knew, always pricking away with the poison needle.

'I'm sorry for ambushing you, but there's something I need to tell you.'

'I'm all ears. The car park adds a nice … mysterious vibe in a vaguely covert manner.' She put down her full briefcase, tilted her head and waited.

'Right.' Warlow tried to shake off the irritated bewilderment she always instilled in him and got down to it. 'I've just got off the phone with Povey and Tannard. They've been doing some preliminary ballistics up at Milton's house—'

Goodey's slight frown stopped him. 'They know that I am now running the investigation?'

It was an odd question that took Warlow unawares. 'I don't know. That may not have got to them yet. What does it matter?'

Two-Shoes's gaze reverted to that defiant mistrust that she always seemed to carry with her. 'It matters because there are protocols that need to be followed.'

Not this. Not now.

Warlow composed something in his head that he hoped might pacify her paranoia once again. It was a lie, but a necessary one. 'They were ringing me to ask about Gil. I probed them on progress. Early days, as I said.'

Two-Shoes's smile took on that odd shape unique to her. Half knowing, half smirk. 'I don't believe you.'

'Believe me or don't. What's important is what they told me.'

'That's where you and I differ, Evan. What's important is that I have not been informed directly.'

'Jesus Christ, Pamela. Tannard is of the opinion that Milton's story is not kosher. The bolt that hit him was not shot from the garden as described. It looks like it might have been shot from inside the house. Milton can't—'

'Why are you doing this?' Two-Shoes spat.

And Warlow now saw nothing but defiance in her eyes.

'Doing what?'

'Obfuscating.'

'Obfuscating? Did you not hear what I said? Milton's story doesn't hold true. I've been toying with scenarios. It's possible he's confused, but equally possible that he's protecting someone—'

Goodey drew her lips back slowly in an expression Warlow had not seen before. The words that emerged next were screamed out at full volume. 'Stop. Stop. Stop this minute, you noisome, pathetic little man. Are you saying Hugo Milton killed all four victims?' She caught herself then. Reigned in the anger to a manageable level, dropping it to a disparaging, serpentine hiss. 'Milton is one of our experts in both cases. Someone who volunteered his services.'

'That's the point. I'm not suggesting he did it, but of all the people who might influence and manipulate—'

Two-Shoes's face had become ugly in her rage. Her voice went back up to eleven on the dial. 'I am not interested in your opinions, detective chief inspector. Milton the killer? Stop. Stop this nonsense.'

Two people walking towards their cars turned to stare. Goodey saw them and laughed but continued, still loud, but at slightly less than screech volume.

'Shall I tell you what is going to happen now? You are

going to enter the building behind me. I am going to run a briefing, and you are going to keep quiet. Allanby can contribute, but you will not. Not one word, do you understand?'

Warlow stared at her. 'No one is trying to undermine you here, Pamela—'

'DO YOU UNDERSTAND?'

Warlow held his ground. 'No. No, I do not understand.'

'No. I don't think you do, do you? Because climbing down off your ivory tower must be so difficult for someone like … you. And I'm certain you believe you possess the means to repel all borders. I'd wait until I tell the Chief what you and Allanby have been up to. How you're screwing up the case. Screwing being very much the operative word when it comes to you two. Don't think I hadn't noticed. I imagine you two cooked up this whole debacle between the sheets. Disgusting.'

Warlow sensed the anger like a red tide rising over his neck. But Two-Shoes had not finished.

'Now, you will follow me in. And there will be no mention of any ballistics from Milton's property until I have seen the actual report. Do we understand one another?' She turned on her heel.

'What's between Jess and me has nothing do with this case!' Warlow spat out the riposte.

Two-Shoes pivoted back, still with that unnatural grin on her face. 'She's ten years younger than you. You should be ashamed of yourself. We can all see what's happening here, and it's repulsive. I'm afraid this case will not go so well for you or your … girlfriend.'

Warlow was genuinely stunned. He wanted to run after her and hurl abuse in her face. But he didn't. He couldn't. Instead, he let Goodey march off with a smile of satisfaction replacing her anger, while he stood rooted, unable to comprehend the blistering animosity he'd just witnessed.

———

In the midst of their mutual anger, neither officer saw the man, not twenty yards away, cigarette in hand, peeking at the two of them from behind his dirty grey van. They didn't see the grin spread across his face as he stuck the cigarette in his mouth. With both hands free, he scrolled through his contacts, found what he was looking for, and held the phone to his ear. Removing the cigarette from his lips, he exhaled a plume of blue smoke while waiting for the call to connect.

'Hi, yeah, it's me, Lloyd. I might have something interesting for you.'

———

Warlow walked around the car park to allow his thermostat to reset before heading for the Incident Room. To witness firsthand the intense resentment that Two-Shoes clearly harboured towards him was ... sobering.

Inside, the Incident Room felt unfamiliar. Many more people had joined the ancillary team. He nodded to Superintendent Braebern; a man younger than Warlow but for whom he had respect. With him were two officers he knew only vaguely.

His own team was crowded around Rhys's desk, waiting for the show to begin.

Jess threw him a questioning glance. He made an effort to smile in response but was unable to and observed her brows fold. But Two-Shoes had the floor.

Warlow barely heard her speak as his mind tumbled around their confrontation. But a few sentences of self-deprecating aggrandisement filtered through.

'The Assistant Chief Constable requires a stable hand at the helm. I like to think I bring an added dimension of detachment to the investigation, too.'

She paused between these egotistical dictums, and he wondered if she was hearing applause in her own head.

To Warlow, it sounded like puffed-up nonsense.

'Moreover, our stance is that increased emphasis should

be placed on the information outlined in the letter sent to senior officers by a person who may have knowledge of the investigation. These require further analysis, though we already know that the most recent one was posted in an isolated post box in rural Herefordshire. With all that in mind, I have arranged for Dr Mary Lansdown to visit the scenes in Mid-Wales where Kirsty Stuart and Gerald Nash were attacked. She is an expert in ancient history, and I would value her input on the significance of the chosen sites. We have limited resources, so DCI Warlow will accompany her today at 1:30pm. An order, not a request.'

She looked over at him and offered one of her smiles. The kind that left Warlow cold.

'Pleasure,' he said. 'I'll take DC Mellings with me.'

For a moment, it looked as if Two-Shoes might object on the principal that taking Gina had not been her idea. But then she gave him a slight nod, like you would to a dog come to heel, and turned back to Jess. 'DI Allanby, can you run through the actions for today regarding the attack on Sergeant Jones?'

Jess threw Warlow one last questioning glance before outlining the planned interviews and the fact that Christopher Messenger had yet to respond.

'Where does he live?' Two-Shoes asked.

'Somewhere in Herefordshire, ma'am.'

Two-Shoes looked up as if a light bulb had gone off in her head. 'Evan, since you'll be up that way, perhaps you could visit. To make sure all likely miscreants are accounted for.'

It was nowhere near where they'd be, and she knew it.

'And, as for interviewing Lloyd Coombs and Stuart's partner, um …'

'Amanda Beech, ma'am,' Rhys said.

'Beech, yes. We'll divide things up. That way, we can get through them more quickly. Superintendent Braeburn can help with Beech and DI Allanby with Coombs?'

Wojak, through his solicitor, had finally agreed to come in the next day.

Forty-five minutes after it had begun, the meeting broke up. Two-Shoes and Braeburn headed for the SIO room while Jess pigeon-holed Warlow.

'What's wrong? Is Gil okay?'

'Gil's fine. I had a set-to with Two-Shoes in the car park. The chaperoning duty is her getting me out of the way.'

'Why?'

Warlow shook his head. 'The chip on her shoulder gets bigger every time we meet. The politics in this place are toxic.'

'Always have been, like every other Force. But there's something else, I can tell.'

'There might be, but it's not for here. As it is, I've been given a gagging order.'

'About what?'

Warlow thought about getting Jess involved. Two-Shoes's warning still rang in his ears, but you could not brush evidence under the carpet. 'Is there anything you need to speak to Tannard and Povey about?'

'I can find something.'

'Then do that. Say that I had to go somewhere, and you're picking up the thread. All that is true. But don't let Two-Shoes hear you. I hope you've got your eggshell-treading shoes on.'

'Don't you?'

'Never owned a pair.' He toyed with the idea of taking a walk with Jess out into the stairwell of secrets. An area where personal calls and discussions were usually held away from prying eyes and ears. But it was now approaching 11:30, and the journey up to the Elan Valley would take a couple of hours. He called over to Gina. 'Get your coat. It's you and me again, I'm afraid.'

'Looking forward to it, sir.' Gina, God bless her, made it sound like she meant it.

Warlow chastised himself silently. She probably did mean it, and he had no right to be snide about it, even in his own head.

Warlow turned back to Jess. 'Christ, I used to think we

were all on the same team. But I'm having my doubts. You and Rhys hold the fort.' He nodded towards the SIO room. 'I'm sure General Custer in there will have a cunning plan.'

CHAPTER THIRTY-SIX

WARLOW SET off north with Gina once more in the passenger seat. They'd gone no more than a couple of miles before the DC spoke up.

'Sir, is everything alright?'

'No, it is not. One of my officers has been attacked, and I am being sent on a wild goose chase into the desert of Wales.'

Gina looked as unhappy as Warlow sounded. 'Is every case like this, sir?'

Warlow sighed. 'No. Not if I have anything to do with it. Normally, you get leads to follow and you chase them to their natural conclusion. Not hurdles to jump over like some mad steeplechase.'

'Isn't that what Superintendent Goodey is doing with the letters, though, sir? Following the leads?'

'There's a difference between following leads and being led by the nose ring. And I'm delighted you have never been tempted in that direction, Gina. From anywhere further than four feet, nose rings just make people look like they have a permanent cold. But, as for Superintendent Goodey, she's reacting to things out of her control. Which is exactly what the letter writer wants.'

Gina sat back, staring out of the window. 'We'll be passing the hospital in a minute, sir.'

'Nothing gets past you, DC Mellings.'

She smiled at the snark. 'I was wondering if I could call in on Gil for a minute. Rhys's Aunty Loveen made some of her savoury scones. I said I'd drop them off if I could.'

'Not from a bridge, I hope. If they're anything like the ones I've tasted, they're heavy enough to cause some real damage.'

'I've seen Rhys eat four and then go for a run.'

'Yes, well, that boy has more than one stomach, like an ox.'

Warlow considered the request. He'd tried to reassure the team that Gil was okay and as well as expected. But it would do no harm for the others to get more reassurance. And the simple act of kindness from a bright spark like her would certainly please Gil.

'Why not?' Warlow flicked the indicator to change lanes on the dual carriageway. 'It will add ten minutes to our journey, but the Elan Valley is not going anywhere. But I'll wait in the car. He's already seen enough of me and if I turn up again, it will only confuse the old bugger. Oh, and while you're in there, check on Milton, would you? I completely forgot this morning.'

———

HAVING HAD a cryptic message from Warlow regarding Povey and Tannard, Jess left the Incident Room and headed for the stairwell of secrets to give the latter a ring.

'DCI Warlow has been called away. He suggested I call you.'

'He's told you about the bolt?' Tannard asked.

'What bolt?'

'He hasn't told you, then.'

'He asked me to give you a ring.'

'We're still not finished with analysis—'

'But you obviously felt something was important enough to have contacted him. Now he thinks it's important enough to tell me to contact you. Hang on, he's just sent me an email. One redirected from you, it looks like.'

'That means he's sending you the vector analysis.'

A moment's silence followed as Jess opened the PDFs that came with the email.

'By vector analysis, do you mean these drawings with red lines on them?'

'I do. OK, let me take you through them.'

RHYS HARRIES HAD an alert set up for when Lane posted anything new. Apart from the pieces he wrote for the newspapers, he ran what was effectively a blog once he was on a story, and now Rhys saw that he'd posted an update entitled,

---

"Crossbow Killer Investigation Takes Bizarre Twist."

Rhys's scalp prickled as he scrolled down.

In what can be described as a farcical turn of events, police investigating the murder of four people, and the near-fatal attack on one of their own officers, today opened up a new line of inquiry. And, like a worm eating its own tail, officers have turned their attention to the expert co-opted into the investigation. Hugo Milton, a medieval weapons expert who describes himself on his website as a man born a thousand years too late, has been aiding police on the kinds of weapons used in both the most recent killings and in the Bowman case.

Having obtained a diploma in history from Aberystwyth University, Milton has also been an advisor on films and TV programmes involving medieval warfare such as The King's Sword, The Iron Throne, and The Army Under the Mountain, as well as advising on video game action sequences. Initially, Milton worked as an analyst for an Investment Bank but abandoned the profession to pursue his interests. He has written several articles for non-scientific journals and is a frequent contributor to online interest groups.

Along with Sergeant Gildas Jones, a Dyfed Powys police detective, Milton was injured in an attack at a property near the royal estate of Llwynywermod on the edge of the Bannau Brycheiniog National Park. Police could not comment on whether Milton is now a person of interest in the killing of Kirsty Stuart and Gerald Nash by crossbow bolt. But we understand that recent evidence suggests he may have questions to answer.

'Shit,' Rhys muttered and swivelled in his chair to search the room. No one was jumping up and down. No one staring bewildered at their screens. But it would only be a matter of time before this became common knowledge. He needed to speak to DI Allanby. Not finding her, Rhys got up and, as nonchalantly as possible, wandered out in search of her.

He met her as she was on the way back to the Incident Room.

'What's wrong, Rhys?'

'Lane, ma'am. He's written something about Milton—'

'Milton?' Jess didn't hide her shock. 'That's twice I've heard his name in as many minutes. I've just been talking to Tannard about him.'

'Then you need to see Lane's article, ma'am.'

'Right, let's have a look.'

Rhys hesitated. 'Aren't we supposed to be interviewing Lloyd Coombs, ma'am?'

'We are. But he is insisting on waiting for his sister and is happy to sit in his van and smoke until she turns up, according to the duty sergeant. That gives us a bit of time.'

———

GINA KEPT her word and was back in the Jeep fifteen minutes after she'd left it. Warlow got going immediately.

'How was he?'

'He seems in good spirits, sir. Though there was a bit of sad news. Apparently, the doctors had been in and told him he'd never play the piano again.'

'Said that with a straight face, did he?'

'Yes, Why?'

'Because the bugger has never played the piano in his life, that's why.'

Gina smiled and nodded slowly. 'He told me to thank Rhys's aunt for the scones and that he hoped she'd still be able to deep-sea dive now that she'd given him all her ballast.'

'Dense, the scones, were they?'

Gina nodded.

'Oh dear. Right, we need to plot our journey. Round trip. We'll grab a sandwich in Llanwrtyd on the way up. Meet with the historian, then come back via Leominster to chat with Messenger, through Hay to Brecon.'

'To think that's all on our patch, too.'

'More or less.'

Gina went quiet again while Warlow searched for something to listen to. 'We'll make the most of the radio because we'll lose the signal later, and then we'll have to listen to my choice in music.'

'Rhys says you have good taste, sir. Some real bangers.'

'Yeah, I'm sure that's what he said.'

'No, he did. He says it's an education. But, sir, you said we were on a wild goose chase. Isn't that frustrating for you?'

Damn these youngsters and their candidness. Molly was the same. 'Yes, it is. This case is complicated. Has been from the outset with all that baggage from twenty years ago, bogging us down.'

'Rhys says that sometimes, there's a point when the smoke clears and you can see where the source of the fire is.'

'He's right. But we're still in the thick smoke for now.'

'Oh, and I asked about Mr Milton, but he's gone home. Discharged first thing this morning.'

'Has he now? Probably fighting the Battle of Agincourt on a tabletop with those little plastic soldiers.'

'Sounds …'

'Mad, yes. Okay—'

The opening chords of *Jet Airliner* came through the speaker. And a smile formed on Warlow's lips. 'Ah, the Steve Miller Band. A banger on order. Now we're talking. Think of some questions we can ask the historian.'

'Rhys has given me some.'

Warlow threw her a glance. 'Such as?'

'Equality. Apparently, there were priestesses. Though Rhys says we shouldn't call them that. Not anymore. He wanted to know if they were the ones that did the sacrificing.'

Warlow shook his head. 'Right, that'll be my first question.'

But of course, it wasn't. Because neither he nor Gina ever met the historian.

———

FIFTEEN MINUTES after Rhys had found Lane's exposé on his blog, Jess had been summoned to the SIO room. Two-Shoes, almost white with fury, had also found the piece. She demanded to know if Jess had been responsible. Had Warlow put her up to this?

Jess truthfully answered no to both questions.

Shortly afterwards, once Jess was dismissed, Two-Shoes marched out of the Incident Room with a face like an earthquake about to erupt. She'd glanced at both Rhys and Jess's screens as she walked by.

Rhys had a map of the Elan Valley up on his monitor. Jess's screen showed her halfway through an email she'd been composing.

Once the superintendent was out of the room, both officers clicked their respective mice, and their screens changed.

Rhys's revealed a profile of Milton from a couple of places, including one where he used to work.

'But for God's sake, do not let the superintendent see what you're doing,' she'd warned him on her return from Two-Shoes's rant.

'Should we forget about him, then, ma'am?' Rhys had asked.

'No. Evan wants us to do some digging.'

'Has he asked you, then, ma'am?'

'Not in so many words. But he's given me a big nudge in that direction.'

CHAPTER THIRTY-SEVEN

WARLOW PULLED up to the very same café that Samantha and Lloyd Coombs had stopped at on their journey back from Carmarthen on Saturday. One problem of being in the throes of a case like this, where travel meant you spent such a long time in the car, food on the go could sometimes not be the healthiest. On the flip side, if you avoided the franchises, you sometimes got to taste some good, homemade fare.

Warlow ordered halloumi and sun-dried tomatoes on sourdough, and Gina got some falafels in pitta bread. Both to take away.

Warlow let Gina eat first and then, as they headed towards Beulah, she took over the driving, and he bit into his sandwich. He knew better than to drive and eat at the same time with a younger officer in the car. The dirty looks he got from Rhys were bad enough.

After consuming three bites, his phone rang, and he glanced at the caller ID. Immediately, he stopped chewing.

'Drinkwater,' he said to Gina through a half-eaten mouthful of sandwich. 'You'd best pull over since we have a signal. It gets patchy from here on up.'

Gina pulled into the garage in Beulah. The only convenience store for miles.

Warlow took the call. 'Afternoon.'

'Are you alone?' Drinkwater's voice sounded ominous.

'No, but I can be.' Warlow exited and walked towards the back of the lot.

'Have you seen it?'

'Seen what?'

'The poison Lane has printed this time?'

'Bleddyn, I'm in Beulah. I've been driving—'

'Only I wondered if you'd proofread the bloody thing for him.'

'Pardon?' Warlow stopped to look out at the view.

'Lane says there's been a fresh development. He says we're shifting our attention towards a new line of inquiry.'

'What line?'

'What line? What line?' The repeated words got a little higher in pitch, along with the volume in Drinkwater's voice. 'Milton. Christ, Evan, I am well aware that you believe we are all fools. All of us except you. And Sion is always asking us to make exceptions. But this time … this time you've gone too bloody far.'

He considered denying the "we are all fools" accusation, but let it stew because most of the time it was true. 'What exactly are we talking about here? What about Milton?'

'Milton is apparently our new most wanted, according to Lane.'

'What?'

But Drinkwater was beyond reason. 'Don't … don't pretend this wasn't you.'

'Wasn't me what?'

'It's one thing to spout off your extreme theories to Pamela, your superior officer, but to leak it to the press … the ACC is apo-bloody-plectic, as it were. And to do this simply because Pamela wouldn't indulge your theories.'

It wasn't so much a red mist that was descending over Warlow's mind, more a deep purple fog.

Drinkwater kept talking. 'I've done my best to defend you over these last years—'

'Stop,' Warlow ordered. 'Just stop. Are you saying that Lane is accusing Milton?'

'As good as. And no one has ever mentioned him except you.'

Silence grew in the space between the two men.

'Well?' Drinkwater said.

'There are anomalies around Milton's report about the attack on him and Gil. Povey told me that. Tannard confirmed it. And in an investigation like this, all anomalies need to be looked at. And of course, Milton knew about the records. He could have set the fire. But I have not spoken to Lane.'

'Then who has? Pamela?'

'You tell me. She and Lane were once best buddies.'

'I will pretend I didn't hear that.' But Warlow's accusation must have stung. Both Drinkwater and Goodey had been neck-deep in the crapfest that led to Catrin Richards almost being buried alive thanks to their misguided interactions with Lane.

'Okay. Then have you asked Lane who his source is?'

'Of course not. He'd laugh in my face.'

Like I want to do, Warlow thought.

'Pamela thinks … Did you write that letter implying sacrificial nonsense to yourself, Evan?'

This time, Warlow was so lost for words, all he could not think to say was a gruff, 'No.'

'The ACC wants to suspend you pending an inquiry.'

Warlow spat out a laugh. 'Jesus.'

'But that would only add fuel to the fire. Leave us with yet more egg on our faces, as it were.'

Warlow heard Gil's voice in his head. *'And that would be no yolk.'*

'I've suggested a period of gardening leave. Until this case is over. Until Pamela sorts it out.'

The amazing Pamela, who, no doubt, was sitting somewhere in the background, nodding with those doll-like features, egging (more yolk) Drinkwater on.

'Fine by me,' Warlow said. 'Do you still want me to babysit the historian?'

'No, we've cancelled her visit. But we can't get hold of

Milton. He's left the hospital, and he's not answering his mobile.'

'He said he'd lost it somewhere in the garden. And he doesn't have a landline.'

'That is the reason he is incommunicado. You are up there. Get to his place, find him, explain, and apologise.' It sounded as if Drinkwater forced the words out through gritted teeth.

'For what?'

'For a cock-up. This man has been more than helpful. And, may I remind you, he's been shot at. Now, if he's become a little spun around by the trauma of that near-death experience, who could blame him? How far away are you?'

'Twenty minutes.'

'Get on with it, then. Ring me when it is done. And consider that your last act on this case, Evan. Don't make things worse than they are.'

Back at the Jeep, Gina was drinking water from a bottle. She sensed his mood had changed.

'What's wrong?'

'Change of plan. We're going to find Milton.'

'Why?'

'We're doing a food delivery.'

'A what?'

'A big steaming pile of humble pie.'

Gina thought it wise not to ask any more questions at that point. But Warlow believed she had the right to be informed.

'There's a little commotion going on back at HQ. Tannard has done some preliminary ballistics work on the bolts fired at Gil and Milton, and something doesn't add up.' He explained roughly what Tannard had found.

'Is it possible Mr Milton became confused about where he was in the garden when he was shot?'

'Of course, it is.'

Gina nodded, following his logic. 'Definitely needs explaining.'

'It does. But involving Milton in any way has not gone

down well with our chief investigator. It's like I'm suggesting sacrificing a sacred cow.'

'Right.'

'And the cherry on the cake is that Geraint Lane has somehow got hold of all of that and put it out into the world.'

'Oh, my God. How?'

'The man is either psychic or has insider knowledge. And so, we are tasked with finding Mr Milton and apologising for unfounded accusations that no one, bar Lane, has yet made.'

'Can we ask him about the ballistic anomaly, too?'

Warlow grinned. 'Ah, I suspect that if the Chief Superintendent was aware that we were even discussing that, he'd have a fit, as it were.'

'But that's mad, sir.'

'It is.' What he didn't tell her was the rest of it. About vindictiveness. Of how now even suggesting a novel idea to Two-Shoes looked like desperate mud-raking on his part.

Or obfuscation.

'But you know what? Milton is an expert in reenactments. Perhaps he'd be willing to give us a bit of a demonstration. What do you think?'

Gina grinned.

———

TWENTY MINUTES LATER, they pulled into Milton's property. They'd both been there before, and so the overgrown courtyard held no surprises. The only difference this time was the positioning of Milton's Land Rover that sat on the opposite side of the garage. The crime scene techs had gone, too, and the place looked eerily quiet. The garage door was open, revealing its bizarre weaponry display, including axes, wicked-looking halberds, bows stacked up against the walls.

'Does he have a licence for all those,' Gina muttered as she got out.

Warlow picked up on her grimace. 'What's wrong?'

'I remember how the place smelled last time, sir.'

'Got any polo mints?'

'No. But I'll manage, sir.'

White clouds formed the canopy to an almost still day. Weather like this seemed to hold its breath as it decided what to send next to the unsuspecting earth below.

They had to knock twice. Milton, his hair wet, had once again opted for his tunic, but his legs were thick and bare below the knee. He'd wrapped cling film around his bandaged thigh, and he wore walking sandals on his feet.

'The King's guard again? I am popular these days.'

'Mr Milton,' Warlow said. 'Still haven't found your phone?'

'Not yet. None of your lot managed to either, am I right?'

'They did not.'

'Come in.'

Warlow couldn't resist a glance at Gina and the deep breath she took before stepping over the threshold.

Milton led them through to the kitchen at the rear of the house. No need for the guided tour this time.

'Tea?'

Warlow agreed to that. A difficult conversation was to be had and lubricating the words could do no harm.

Milton indicated two wheel-back chairs, and the officers sat.

'Mr Milton—'

'Evan, surely by now it can be Hugo.'

'Hugo.' Warlow gave a single nod. 'I realise you are not a person too troubled with the modern world and all its quirks, but I'm here to explain about some developments in the case which unfortunately involve you.'

'Me? Apart from being shot, you mean?'

'I do, though it is related to you being shot.'

A kettle boiled. Tea was made, milk and sugar added where needed. All as Warlow explained the circumstances of their visit.

'And you say that this man, Lane … he's implying that you are now investigating me?'

Warlow kept his voice even. 'It's all been blown out of proportion. As mentioned, the bolt that was found in the garden … It's a small thing that our scientific investigators picked up on. The trajectory prior to impact.'

'Oh, but we must look at that. It's fascinating.' Milton got up and walked to the kitchen window, looking out into the garden. 'I seem to remember that they found the bolt to the right of that target.'

Warlow and Gina joined him. There had not been a target at the bottom of the garden the last time he had been here.

'Oh, I've only today placed that. Getting in a bit of practise, you understand. And Superintendent Goodey has asked me to test other bows which I am expecting delivery of. I have a couple in the garage already. But the bolt that struck me – yes, to the right of the target.'

Warlow caught Gina's glance. Without even having to ask, Milton was asking all the right questions and doing their job for them.

'I even have some drawings.' Warlow fished out his phone.

'Excellent. First, let me show you where the bolt was found.'

CHAPTER THIRTY-EIGHT

THE INCIDENT ROOM had gone silent. Jess felt none of the energy that usually pervaded the place. And that was purely due to the style of leadership. As Warlow and Gina pulled into Milton's property twenty-eight miles away, Jess studied the line drawing Warlow had sent her, blown up on her monitor screen, showing where they'd found the bolt in Milton's garden. The line tracing clearly pointed towards the back door. The idea of a deflection had occurred to her, as well. But the angle looked very large. Almost forty-five degrees if the shot had been loosed from near the garage and if Milton had been standing anywhere near the back door.

She checked his statement:

'I was in the garden, and I detected the sound of a snapping twig. Next thing, there's a pain in my leg and see it's bleeding. Just before that, I heard the click of the trigger mechanism. I suppose recognising what that sounds like might be what saved me, because I've been exposed to hundreds of crossbow shots. I turned and ran back into the house. Adrenaline kicked in. Only once I was inside did I look at my leg and it clicked I'd been hit. A glancing blow, but painful enough. And it bled profusely.'

Why had the shooter aimed low?

Jess, like Warlow, was intrigued. Had they wanted to incapacitate him before coming in for the kill?

Also, like Warlow, she couldn't help but feel that something was off.

'Ma'am,' Rhys called to her from his desk. 'I think you need to see this.'

She walked over and stood behind the acting sergeant. 'I'm on the Corvi Albi official site, ma'am. White Crows.'

'Which is?'

'Medieval reenactment society in the Midlands. From Vikings through to the Middle Ages, it says. This is where Milton told me he'd been when Stuart and Nash were killed.'

'And?'

'And this was a three-day affair. Reenactments across several eras over that period. But, on the evening of the first day, a storm hit. The ground became totally waterlogged. So much so that they had to abandon the actual battles.'

Rhys looked up at Jess. She said nothing.

'Thing is, ma'am, Milton has never been a suspect. I mean, why would he be?'

'There's a but coming, isn't there?'

'The Corvi Albi have been around for a long time. Milton was a founder member. His name is everywhere. And they keep records. Twenty years ago, when the Bowman case happened, the Internet was not like it is now, but the Corvi Albi site has archives, and they have a Facebook page. It looks like a log or diary of meetings was kept by various secretaries. They've digitised those now, and they are accessible.'

'What are you saying, Rhys?'

'The big reenactment weekend is the same every year. The third weekend in March. I checked the log for the day that the Bowman killed his first victims, ma'am. It was a Sunday. The Corvi Albi were at their combat jamboree in Hereford. But guess what?'

'Don't tell me, rain stopped play?'

'Exactly, ma'am. Same sort of thing. The ground got too wet for people to stand there and fight in the melee. It was called off. Bit of a coincidence.'

'That's a "C" word.' Jess hissed out the sentence.

'I am aware, ma'am. And I've been thinking about the bolts that were used in the Bowman case. They were French. Not commonly found in the UK. But Milton was a European lawyer then. BND is an investment bank with offices in London and Brussels. He spent a lot of time in Brussels.'

'That's not in France.'

'No, ma'am. But it's a damn sight closer than Wales is.'

Jess could sense her pulse throbbing in her neck. Rhys wore an unhappy expression.

'Come on,' she said. 'What else is there?'

'Little things he said, ma'am. He's much more than a hobbyist. I genuinely think he wishes he'd been born a thousand years before, or even longer. I realise that this makes no sense because he was shot at, like Gil.'

Jess's eyes widened. 'He was, but with hardly any damage. A glancing blow. And what better way to shield yourself from any suggestion of involvement than by becoming a victim …' Thoughts were coming fast now. Too fast. 'Except he hadn't bargained for a bolt getting stuck in a willow tree.'

'What?'

'Ring Gina. Ring her and tell her to stay away from Milton. I'll ring Evan.'

'But—'

'Do it!'

———

Warlow, Gina, and Milton walked out of the back door and through to the garden. At the rear, a piece of tape was still attached to a thin willow trunk. 'There, do you see?'

'I do.' Warlow leaned in.

'Now, let me get a coat, and I will walk you through exactly what happened once again.'

'That would be really useful,' Gina said.

'If you two come back into the centre of the garden, I'll be able to direct you from the kitchen door.' Milton talked over his shoulder as he strode back inside the house.

When he was gone, Gina turned to Warlow. 'Looks like we'll get our answers anyway, sir. A reenactment.'

'Yeah. He's been remarkably cool about it all.'

Warlow looked across at the garage and tried to imagine someone wielding a crossbow coming towards him.

Tannard had been right. A shot from there would have gone in a totally different direction.

But Milton seemed confident.

Gina glanced at the target and the arrows protruding from the circles. 'They look more like arrows shot from a longbow, sir.'

'Well observed, Detective Constable.' Milton spoke from the open door from where he emerged.

Both Warlow and Gina took a second to pick up on the glee in his voice and the fact that he was holding a longbow in his hands, with the string drawn back and tensed with an arrow pointing at them.

Both officers' phones went off at exactly the same time.

Gina reached for her pocket.

'I wouldn't if I were you,' Milton said and stepped out into the garden, bow raised, the arrows' trefoil hunting point glistening in the daylight.

———

'NO ANSWER, MA'AM,' Rhys said.

'Me neither.'

'Bad signal?'

'Who knows?'

Rhys began scrolling through his phone. 'I have Gina's phone on a FindMy app.' His fingers enlarged the image. 'She's in the countryside, near Myddfai …'

He looked up, colour draining from his face. 'That's where Milton lives.'

Jess shot to her feet and started for the door. 'Grab your coat, Rhys.'

He needed no further invitation as he hurried with Jess out to her Golf.

———

'OF COURSE,' Milton said, 'you could run for it. However, if you are familiar with longbows compared to crossbows, you'll understand that they are faster to load. Much quicker. A trained longbow archer could fire ten or more arrows per minute. Less than six seconds between shots. A crossbow is much slower, takes twice as long.'

Milton moved sideways. 'Now, I am twenty yards away. You could rush me. One of you would die, the second might survive or might not. Depends on how fit you two are.' He stepped back another two yards. 'Now, the odds are very much in my favour.'

Warlow, though his throat had dried up, found some words. 'What's going on?'

Milton's face stayed next to the tensed bowstring.

'What's going on is that I miscalculated. But then, you are aware of that. You know my story doesn't quite hold true. I thought your Sergeant Jones had put two and two together and that was why he came. But that was not the case. Like I say, I miscalculated. But then, why not use the opportunity to throw dust in your eyes.'

'You shot Gil?' Gina said.

'I did.'

'But—'

'Think about it. Think.'

'You shot yourself,' Warlow said.

'Very good, DCI Warlow. Very good. I held the crossbow with the bolt against my thigh. Awkward shot, almost in reverse. Hurt like hell. But I should have aimed it east, not south. Then I "rescued" your sergeant.'

'You bastard.' Warlow took a step.

Milton tensed the string a little more. 'Uh-uh.'

Warlow stopped.

'Why?' Gina asked.

A smile appeared on the face holding the bow. A wild face behind the strands of long hair hanging down. As if the face and the man it belonged to came from another time and place.

'Because I needed to know how it felt. Reenactments are one thing, but I needed to see it. To experience it. Be one of the few people alive who has actually killed with a crossbow. Each of the four times it was different. The actual death. And now I'm going to understand, truly understand, what it's like to kill with a longbow. It isn't pretty. But you'll find out.' An unpleasant smile appeared under the curtain of hair.

Warlow stepped in front of Gina but kept his eyes on Milton. He whispered words for her ears only, 'If he fires, you run, do you hear me? Do not wait. You run and do it zig zag towards the trees behind.'

'No,' Gina wailed softly.

'Five seconds,' Milton said. 'That's how long I take to reload and aim, remember?'

'What is wrong with you?' Gina said, and her voice came out as half a sob.

'Me? Look around you, DC Mellings. We haven't really moved on much, have we? Civilisation is lying to itself. Some places are still in the Dark Ages. Medieval cultures and practices are evident in every direction you turn. Places where they cut off your hand if you steal, stone you if you cheat, use charms to treat AIDS, hide women away like wrapped-up parcels. We're in the bloody minority here. And soon, this country is going to be back where it was. We're being overrun because when they come here, they don't change. You would do well to learn a little history and take up the bow.' He made a noise that might have been a quiet giggle.

It turned Warlow's stomach.

'And no one ever considered me. That I might be the one. They'd rather chase fairy tales in letters. None of your lot even asked me where I was when the shots were fired. Until now.'

'There is no point in killing us,' Warlow said.

'Oh, there is. There is all the point in the world.'

He raised the bow and once again, Warlow sensed that here was a man who could not be swayed by argument or logic or threat. A man whose faculty for reason had slipped way beyond that.

Milton was corrupt. Seduced by a depraved longing and yielding to that longing again. Warlow saw imminent death in the man's eyes and in the final tensing of the bowstring.

He turned his back in a half crouch, put an arm up to cover his head, his pulse roaring in his ears. 'Gina … run.'

Warlow heard two noises. Two faint clicks, impossibly close together.

He had a millisecond to wonder if longbows had triggers these days before the thrum of the arrow being released met his ears. But the sickening thud of projectile meeting flesh and the shrill and agonising scream of pain that followed came neither from Gina nor Warlow.

The DCI pivoted and dropped his arm.

Milton no longer stood in the garden, instead he was writhing on the ground where he had fallen, a mixture of moans and desperate pleading peppered by screeches of pain emerging from his open mouth.

The bow and arrow he'd been holding lay scattered on the ground next to him. His hands were now fluttering around the four inches of crossbow bolt protruding from the left side of his chest at the bottom end of his rib cage. 'Please … please … oh God … please help.'

But Warlow didn't move immediately because his eyes flew across to the figure holding a crossbow with shaking hands, horror etched on her distorted features.

There had been a first click. There had been a trigger. But not from Milton.

Samantha Coombs only had eyes for the monster she had just shot.

'You! You!' She hurled the words at Milton. Then she let the crossbow fall and ran towards the man.

Warlow moved then. 'Gina, go to him. Call this in.'

Samantha moved quickly, but Warlow intercepted her. 'No, you can't.'

Though she wasn't large, she fought him like an animal. 'Let me go. Let me go.'

'You can't.'

Her wild eyes looked up into Warlow's, her expression incredulous. 'You heard him. He killed my dad and all those other people.'

Her mouth became a snarl. Saliva sprayed as she screamed. 'He has to pay. He doesn't deserve to live.'

Warlow struggled to hold her back. He got behind her, one arm around her chest as she lurched and thrust herself towards the still screaming Milton.

Gina was at the fallen man's side, trying, and failing, to calm him down.

Milton was sheet white. 'It hurts, Jesus fuck, it hurts. Take it out. Take it out, please.'

'I can't do that,' Gina tried to explain. 'I can't. It'll make things worse.'

Milton replied with an incoherent moan.

'I hope it does hurt, you bastard,' Samantha screeched. 'I hope it hurts forever.'

'Gina?' Warlow yelled.

Gina had her phone in her hand. 'Ambulance is on its way, sir.'

'He doesn't deserve an ambulance.' Samantha kicked out at Warlow and caught his shin. The blow made him almost lose his grip.

'Right, come on.' Warlow dragged her away, back along the path between garage and house towards the Jeep.

'Let me go! Let me go!'

At the car, he swivelled her around and pinned her back against the vehicle. 'Samantha, listen to me—'

Still, she writhed and fought. 'How can you side with him?'

'I am not siding with anyone. You just shot a man. And I know he was about to shoot me and my officer, and I'll make sure everyone knows that. But we can't make this worse. If you go near him now, it will be much, much worse.'

'I don't care. What he's done to me ... what he did to us all ... I want to kick him ... I want to grab that arrow and twist it in. He's a monster. He's ruined lives and just watched us all suffer. My brother, my mother …'

It broke, then. The uncontrolled rage that had turned her into a wildcat. It broke, and she somehow shrank in Warlow's grasp as tears of horror and wailing grief overtook her. Most of what she said after that, as she buried her head in Warlow's shoulder, he could not make out. But one sentence, spoken in hushed tones of harrowing disbelief, he would remember for a very long time.

The wailing subsided, and Samantha Coombs looked up into his face.

'Because he wanted to know what it felt like to kill them. Because he wanted to know how they died … oh God … What makes someone like that?'

'We'll never know,' Warlow muttered.

Samantha sobbed again and buried her head once more.

CHAPTER THIRTY-NINE

J ESS AND R HYS arrived at Milton's house before the ambulance. Rhys helped Gina make Milton as comfortable as they could. Not a straightforward task as Milton remained in constant moaning agony.

Warlow put Samantha into the backseat of the Jeep, contemplating what she'd done in a moment of anger and, for Warlow and Gina, liberation.

She'd gone into shivering shock as the post-adrenaline rage subsided.

Response vehicles were on their way, as was the whole circus that came with a major incident. They'd had enough practise in these last few days.

Jess volunteered to talk to Two-Shoes but, by that time, the blue touch paper had been well and truly lit and wheels were already in motion. The call was brief, as the superintendent was herself on the way. Notably, she did not enquire after Warlow's well-being.

'I'm gutted,' he said when Jess relayed that little gem.

'I bet you are. Though she asked after Gina.'

'Of course, she did. But I am still persona non grata as far as she and Drinkwater are concerned.' He relayed the call he'd taken from Drinkwater in the petrol garage in Beulah. A memory that irked still.

Jess's mouth became tight as she listened and uttered, 'God's sake,' to confirm her disgust.

Warlow remained remarkably unruffled. 'No, that's okay. I don't mind admitting to you that I won't be sorry to see the back of this case.'

They were standing in the courtyard as the ambulance finally arrived. The paramedics' first port of call was Milton, but Warlow insisted they have a look at Samantha Coombs too, once the injured man was stable.

After that, there was little to do but wait for the show to open. Jess explained how Rhys had pieced together the circumstantial evidence that put Milton in the frame.

Warlow checked his phone. The text from Jess that she sent just a minute too late for it to be of any use, read:

> Milton involvement increasingly likely. Be
> aware.

'What are his chances, do you think?' Jess asked five minutes later as they took Milton away.

'No idea. Half of me hopes he doesn't make it.'

Jess frowned.

'Yes.' Warlow held up his hand. 'That makes me sound as big a monster as he is. But if there's a trial …' He shook his head. 'I would prefer not to have a monster smirking in the dock. But more than anything, I don't want the relatives to have to sit through him describing how their loved ones died.'

His nostrils flared as he exhaled. 'God knows what the trick cyclists will make of it all. Imagine chasing down what makes him tick. Be like a plumber backtracking a leaky sewage pipe.'

'Rhys believes that maybe the cancellation of the reenactment, which was the only common factor, could have somehow been a trigger,' Jess said.

'That's another rabbit hole I'd rather avoid.'

Gina and Rhys joined them.

'Where's Samantha?' Gina asked.

'Still in the Jeep. We'll get her transferred to custody in Ammanford.'

'Okay if I sit with her, sir?' Gina asked.

'Go ahead,' Warlow said. 'Thanks, Gina.'

She smiled and walked to the car.

Rhys didn't move, but followed her with his eyes, looking very troubled.

'You okay, sergeant?' Jess asked.

Rhys's good-natured smile struggled to make an appearance as he turned to Warlow. 'Gina told me what happened, sir. He was going to shoot you with a bloody arrow.'

'He was.'

'She said you stood in front of her, sir.'

'He kept on about how there'd be five seconds between shots. Gina's fit. Fitter than me. She'd have made the trees in the time it took to reload, or whatever the hell it is they do with arrows.'

This time, it was Jess's turn to go pale. 'For God's sake, Evan.'

'It was the most pragmatic approach.'

But Rhys hadn't finished.

'Thank you, sir,' he said, his eyes moist.

'Stop that, now,' Warlow said, but gently. 'You would have done the same.'

'Maybe. Who knows?'

'*I* do.'

Rhys held out his hand. Warlow shook it.

'I have told Gina to make sure she has her stab vest on when she's out with you, sir.' This time, the words were accompanied by a faint smile.

'Don't worry, I've always got a cunning plan.'

Their attention turned to the drive where a response vehicle, siren on, sped down and came to a skidding stop on the gravel.

'Cavalry's here, then,' Jess said.

'Yeah. Once they have Samantha in custody, I'm leaving this one to you, Jess.'

'What?'

'I'm just following orders.'

'What orders are those, sir?' Rhys asked.

'Weeding.'

———

Warlow left them to it. But he had a report to write up. He did that sitting at a desk in the Incident Room at HQ. Later that afternoon, he made his way back to the hospital to visit Gil. The sergeant listened to the whole sorry tale, showing no emotion. When he'd finished, and Gil had remained oddly calm throughout, Warlow felt the need to comment.

'You don't seem that surprised?'

Gil made a noise like a tyre deflating. 'Are you? If you are, where have you been for the last ten years? We're becoming inconvenient, Evan.'

'Who are we?'

'You and me. If you hadn't realised, we're being written out of the script. There are those out there who can't foxtrotting wait for us go from heroes to zeros. Just flick on any film or TV programme.'

'That's fiction,' Warlow objected.

'Yeah? Well, I'm just waiting for Bond to end up a burnt-out old has-been, slumped in a bus shelter, being shown the error of his ways by a bright young—'

'Don't say it.'

'I know. Someone is listening. On our phones, or walls, or perhaps we've even had some bloody device transplanted at birth. *Arglwydd Mawr*, it's cultural totalitarianism, I'm telling you.'

'You're not still on those meds, are you?'

Gil grinned. 'Wish I bloody was. *Iesu bach*, they were good stuff.'

'Is that what this is all about? Really? All that critical cobblers they teach in universities these days.'

'All I know is I'm thinking of changing my name to Winston Smith. Face it. We're the wrong colour, have the wrong chromosomes, are the wrong age. We are gammon-flavoured dinosaurs.'

'Which are you, then? T-Rex?'

'I'm more the one with the thick armour and horns. Hamteratops, to keep with the gammon trope.'

'I presume that's one you made up?'

Gil grinned.

'What about me?'

Gil tilted his head in thought. 'Too small to be a T-Rex, but raptor, mid-size. Nippy and deadly.'

'That sounds like a pair of ninja dwar … persons of short stature.'

'Please, enough of your stereotyping language.'

Warlow smiled. 'Alright, nippy and deadly, it is. I'll take that.' He helped himself to some grapes. 'Don't mind, do you?'

'Get stuck in. Three bunches there. I'll be passing pure Chardonnay by tonight.'

A text from Jess came through on Warlow's phone:

> Milton still in surgery. Liver and spleen damage plus the bolt struck a vertebra.

He showed it to Gil.

'Looks like I was lucky, then.'

'I'd buy a tenner's worth of lottery tickets if I were you.' Warlow put his phone away.

'Has anyone spoken to you since Milton threatened to kill you? Drinkwater, or the ACC?' Gil asked as he reached for some water with his good hand.

'No. And long may that continue because, the way I feel now, I'd probably say something stupid.'

Gil studied Warlow for a disconcertingly long time before he eventually asked, 'Not thinking of chucking it in, are you?'

'Two-Shoes could make life very difficult for Jess. If I'm out of the picture, she has no ammunition.'

Gil considered his response for a long time and then said, 'Right, go home. Drink some wine. Talk to your dog.'

'That's exactly what I'm going to do.' Warlow got up and made for the door, adding, 'Keep me informed.'

When he'd gone, Gil found his phone and, using his one good arm, dialled Sion Buchannan.

———

THE DAWES, two dog lovers who'd been Cadi's sitters ever since Warlow had rejoined the Force, were surprised to see him so early. But Cadi, like a demented wiggling bee, had no such reservations.

At Ffau'r Blaidd, Warlow changed into outdoor gear, got Cadi into the back of the Jeep, and drove up to one of their favourite beaches. It took fifteen minutes to Ceibwr, a mixture of sand and pebbles with a stream running down from the hills.

Too early for people to be walking after work, so he found the spot empty, as it often was. He threw a ball for the dog a dozen times, and she splashed at the water's edge, returning with a sandy snout to deposit the prize at his feet for another run. They walked up and down the stretch of sand and saw no one bar the odd dead jellyfish which Cadi found most interesting.

Warlow let his mind wander but found no answers up any of the blind alleys he meandered into.

The day remained dry but grey, the offshore breeze strong enough to make Cadi's ears flutter.

Warlow found a sheltered spot to sit on a boulder and toss pebbles into a pool. Cadi watched him with great interest, sitting close, within fondling distance as was her way, tempting Warlow to reach out and touch her head inter-mittently.

The dog remained content with that, and so did the man. There was a lot to be said about the simple pleasures in a world complicated by fickle human interaction.

Calmer after the walk, Warlow returned home to make himself some supper.

Jess rang, and they spoke briefly, but she got called away.

He knew the score. They'd just found a serial killer and there would be a great deal to do. Her last text came at 21.20.

> Finishing off in Ammanford. Samantha Coombs, still very shaken. There'll be no interviews tonight. But in early tomorrow. Don't wait up.

He texted back:

> I'll be down in the garden room.

> Good idea. So I won't disturb you. See you later

Warlow slept pretty well considering, even though he heard Jess pull up at around one.

They met over a coffee just before 7am. Warlow was up and Cadi fed. Jess, tired-looking but fresh from a shower, entered the kitchen and put her arms around him as he sat at the breakfast table.

'Are you okay, Evan?'

'I am. Honestly.' He turned and kissed her gently on the cheek. 'How about you?'

'Fine, but you staying away like this is mad.'

'Only bad things will come from me being around Two-Shoes at the moment. I'd only say something I'd regret.'

'While she gets to say whatever she likes?' Jess was being angry for his sake.

Warlow shook his head. 'How did it go after I left?'

Jess went to the cupboard and took down a bowl. 'As expected. We're interviewing Samantha this morning with her solicitor. Two-Shoes wants Braeburn to do it.'

'He's good.'

'I know. But it should be you. You broke the case.'

'No, you and Rhys did.'

'If you hadn't pointed us towards Milton—'

'That was down to Tannard.'

'Okay. Team effort. I'm happy with that.'

'So am I. That's what's in my report.'

Jess spooned yoghurt into her bowl. 'My God, Two-Shoes should be happy with it as well. But she isn't. I could see she was seething. I think she was pissed off that we'd actually found him.'

'What about him? Milton?'

'Still in ITU. He needed a lot of blood. High-risk of infection because the arrow went right through his intestines as well. They're probably going to transfer him to a rehab unit because there's likely spinal damage.'

'Jesus. Is he talking?'

'Not yet.'

Warlow had a newspaper site up on his iPad. Jess glanced at it, and her eyebrows went up. 'Not your usual breakfast routine.'

'Don't normally have time. Today, I do.'

Jess sighed. 'You should be coming with me.'

'There's no point. In fact, I'm toying with going away for a couple of days. I've spoken to Tom. Thought I'd pop up to London and see him. You're going to be busy anyway, and Cadi can stay with the Dawes.'

'If it's what you want?' She sounded deflated.

'It is. I need to get away. I require some time to contemplate.'

'Isn't that what Two-Shoes wants?'

Warlow realised that he could have opened up to Jess then. Told her of Two-Shoes's threat. But he didn't. He genuinely needed to reflect on all this thoroughly.

Jess glanced at her watch. 'We should talk, but I need to go in five minutes.'

'Right, well, sit down and eat your breakfast.'

'Yes, sir,' she said and smiled.

It made her look stunningly attractive.

Warlow almost winced from the pain it caused him somewhere deep in his chest.

CHAPTER FORTY

FOR ONCE, in the car and in the quiet carriage of a Great Western Swansea to Paddington train, Warlow found time on his hands. And with that came the opportunity to confront the problems that life was so bloody good at throwing in your way.

Often, in the job, he'd come across people, victims most often, who wasted time and effort, sometimes years, in attempting to rationalise the irrational. Human nature could be a bugger that way.

And now he was playing exactly the same self-destructive game.

How on earth had it come to this?

More often than not, the answer lay with other people. People with agendas that brooked no logic, driven instead by the chaos that governed the actions of the mad and the bad.

Warlow had already concluded that perhaps Milton was a hybrid of the two.

But Two-Shoes, whom he also now considered an enemy, didn't quite qualify as mad or bad. Nonetheless, she embodied someone, similar to Milton, who had gone astray in some of her actions. Let fixed ideas, immutable fixed ideas, run her motor. And on more than one occasion.

——————

In London, Warlow had a wander around old haunts and called up an old friend.

Bob Regis had been a new DI when Warlow had made it to the big smoke as a green detective sergeant. Regis had since retired but, unlike Leach, remained fit and well and grandfather to a budding young footballer making waves in Tottenham.

Regis lived in Belvedere at the end of the newly constructed Elizabeth Line. A feat of engineering that added almost twenty percent to Regis's modest semi's value overnight on completion.

'Fifty minutes to Oxford Circus,' Regis had said. 'I'll meet you in town.'

Warlow bought the coffees. Not at Oxford Circus, but at a little place on Marchmont Street. Not the original café they'd frequented all those years ago as colleagues, but close enough. There, they swapped insults and reminisced after people from the old days, now either dead or retired, mostly. Like a morbid roll call.

Regis listened open-mouthed as Warlow told him about Milton and his close encounter of the terminal kind with the sod.

'When all this comes out, you'll be hounded by the hyenas.'

'Yeah, well, the dog sees them off if anyone comes down the lane.'

'Really?'

'No, not really. She'd invite the buggers in for a cup of tea.'

'Labradors.' Regis snorted. 'We've had a couple. Don't have a nasty bone in their bodies. So, what are you doing here? If you're involved in that crossbow case, I'd have thought it would be full on by now.'

Warlow explained. About the gardening leave. About the incomprehensible antagonism that Two-Shoes had demonstrated towards him. Regis listened with the odd sympathetic nod until Warlow finished.

'I think I've met Goodey before,' Regis said.

'Really?'

'Yeah. her type anyway. Both sexes. If you pardon my French.'

'Always do.'

'All they ever see is the next rung on the ladder.'

They ordered second cups. Halfway through and munching the free tiny Biscoff biscuit that came with it, a random thought wafted through Warlow, lingering just long enough to attract his attention.

'There is one more thing I wanted to run past you.'

Jeeze Denise, Warlow's deceased ex, had died of alcohol-related complications. She'd left a sizeable legacy for him and her sons. She'd also written him a deathbed letter in which she mentioned a visit from someone an unspecified number of years ago after they'd broken up. She'd hinted that she'd been quizzed about Warlow, and about whether he ever talked to her about someone called Fern.

'The trouble is, her brain, by that time, was mixing up the words. I should let it all go, but I can't. Fern mean anything to you?'

Regis shook his head. 'Don't ring any bells.'

'No, nor with me. But it might not be Fern because, thanks to the vodka, marbles were already being lost by this stage and occasionally there might be a twisted link between the words she used and the words she had in mind. For a time, I wondered bough, or branch or even trunk. But it didn't get me anywhere.'

'I enjoy a good crossword,' Regis said. 'I'll have a think. But I'm sorry to hear about Denise. And since, have you dipped your toe?'

'Funny you should ask.' A wistful smile crept over his lips. 'She's a copper and my DI.'

'Christ, Evan, you don't mess about, do you? Talk about making a rod for your own back. You remind me of those bloody gymnasts that like to add a maximum difficulty to their tumble tosses.'

Warlow grinned. 'Interesting analogy, Bob. But I'd be grateful if you have a ponder about Fern.'

'A case, you reckon?'

'I don't know. It may be absolutely nothing. But …'

'Okay. I'll let it simmer.'

———

JODIE COOKED them all something aromatic from a Persian cookbook with lots of chickpeas. Delicious, but Warlow suspected he'd pay for it later. Luckily, he slept on the couch and disturbed no one when the brass section in his intestines started up at 1:45am.

He had not troubled his hosts with the real reason for his visit, either. Accumulated leave seemed like a good enough excuse for them.

When Sion Buchannan rang him at 9:30pm on his second night in London, Warlow stood at the bar of Tom's local, buying a pint for the two of them. Just the one, as Tom would be in the operating theatre at 8am. When the call came through, Warlow signalled to Tom to collect his beer from the bar and took himself and his phone outside.

London was always warmer in March than West Wales and certainly less wet. There were people in warm coats outside on the pub pavement and clustered around a couple of tables. Hardly balmy, but Londoners never minded a bit of alfresco drinking, even in the rain and fog.

'Sion?'

'I'll keep it brief, Evan. Can you come in tomorrow?'

'I'm in London.'

'That's okay. Just give me a time. We need to see you.'

'What's it about?'

'A lot of things. All of them need to be face to face, though, I'm afraid.'

'Is it about Jess and me?'

'That's part of it. I'm not privy to it all. I've been asked to set it up, that's all.'

Not like Buchannan to be coy. 'Okay, I'll see if I can get an early train. Say 1pm for the meeting to be safe?'

'Fine.'

Warlow waited, but a taciturn Buchannan said nothing else.

'So, should I wear a stab vest?' Warlow asked.

'Might not be a bad idea.' Were Buchannan's last words.

He batted away Tom's questions about the call with "Work" as an answer. When he phoned Jess at ten to tell her he was coming back the next day, she sounded pleased, but genuinely ignorant regarding the meeting.

'What do you think they want to see you about?' Jess asked.

'I feel the wart-encrusted hand of Two-Shoes at play.'

'Oh, God. She's been difficult to work with. In the end, she didn't let me anywhere near Coombs. I've been handling the search of Milton's place. It's full of junk, though Tannard got very excited about his printer. She thinks there's a good chance it printed the letter he sent to you.'

'No surprises there.'

'I'm missing you, Evan.'

'Me too. Missing you, I mean. Not missing me. I'm still there every time I look in the mirror.'

She laughed. Warlow liked the sound of that. He'd miss it if it wasn't there …

He cut the power to that idea pdq.

'Molly okay?'

'Yes. She's worried about you going away. She thinks you're getting cold feet.'

'My feet are nice and warm, thanks for asking, tell her.'

As lies went, this one might qualify as dirty grey, if not actually white. A bit like Lloyd Coombs's van.

———

THE MEETING TOOK place in an interview room in the admin block at HQ. A quieter part of the building, a room reserved for interviewing candidates for the more senior posts. But it would do as a place to end careers, too.

Warlow sat outside the room, like a kid outside a head-teacher's office, wondering why he allowed such thoughts to bother him. He knew his tenure had always been precarious. Brought back to a consulting role from retirement initially, he ended up being re-employed to run a rapid response team.

In a sense, staff shortages were more a reason for his continued employment than any imagined success rate in the cases he and the team dealt with.

Now he was simply being negative. Letting his anxieties dominate. But such was the vibe. Because now here he sat, outside a room, with palms as moist as a rookie DS applying for his first Inspector job. But his nerves were nothing to do with his predicament. His worries were all for the others. Jess, Gil, and Rhys, especially. Gina would find her own way. But the others … if any of them suffered because of his … what?

His insight troubled him even more.

Was it his arrogance? The way he treated others? He knew he could come across as gruff and undiplomatic. And in these days of offending people with the wrong word, hint, or even thought, perhaps they were all good reasons for dismissal.

The door opened, and Sion Buchannan, his stooped gait a learned habit borne of knocking his head on too many ceilings and door headers, looked down.

'Sorry. The Chief Constable got held up.'

'Chief Constable?'

'It's like Navarone in here. All the big guns. They're ready for you.'

Four people sat behind a long desk. All in uniform, bar Pauline Garston. None of them needed any introduction. Besides Buchannan, who took a seat at the end to make it five, the dynamic duo of ACC Reeves and Superintendent Drinkwater sat with slightly forced smiles. In the middle of them sat Gillian Kerr, Chief Constable. He'd met her just the one time. She had been appointed shortly after his retirement, and their paths had crossed only briefly on his return. But she clearly had the chair.

And no Pamela Goodey.

'Thanks for coming in, Evan. I hear you had to come from London. I'm sorry about that. Your son is there?'

They were lulling him with soft soap before they slipped in the knife.

'Yes, my youngest. He's training to be a surgeon.'

Warlow put Kerr at a year or two older than him. She had her jacket off, as did the others. The radiators were on and made the room stuffy.

'I'm going to speak,' Kerr continued. 'Not so much a prepared statement, more of an outline of my opinion after having discussed with my colleagues the events leading up to your … absence.'

Good word, absence. Not suspension, not even gardening leave. Simply away from where you were meant to be.

'You were leading the investigation into the killing of Stuart and Nash. We are all aware that you and your team, in conjunction with crime scene investigators, were responsible for the aspect of the investigation that led to the identification of Milton as the man responsible for all four killings. Prior to that, because of the high profile of the case and press interest, some of my colleagues felt that not enough progress had been made quickly enough initially and placed Superintendent Goodey in charge of the investigation. Am I right so far?'

'Spot on, ma'am,' Warlow said.

'I understand, too, that a journalist published sensitive information regarding Milton before we had any firm evidence. And that Superintendent Goodey accused you of leaking that information. Is that correct?'

'It is. However—'

Kerr held up a hand. 'If you could just let me finish. The woman who shot Milton, Samantha Coombs, did so because she heard Milton admit to killing her father. She'd gone there to confront him and overheard him in the garden. She saw he was holding you at bowpoint, if that is the correct term. She sourced a weapon from one of many he had in his garage, a crossbow, one already loaded. I presume he was testing these weapons or intending some target practice. However, she also saved you and a junior officer from significant harm from Milton, who was threatening you with a deadly weapon.'

Warlow nodded.

'During her statement, Samantha Coombs explained how she had been alerted to Milton's involvement by her brother.'

'Her brother?' News to Warlow.

'After the attack on Sergeant Jones, in which Milton also induced a self-inflicted wound from a crossbow, Lloyd Coombs had been asked to attend by your investigative team in order to re-establish the movements of persons of interest in that aspect of the case. Coombs was here, awaiting his sister's arrival. He admitted to overhearing a heated exchange between you and Superintendent Goodey in the car park.'

Warlow stared at the panel. Buchannan's eyes glittered. Drinkwater and Reeves looked as if they might vomit. Pauline Garston, the only one smiling, kept her gaze aimed towards her hands on the desk.

'Lloyd Coombs told us he heard Superintendent Goodey, and not you, explicitly say, in a very loud voice, that Hugo Milton killed all four victims. He relayed that information to the journalist and his sister, who was within ten miles of Milton's property, when he rang her.'

Warlow could only blink at this revelation. Something inside him wanted desperately to say, 'Foxtrot. Foxtrot, Sierra.' Instead, he swallowed and said something else. 'Superintendent Goodey made a point during our discussion, ma'am. Something I ought to have officially reported. About DI Allanby and I.'

The Chief Constable nodded.

'That's already come out in the wash,' Buchannan said before Warlow could say more.

'And there are considerations,' Kerr added. 'But because your collective efforts have been successful up to now, I have no reason to make that a problem. Do you?'

'We're all grownups,' Warlow said.

'Superintendent Goodey is no longer leading the investigation. It is a joint effort now. We will need a task force and Superintendent Braeburn has been asked to review the Bowman case now that we believe we know who the perpetrator is. As regards your relationship with DI Allanby, Superintendent Buchannan will continue to advise me regarding any performance-related issues.'

'What does that mean in English?'

'Do not bring your dirty washing to work, Evan,' Buchannan said.

Out of the corner of his eye, Warlow saw Drinkwater take a sip from a plastic glass and grimace. He wondered if he was trying to swallow back a little bile.

Kerr steepled her fingers together on the desk. 'The Stuart and Nash case progresses, and we'd like you to resume and follow through. The hard work is yet to be done, as you know. Milton is not yet fit to be interviewed.'

'When do I start?' Warlow said.

That broke the tension.

Kerr hadn't finished, though. 'And on a personal note, I'd like to apologise. Superintendent Goodey was out of order.'

Warlow nodded.

Kerr smiled. 'Then let's all get back to work, shall we?'

She glanced at her colleagues, who all nodded, taking their lumps as they deserved to.

CHAPTER FORTY-ONE

THE ROOM EMPTIED. First out of the door were Drinkwater and the ACC. Warlow half fancied he saw tails between their legs. The Chief Constable and Garston and Buchannan hung on for a few informal words.

Kerr approached and shook Warlow's hand.

'Jess came to see me this morning,' she said with an amused and knowing smile. 'She's a straight talker.'

That would be her epitaph. 'Dare I ask what she said?'

Kerr tapped her nose. 'But the relevant bits were that you were hard on yourself, allergic to your own emotions which you keep in a glass jar with the lid screwed down tight, and are as straight as an—'

'Please don't tell me she said arrow?'

'No. That was my clumsy idiom. Jess is more direct. What she said was that you were very good at your job, irrepressibly honourable, and … unconventional in your approach. An approach that sometimes triggered a variety of irritated responses from some more … traditional sources.'

'She said all that?'

Kerr's smile answered his question before she even spoke. 'I'm still paraphrasing. Bottom line, a glowing report from someone who respects you for the job you do. And one not in the slightest tarnished by emotion. I see great things ahead for her.'

'I'll tell her that,' Warlow replied.

She made meaningful eye contact and kept it as she spoke. 'Do. Just keep doing what you're doing, Evan. Quietly, efficiently, successfully. Three of my favourite words.'

She turned away, retrieved her jacket, slid it on, and left with a bundle of notes in her hands.

Pauline Garston shook Warlow's hand, too.

'Thanks for finding him.' Her words were full of some unspoken emotions, relief chief amongst them. 'You know, I spoke to Leach about Milton. He'd volunteered his services back in 2001. We had not approached him. I said we had to vet him properly and that would've involved all kinds of checks. But Leach, as we know, was fixated. He said we ought to accept gifts when they turned up on the doorstep.' She shook her head.

Cases such as this were riddled with near misses. She had nothing to apologise to him for, but he hoped she'd be kind enough to forgive herself. Then her features softened. 'By the way, Jess put her head on the block for you, visiting the Chief Constable. You are a lucky man.'

'I am,' Warlow said.

'I suspect the rest of your team would have done the same, given the chance.'

And, of all the things said to him, those last two statements from Garston meant the most.

———

Buchannan and Warlow walked back to the superintendent's office where the DCI took his leave.

'Thanks, Sion.'

'I did nothing. I told the ACC that you'd already spoken to me about yours and Jess's relationship and that I felt it was something that did not need sending up the line. It's what normally happens with these things. The ACC and Bleddyn Drinkwater disagreed. But Jess beat them to it.'

For a few seconds, Warlow didn't know what to say. While in London, he'd tormented himself with the conviction they'd force him to make an unpalatable choice of the Hobson variety. It hadn't occurred to him for one moment that he might have allies to fight his corner. That knowledge was humbling. He'd have a lot of people to thank. But some to still despise.

'I've got to ask. Where is Goodey?'

'The message is, if she wants to move up, she'll need to move elsewhere.'

'But she's still around for now?'

Buchannan shrugged. 'Like Covid, she'd be difficult to eradicate completely.'

'Avoidance the best tactic, then?'

Buchannan nodded.

'I appreciate you fighting our case, Sion.'

Buchannan straightened his back. 'Don't forget, I am now officially your relationship manager so …'

'Do you still want photos?'

Buchannan grinned. 'Ah, that's the tone lowered nicely. No, thanks. I'm certain you'll keep each other in check.'

———

WARLOW MADE it back to the Incident Room at 14.17. He pushed open the door. The place buzzed with activity, its missing mojo back from vacation with a healthy glow.

Jess looked up from her desk, smiled, and raised one questioning eyebrow.

Warlow mouthed, 'Thanks,' and held a thumb up.

'I've pressed the button on the Rosebush cottage by the way,' Jess said.

'Great stuff.' Warlow grinned.

Then Rhys saw him. 'Hello, sir. How was the conference?'

'Yes,' Jess said, a little too enthusiastically. 'How was it? And how come you get to go to a conference in London in the middle of a murder enquiry, anyway?'

A conference. Warlow mentally joined the dots. Another

little white porker to explain his absence. Okay, he could accept that.

'Boring,' Warlow said. 'Right, who's for a cup of tea?'

Gina's hand was the first to go up. She glanced at Rhys, who pushed up from his desk with a resigned expression. He knew better than to suggest that the junior officer, especially a female junior officer, and partner in more senses than one, should make the tea.

Warlow stopped him with a raised hand. 'No. I'm making the tea. Plus, I have biscuits. £1 special in the garage in Neath. You're not the only one with an eye for a bargain, Rhys. My treat this time.'

The irony was not lost on him that they would've been *his* solace had things gone pear-shaped. A commiseration for having been drummed out of his job so that Jess could progress. He'd made that decision, and it had been an easy one in the end, though she need never know. Now, instead of sacrificing either his relationship with Jess or the job, he was going to sacrifice the biscuits on the altar of muted celebration instead.

'Hobnobs,' Rhys said as he glimpsed the packet and pumped his fist.

Gina rolled her eyes. 'The simple things.'

'What are we celebrating, then, sir?' Rhys asked.

'A weathering of the storm, sergeant. And, as someone once famously said, *Ni Yma O Hyd.*'

'Great anthem, sir,' Rhys said.

'What am I missing?' Jess looked a little bemused.

Warlow shrugged. 'Rough translation is, *We're Still Here.*'

'Despite everything and everyone,' Rhys added.

'We'll get Gil to sing it for you when he gets back to work,' Gina said.

'He would, too.' Rhys grinned.

'Then I'll look forward to it.' Jess beamed.

'So we should we all.' Warlow handed Rhys the biscuits. 'Keep looking forward because what's done is done.' He held Jess's gaze for a couple of seconds and added, 'Look back and smile on perils past.'

'Who said that, sir?' Rhys asked, as Warlow suspected he would.

'Scott.'

'The bloke who explored the Antarctic?'

'No. Ivanhoe? Rob Roy?'

Rhys shook his head.

'Walter Scott wrote both and a ton more. Come to think of it, you should read Ivanhoe to get a handle on Milton and his weapons, since it's set post-Crusades.'

'Is it on Netflix, sir?'

Warlow smiled or at least his lips made the right shape, decided wisely not to answer, and instead raised both hands in a gesture of ignorance and surrender combined, before turning towards the door and leaving them with one last word as he headed for the kettle. 'Tea!'

ACKNOWLEDGMENTS

As with all writing endeavours, the existence of this novel depends upon me, the author, and a small army of 'others' who turn an idea into a reality. My wife, Eleri, who gives me the space to indulge my imagination and picks out my stupid mistakes. Tim Barber designs the covers, Sian Phillips edits, and other proofers and ARC readers sort out the gaffes. Thank you all for your help. Special mention goes to Ela the dog who drags me away from the writing cave and the computer for walks, rain or shine. Actually, she's a bit of a princess so the rain is a no-no. Good dog!

But my biggest thanks goes to you, lovely reader, for being there and actually reading this. It's great to have you along and I do appreciate you spending your time in joining me on this roller-coster ride with Evan and the rest of the team.

CAN YOU HELP?

With that in mind, and if you enjoyed it, I do have a favour to ask. Could you spare a moment to **leave a review or a rating**? A few words will do, but it's really the only way to help others like you discover the books. Probably the best way to help authors you like. Just visit my page on Amazon and leave a few words.

A FREE BOOK FOR YOU

Visit my website and join up to the Rhys Dylan VIP Reader's Club and get a FREE novella, *The Wolf Hunts Alone*, by visiting the website at: **rhysdylan.com**

The Wolf Hunts Alone.

One man and his dog... will track you down.

DCI Evan Warlow is at a crossroads in his life. Living alone, contending with the bad hand fate has dealt him, he finds solace in simple things like walking his neighbour's dog.

But even that is not as safe as it was. Dogs are going missing from a country park. And not only one, now three have disappeared. When he takes it upon himself to root out the cause of the lost animals, Warlow faces ridicule and a thuggish enemy.

But are these simply dog thefts? Or is there a more sinister malevolence at work? One with its sights on bigger, two legged prey.
A FREE eBOOK FOR YOU (Available in digital format)

Only one thing is for certain; Warlow will not rest until he finds out.

———

By joining the club, you will also be the first to hear about new releases via the few but fun emails I'll send you. This includes a no spam promise from me, and you can unsubscribe at any time.

AUTHOR'S NOTE

This story almost didn't see the light of day. Just three months after I finished writing it, a horrifying true crime case made headlines involving a crossbow killer. When something like that happens, as an author, you can't help but think twice. Readers might assume it's in poor taste to publish a book that appears to capitalise on such an event.

Of course, I know I wrote this story before those real-life events occurred. And, realistically, my writing about something that later happens doesn't create any connection between the two—that would be absurd. Still, I feel it's important to explain this to you, the reader, so there's no misunderstanding.

As for the locations in the book, they are all real, including the estate previously owned by the new King. To my knowledge, it's still not necessary to have a license to own a crossbow in the UK.

Regarding motivation, well, there are some very strange people in this world. So, stay safe out there.

All the best,

Rhys

P.S. For those interested, there is a glossary on the website to help with any tricky pronunciations.

READY FOR MORE?

DCI Evan Warlow and the team are back in…

One Less Snake

Power leaves a smoking trail. Death finds the end of it.

In the picturesque coastal town of Solva, Wales, a morning walker stumbles upon a horrific sight - a charred car wreck containing a body at the bottom of a quarry.

DCI Evan Warlow's investigation into the death of controversial ex-politician Matt Gittings reveals a sinister underbelly of drugs, corruption, and revenge. As his team races to connect the dots between Gittings' sordid past and his violent end, they become targets themselves.

With a killer watching their every move and a journalist threatening to expose their operation, Warlow must decide who to trust before it's all too late.

www.ingramcontent.com/pod-product-compliance
Lightning Source LLC
Chambersburg PA
CBHW050549190726
48283CB00007B/2067

* 9 7 8 1 9 1 5 1 8 5 3 8 9 *